# HEALING LUKE

# BETH CORNELISON

SOURCEBOOKS CASABLANCA™
AN IMPRINT OF SOURCEBOOKS, INC.®
NAPERVILLE, ILLINOIS

Published by Sourcebooks Casablanca, an imprint of Sourcebooks, Inc.
P.O. Box 4410, Naperville, Illinois 60567-4410
(630) 961-3900
FAX: (630) 961-2168
www.sourcebooks.com

Printed and bound in the United States of America
QW 10 9 8 7 6 5 4 3 2 1

*To Paul and Jeffery*
*with all my love*

# Chapter 1

"HOT REDHEAD AT ONE O'CLOCK."

Luke Morgan raised his gaze from the wetsuit zipper he was working to unjam and scanned the long pier. He spotted the woman in question on the deck of her boat, where she soaked in the Florida sun. He sent his brother a smug grin. "Nice, huh? Her name's Kelly."

Aaron turned a startled glance his way. "You've already met her?"

Satisfaction swelled in Luke's chest, and his grin widened. "Yep."

His older brother arched a golden eyebrow. "And what's the scoop?"

Purposely making his brother squirm, Luke turned his attention back to the stuck zipper on the wetsuit. "The scoop is we've got twenty high school seniors who expect to go snorkeling in fifteen minutes, and you still haven't got that damn engine running. Get your ass in gear, man, and stop gawking at the neighbors."

Aaron's boisterous laugh rang through the marina. "I'll be damned! Little brother struck out!"

"I did not strike out!" Luke frowned, irritated by his brother's assumption. He didn't bother explaining that he hadn't struck out because he hadn't made a move on the redheaded dish. Yet. Aaron would only ask why he hadn't, and Luke wasn't sure he knew.

Just because in recent months he'd given up the one-night stands that left him feeling hollow didn't mean he'd sworn off women completely. But he was restless. He wanted something more, though for the life of him he couldn't say what that something was. No amount of partying with his brother or recreational sex filled the empty space lurking inside him.

Aaron flashed him a cocky grin. "Uh-huh, if you didn't strike out, then when are you going out with her?"

The warm gulf breeze ruffled his brother's blond hair, and the late April sun glinted off the gold stud earring in Aaron's left lobe.

Luke gritted his teeth. He lost patience with the jammed zipper and tossed the wetsuit aside. "Do we have any more small suits in the shop? We may need 'em for the girls."

"You're avoiding my question."

"You're perceptive." He opened a storage bin under a row of seats, and a strong chemical odor wafted up to him. Luke paused and sniffed the air. "Do you smell gas?"

He bent over and peered under the casement around the engine, searching for the source of the suspicious odor. "Aw, hell. We got a puddle of gas back here. The fuel line must be leaking."

"Are you losing your touch with women?"

He shot Aaron a dirty look. He could get a date with the redhead any time he wanted. Women never turned him or Aaron down. They had perfected the "Morgan charm" and had the family's blond good looks on their side, a fact that his brother exploited to the fullest. "Man, do your womanizing on your own time. We've got a problem over here."

Aaron smirked and sauntered across their thirty-foot pontoon boat, used during the summer season to take Destin tourists snorkeling or fishing in the Gulf of Mexico. The family enterprise had started as a hobby for their father and grown into a profitable summer business.

Luke stepped back, giving Aaron room to take a look at the fuel line. Aaron jiggled a few wires and ran his fingers along the rubber fuel hose. "Here's the leak. Find me a wrench."

"Damn. We've got fifteen minutes to get the engine running before we have twenty very unhappy customers." He retrieved the tool box from another storage bin and fished out the wrench.

"Relax, will ya? I can fix it. I just have to do one thing first."

"What?" Luke folded his arms over his chest and watched Aaron cross the boat and hop onto the pier. "Where you goin'?"

"I'm gonna score myself a date tonight with a certain hot redhead. Sorry, man. You had your chance."

"Aaron, come on. Save it for after hours. We've got work to do now," he called to his brother's retreating back.

Huffing his frustration, he carried the wrench over to the engine. He perched on the railing of the pontoon and observed his brother's well-rehearsed routine. A flash of his knock-'em-dead smile. A few flattering words while admiration lit his eyes. The smoothly delivered invitation to dinner or a movie.

Luke expelled a gust of air through pursed lips in disgust. Why hadn't he asked Kelly out earlier when he had the chance?

He watched the redhead reach over to write her phone number on the back of Aaron's hand. His brother had done it again. The lucky bastard. Now he'd gloat and act smug…

Grimacing, Luke slammed the wrench down on a steel rod that anchored the engine in place, creating a loud, metallic clang.

And a spark.

The leaking fuel ignited in a bright flash and thunderous boom. The concussion of the explosion knocked Luke backward and over the side of the boat. A searing pain arced through him. A scalding heat gnawed his right eye.

Then merciful darkness sucked him into an unconscious void.

Aaron held his breath as Luke's doctor approached in the hospital corridor. The man wore a grim expression, and Aaron's gut clenched with dread.

Their father, Bart, his own face dark with worry, stepped forward to meet the doctor in the middle of the hall. "Well? How is he?"

"He's actually quite lucky." The doctor tucked a pen into the already-full pocket of his lab coat.

"Lucky?" Aaron gave a derisive snort. "Exactly how do you figure that, doc?"

"Quiet, Aaron," Bart warned in a sterner tone than Aaron had heard his father use in years. "Go on, doctor."

"Well, if he hadn't landed in the water after the explosion, the burns almost certainly would have been more extensive, more serious. As it is, many are only first degree burns that will heal quickly. The second degree burns are what is called mid-dermal partial thickness burns and are concentrated on his hand and chest."

"How bad is a mid-partial whatever-you-said burn?" Aaron asked, a sick feeling roiling in his gut. "Will he be scarred? Can he get those skin grafts they talk about?"

"I won't lie. Any second degree burn is serious and poses a number of challenges. The mid-dermal second degree burns Luke has generally heal well and leave less scarring than those that affect deeper tissue levels. But he'll still need debridement and an aggressive treatment to prevent infection. He'll have some scarring, but we have ways to minimize scars."

Aaron's mind reeled as the doctor continued. He caught terms like silver sulfadiazine cream, and occlusive dressing, and compression garment, which all meant little to him. Except that Luke had a hell of a road ahead of him.

As the doctor continued, Aaron vacillated in wild mood swings between relief and guilt that he hadn't been the one who'd been injured.

*Damn it, no one should have been injured! If he'd fixed the leak when Luke found it...*

"Yes, I'm afraid it's extremely painful." The doctor's remark pulled Aaron's attention back to the debriefing. He shuddered when the doctor described how the dead tissue of Luke's burns would be scraped away with a stiff brush and high-powered water in debridement therapy.

Aaron swallowed a groan. Painful indeed.

"How much of his vision did he lose?" Bart asked, furrowing his brow.

"The jury's still out on what he'll be able to see from his left eye. Most to all of his vision should return as the swelling heals. However, it appears some debris hit him in the right eye. He's lost that eye completely."

"Shit," Aaron snarled under his breath, turning to rest his forehead against the wall and squeeze his eyes shut. Acid gnawed his gut, and concern for his brother, his best friend, weighted his heart like lead.

Luke didn't deserve this…

"Right now my primary concern is the damage to his right hand."

The doctor's dire-sounding comment brought Aaron's attention back to the physician's report.

Bart's face had grown white, despite his year-round tan. "What about his hand?"

"We'll probably have to amputate his thumb. Most of it was severed and repairing the damage isn't likely to be successful. His other fingers have nerve damage, but he should be able to regain full use of them in time. We'll talk later about getting him set up with an occupational therapist."

"Was there any internal damage? To his organs, I mean?" Bart asked, concern darkening his gray eyes.

"No. Not that we've found so far, but we're monitoring him closely."

"Thank God for that much." Bart sighed and ran a hand through his hair.

"That's about it. We'll have to talk more later about what you'll need to do for him once he leaves the hospital. Someone will have to change his bandages daily for a while, that sort of thing. For now… any questions?"

"No, no questions." Aaron crossed his arms over his chest and heaved a deep breath of despair.

Bart shook his head, an expression of shock and anguish making him look years older.

"Then I'll go make arrangements for his amputation surgery."

"Thanks, doctor." Bart shook the physician's hand as he left.

Poor Luke. Damn it, it wasn't fair!

For a horrible moment, when Aaron had pulled his brother out of the water, he'd feared Luke was dead. And he'd wanted to die himself.

Guilt and grief consumed him. He could have prevented this if only…

Aaron followed his father into Luke's room and winced at the sight of his brother's bandaged face and arm. His gut tightened, but he forced a smile to his lips when Luke opened his unbandaged left eye. Luke's blue eye, so similar to his own, was bloodshot, and the lid swollen half-closed. His brother's dark-blond hair had been singed in a few spots, and Aaron nervously combed his fingers through his own hair as he took a seat beside the bed.

"Hey, Dummy," he said, using the playful nickname he'd given his brother years ago.

"Hey, Stupid," his brother returned, using Aaron's moniker. A tiny grin tugged the corner of Luke's mouth briefly, then he closed his eye again with a deeply inhaled breath.

"How do you feel?" Aaron asked tentatively.

"Not bad, really. I've got some pretty wicked pain-killers pumpin' through me right now. All right here, whenever I click this little button." Luke held up the device in his hand that allowed him to dispense more of the drug in measured and regulated doses from a computerized pump. Luke demonstrated with a flourish. "Ahhh, that's better."

Aaron gave a short huff-like laugh at his brother's drug-muddled antics, then stared down at his feet, uncertain what to say.

"We've just talked to the doctor, Luke," Bart said softly.

"Mm."

Their father sighed. "There's good news and bad."

"Mm."

"You're gonna need surgery on your hand. Do you want to hear it now or rest some more?" Bart paused but got no response. "Luke?"

He glanced at Aaron, then back to his injured son. Deep lines of worry creased Bart's brow, and he bent closer to his son. "Luke?"

The light sound of Luke's snore answered him. Bart cast a weary grin to Aaron, then jerked his head toward the door. "Come on. Let's let him sleep. I still need to call your mother and let her know what's happened."

"Like she'll care." Aaron gritted his teeth and slumped back in the chair.

Bart raised his chin a notch and squared his shoulders. Even before his father spoke, Aaron knew that he'd defend his ex-wife.

Rather than argue the point, Aaron shrugged. "You go on. I'll stay here for now. You know, just in case…" He didn't bother to finish.

Just in case what? He didn't know. In all his life, he'd never felt so helpless, so damn useless.

Bart nodded and turned to leave. As soon as the door clicked shut, Aaron gave in to the emotions that had built inside him since he'd watched the ball of fire knock his brother into the Gulf. For only the second time in his adult life, he cried.

Luke was suffocating.

After more than three weeks confined in his house, he needed air. Figuring he could brood over the injustice of his accident as well outside as in, he stepped onto the front porch and glowered at the sky. The sun seemed obscenely bright, and he tugged the rim of his baseball cap down to shield more of his face from the afternoon light.

Taking a seat in a resin chair, he carefully stretched his legs in front of him and propped his feet on a second chair. With a sigh, he leaned back until his chair propped against the front wall of the beach-front house and closed his eyes.

According to his doctors, his burns were healing exceptionally well and showed no signs of infection. At this rate, he could resume normal activities as he felt up to it.

Normal activities.

Luke scoffed at the term as he sucked in the gulf breeze. Nothing about him or his life was normal anymore. He looked like some kind of sideshow freak. The explosion had left him with one eye, a missing thumb, and the certainty that his days of competing with Aaron for women were over.

He'd just gotten semi-comfortable, prepared to settle into a good sulk, when a female voice roused him from his musings.

"Excuse me."

Luke tapped the bill of his cap up a fraction with a flick of his good hand. He peered out at the petite brunette standing at the foot of the stairs, looking at him.

"What?" His tone fell short of polite, but he didn't care. He was in no mood for company.

"Do you know where Gulfside Snorkeling Excursions is?"

He hesitated a beat. "Yeah."

Something in the lilt of her voice or the graceful movement of her body triggered an instinctive awareness inside him. Being in the presence of a pretty woman caused a strange prickle on the back of his neck. No one except his family and the hospital staff had seen him since the accident. He'd made sure of it. Friends had stopped by to commiserate, but he'd had Aaron send them away. He wasn't ready for people to see his disfigurements, and he certainly didn't want their pity.

"Well, could you tell me where it is? I can't seem to find the place." The young woman climbed a couple of steps, moving closer to him.

She was definitely attractive. His stomach clenched. For the first time in his post-pubescent life, he faced the fact that a woman would not like what she saw of Luke Morgan.

He tucked his bandaged, thumbless right hand with the ugly compression glove in the pocket of his sweat pants and reassured himself that his long-sleeved T-shirt covered his burned arm. But the awful black patch over his blind eye made him feel like a ridiculous Blackbeard wanna-be.

"Sir? Did you hear me?" The brunette tipped her head, peeking under the low bill of his cap with her large, lovely eyes.

He searched for a way to get rid of her, to eliminate the source of his discomfort. Angling his face away from her, he feigned interest in the car that rolled by on the street. "You've found it."

"You mean, this is it?" Wrinkling her nose, she pointed to the house behind him.

"No, that's our house. As in, private property." His churlish tone sawed at his conscience.

Clearly the brunette wasn't going away until he gave her what she wanted. Despite the qualms swimming through him, he let the legs of his chair touch the floor. Tender, injured tissue pulled on his chest and sore muscles protested as he sat straighter in the chair. He braced himself for the woman's reaction and reached up to tug his cap back from his face. Raising his chin, he gave her a good view of his face—eye patch, red scars, and all.

To her credit, she hid her repulsion well. In fact, other than a quick flick of her eyes to the patch, and a slight adjustment of her stance, she had no reaction. He admired her for that. The chick obviously had a strong stomach. Or else some fine acting skills.

Tucking a wisp of her pixie-cut behind an ear, the brunette wrinkled her brow in query. "Then where is the snorkeling office?"

Why couldn't she take a hint? He thought his evasive answers said clearly enough that he wanted to be left alone. He sighed heavily.

"The snorkeling office is downstairs. Go down those steps over there." His tone begrudged her the information, but he directed her to the beach access with a lazy hitch of his left thumb. "You enter from the marina."

She took a deep breath and nodded. Sliding her sunglasses from the top of her head to the bridge of her nose, she turned, calling cheerfully, "Thanks. Sorry to bother you."

Damn it, why did she have to sound so chipper? Her grace under his fire chafed at him. He'd acted like the monster he now resembled.

Her hips swayed provocatively as she sauntered down the sidewalk. Hesitating a moment, he weighed his choices until compunction for his rudeness finally won. "Hey! They're not there."

She stopped on the sidewalk and faced him again. "They're not?" Walking back toward him, she pushed the sunglasses back up on her head. "You're sure?"

"Positive." Luke stared at her, knowing she wanted more information. But he made her wait, made her ask for every crumb. He knew his obstinacy carried his bad mood too far, yet her sunny disposition nettled his own sense of defeat and frustration.

Finally, she braced a hand on her hip and cocked her head to the side. "Do you know where they are or when they'll be back? I have a reservation to go snorkeling on the two o'clock trip."

"Alone?" This tidbit intrigued him. Families, couples, or groups of friends comprised the bulk of their business. Rarely, almost never, unaccompanied women.

"What difference does that make to you?" Her tone held umbrage for his prying.

Luke gave her a negligent shrug. "None."

Actually, her willingness to travel alone spoke volumes to him about her self-assurance and poise. The kind of self-assurance he'd had before...

The reminder of his new doubts pricked.

Another taut moment of silence ticked by before she asked wearily, "Do you know when they'll be back?"

"Later." He watched her curl her fingers into her palm in frustration. The brunette's fading grasp on her temper amused him—whether out of some misplaced revenge for his own discomfort or because he rather liked the sparks lighting her eyes, he wasn't sure.

"How much later?"

"Few minutes, maybe."

She relaxed her stance and turned back to stare out at the street. "Mind if I wait, then?"

"Makes no difference to me." When she moved toward another chair on the family's private deck, he tensed. "Not here," he added, stopping her in her tracks.

Her expression, as she slowly faced him, reflected a blend of embarrassment, hurt, and offense. Luke experienced a flash of guilt for his harshness, but he truly was in no mood for company.

Without another word to him, she marched down the steps to the sidewalk accessing the marina. She settled on the top step and cast him a withering sideways glance. Drawing her knees to her chest and resting her arms on top of her bent legs, she turned her gaze out to the beach. Calmly, she watched the activity of the pier and began her wait.

And Luke resumed his brooding.

Pulling his right hand from his pocket, he stared down at the offensive compression glove and bandages that hid his stump. The doctor had wanted to transplant a toe to replace his thumb, but Luke had flatly refused. Having no thumb suited him better than the freakish-looking, Frankenstein-configuration the doctor proposed.

A toe on his hand? *Hell no.* Weren't his disfigurements horrid enough without playing cut and paste?

Aaron had tried to convince him the eye patch made him look like a bad-ass. Luke knew better.

Acid burned in his stomach. He didn't deserve this. Why did he have to be cursed with a broken body the rest of his life? Since returning from the hospital, he'd buried his confusion, his frustration, and his grief under layers of hostility and sarcasm. He didn't like the man he'd become, but it served his purpose. His nastiness kept people away.

Inside, behind closed doors, he could shut out the world. He could mope and fume, and no one bothered him. And that was just how he wanted it.

Aaron and their father, Bart, had learned to give him a wide berth. In fact, Miss Sunshine was the first person to say more than a few words to him in weeks.

Luke glanced over at the steps where she still waited.

While he watched her, the hollow ache he'd known deep in his soul even before his accident reared its head. The solitude he wanted seemed lonelier now than it had just minutes ago. A sense of futility accompanied the disturbing ache. The explosion had likely destroyed any chance of ever satisfying the emptiness that haunted him, and his encounter with the brunette brought that fact home in living color.

The void inside yawned wider, its darkness threatening to engulf him. He couldn't take this inner turmoil any longer. He had to find some peace, some escape… some hope.

❖ ❖ ❖

Abby Stanford watched the peaceful lapping of the waves by the pier and waited for the owners of the snorkeling shop to return. The beauty of the sparkling turquoise water and the wide blue sky soothed her aching soul. Even the quiet thumping of the boats against the wharf and squawk of sea gulls made a refreshing change from the din of traffic and choking exhaust in Dallas. Inhaling the salty scent of the Gulf, she commended herself for making the trip to Destin. Her husbandless honeymoon. She exhaled sharply, battling down the sting of what could have been. This time by herself, time to think, would help her put Steve's betrayal in perspective.

Alone along the white-sand beaches of the Florida Gulf Coast, maybe her broken heart would begin to heal.

*You obviously can't satisfy him the way I do.*

The well-endowed bimbo in Steve's bed had taken malicious glee in her distress. The jibe twisted the blade of Steve's betrayal, sharpening the pain that cut her to the marrow, and feeding her insecurities about her small size and boyish physique.

Renewed grief squeezed her chest, made it difficult to breathe.

Oh, God, she missed Steve. Or rather, she missed the man she'd thought he was. The man she'd fallen in love with in college. The man she'd given her virginity to. The man she'd wanted to spend her life with.

Had that man ever really existed? How could she have been so blind to the changes in him? And how could she move past the numbing disbelief, the surreal disconnected feeling, and the sharp flashes of pain when the harsh truth of their broken engagement crashed down on her again? Even remembering the happy times they'd had caused a bitter ache in her heart. Had it all been a lie?

Abby conjured her memory of the night fourteen months ago when Steve had proposed. The moment had been fairy-tale perfect, dreamily romantic. After a classy dinner in Reunion Tower, enjoying the 360-degree view of the Dallas lights, they'd returned to his apartment. Candles and cut flowers crowded his small living room. Steve had dropped to one knee and professed his love. From his coat pocket, he'd produced a diamond ring engraved with the night's date.

Abby's chest seized with bittersweet pain, remembering her squeal of surprised delight and their shared laughter when the champagne he'd chilled bubbled over onto his sofa.

How could the man who'd been so thoughtful, so romantic, so full of love have had such a complete change of heart fourteen months later?

Acid roiled in her stomach like the waves crashing on the beach, and she determinedly shoved the painful memory aside. This trip was about healing, about moving on. With the relaxation technique she taught her occupational therapy clients, she slowly breathed in the fresh sea air, letting the slow inhalation clear her mind and calm her frayed nerves. Given time, she would adjust to her new circumstances. She believed this mantra, which she used to encourage her patients on a daily basis. Just as her patients could learn to cope with their spinal injuries, she could survive the trauma of her broken engagement.

All she needed was the time to grieve, time to adjust, time to heal.

Abby checked her watch. The rude guy upstairs had said only a few minutes, but it had already been almost thirty.

With her arm, she wiped the perspiration beading on her forehead. The hot sun stung the tops of her legs, the first hint of a burn. Her discomfort and her frustration with her circular thoughts chipped away at her patience.

Cheerful whistling drew her attention to a man approaching the entrance of the snorkeling office from the pier. Abby brushed off the seat of her shorts, assessing the man as she traipsed down the steps toward him. The wind ruffled his short blond hair, and he wore electric-blue swimming trunks that set off the golden glow of his tanned chest. The flash of sunlight on metal called her attention to the stud earring in his left lobe. Generally she disliked earrings on men, but this guy pulled it off with style.

"Hello."

He turned his head to see who'd addressed him.

"Hi there." He added a dazzling white smile to his returned greeting. "Can I help you?"

Abby almost tripped when she saw him up close. The chiseled face, the bright smile, the earring. The total package was so... sexy. Stunningly so. "I... I had a reservation to go snorkeling at two." Snorkeling had been her idea, and when she'd told Steve she'd booked the excursion, his eyes had lit with anticipation. *Awesome, Abby! And let's look into parasailing, too. I've always wanted to try that.*

The sexy blond consulted his large, probably waterproof, watch and winced. "Ouch. Please tell me that you haven't been waiting here for half an hour."

He scrunched up his face, his expression playfully apprehensive and apologetic.

Grateful for the distraction from thoughts of Steve, Abby tipped her head, appraising his charmingly remorseful expression. "I don't like to lie."

"Yikes. That's what I was afraid of." Mr. Handsome rubbed his chin, where the first hint of gold stubble grew, and turned to go into the office.

Abby followed, pushing aside her nagging impatience. Her annoyance probably had more to do with her own situation.

And the ungracious treatment of the guy with the blue baseball cap and eye patch.

Normally, she let jerks like him roll off her back. As an occupational therapist, she dealt with enough grumpy clients to know how to shield herself from other folks' bad moods. Yet the guy had treated her with such needlessly cold disdain that he'd penetrated her usual defenses. Of course, thanks to Steve, her defenses were currently at an all-time low.

"Let me check the books and… uh…" He moved behind a glass counter with fishing gear and snorkeling equipment displayed in the case and dropped his keys next to the cash register. Pausing long enough to flip on a portable radio, he filled the room with the whining guitars of Aerosmith.

"Reservation book," he muttered to himself and began digging through reams of paper and miscellaneous clutter on the shelves lining the wall behind the counter. "I know it's around here somewhere."

Abby took a slow breath, determined not to lose what was left of her composure.

"Hang on just a minute. I'll be right back." He held up a finger and flashed her another brilliant smile. She agreed with a quick nod.

The blond hurried to an open door at the back of the shop. "Luke!" he shouted, ducking his head through the doorway. "Hey, Luke, get down here! Where'd you put the appointment book?"

"I haven't touched it!" a deep male voice called back.

"Well, I can't find it and—"

"That's your problem!"

The blond cast a chagrined smile toward her then pinched the bridge of his nose. He shuffled back to the shelf, muttering under his breath, and continued searching for the missing appointment book. Abby amused herself by browsing around the souvenirs available in the small office while he ransacked the area behind the counter. A movement near the back door caught her attention, and she looked up to find the gruff guy from the porch settling on a wooden stool near the back door. He met her gaze and gave her a curt nod, his expression blank.

"You work here?" She drew her brows together in a puzzled frown. Shifting her gaze to the man behind the counter, she questioned him with her glance.

Her handsome helper seemed equally confused. "You two have met?"

When the surly guy in the cap made no reply, Abby volunteered, "He was upstairs, out front when I arrived, and I asked him directions to the office."

The man with the blue cap turned what Abby considered a challenging glare on the handsome blond.

"So why'd you make her wait outside instead of

helping her?" When the blond received no response other than a grim stare, he scowled. "Luke? Answer me!"

Abby turned back to scan the postcard rack, uncomfortable with the visible tension between the two men. She felt oddly responsible for their disagreement.

"I could ask you the same question, Aaron. What the hell took you so long to get back?" A surprising hostility filled Luke's tone.

With a snort, Aaron turned back to his search for the appointment book. "I had a boat full of fishermen with me on a tour." His tone was quieter now but equally annoyed.

Abby peeked up at the two men from the postcard she'd plucked from the rack at random.

"You remember about customers, right? Working? The business?" Aaron aimed a finger at Luke and narrowed his gaze. "A business you still have a responsibility to, little brother."

"I'm hardly in a position to help." Luke slowly crossed his arms over his chest, and she noticed his bandaged hand and compression garment for the first time.

Coupled with the red scars on his neck and chin, the bandages piqued her curiosity. She'd wondered about his choice of long sleeves in May, but now she began to piece together a broader picture.

"Hell, man, I'm busting my ass trying to take the tours out and keep the office running at the same time. The least you can do is—"

"Is what, Aaron?" Luke snapped, rising to his feet. He assumed a defensive stance, balling his left hand at his side.

Abby shivered at the venom in his voice.

"What exactly do you expect me to do? Take groups out on a boat with an engine that's still blown to bits?

Write up contracts without a thumb?" He raised the injured hand for effect, and her stomach clenched.

No thumb?

She'd guessed Luke's injuries might be partly responsible for his bad mood. She'd worked with enough accident victims at the rehabilitation hospital to recognize his bitterness. Disabling accidents often left people angry and hostile. A sympathetic pang zinged through her chest. She hated seeing anyone hurt. And given her own circumstances, she sympathized with his pain.

Luke's tirade quieted his brother. Abby cast a glance toward Aaron and found him staring at his feet with a tortured expression darkening his face. She saw clearly that Aaron struggled with more than his temper. The suffering she read in his furrowed brow went deeper than the current argument.

Compassion twisted in her chest, squeezing her lungs. The scene before her was all too familiar.

Finally, Luke strode over to the counter where he yanked a black notebook from beneath the cash register. He slapped it on the counter with a thud. "Right where it always is, moron."

Aaron flexed and clenched his fist as if itching to slam it into his brother's jaw. He sucked in a deep breath and blew it out through pursed lips.

Luke's expression softened, transforming to one of guilt, and he pinched the bridge of his nose. "Sorry," he murmured as he stalked back to his stool.

Finally, Aaron looked at Abby, and she quickly turned away, uneasy with the tension between the brothers.

Aaron heaved a deep sigh before he spoke. "Sorry about that, ma'am. What did you say your name was?"

"I didn't." She flashed him an awkward smile as she walked back to the counter. "The name's Abby Stanford."

While Aaron flipped open the notebook and leafed to the right page, she hazarded a glance at Luke. He met her gaze with a penetrating one-eyed stare. The bright cerulean of his uncovered eye bore into her with an intensity that caused a flutter in her veins.

Without shifting his unnerving gaze, Luke removed his cap and raked his healthy left hand through dark-blond hair. He combed his almost shoulder-length hair behind his ears with his fingers before replacing his cap. The whole time, his unflinching gaze held her captive with its piercing heat. Like a blue flame, his gaze licked her, warmed her blood, kicked the flutter inside her up to a whirl. She dragged her attention away from his hypnotic stare. Her heartbeat raced as if she'd just completed her morning jog. Flattening her palms on the cool glass counter, she drew a deep breath for composure.

When she dropped her gaze to the reservation list Aaron studied, she spotted her listing and realized Aaron's problem with finding her name. "Oh, that's it. Mr. and Mrs. Steve Crenshaw."

Aaron glanced up, puzzled. "I thought you said Stanford."

"It is Stanford."

He arched an eyebrow. "I'm confused."

Sighing, she pulled the sunglasses off the top of her head and fidgeted with the earpiece. A sharp pang spun through her for what should have been. "I was supposed to be Mrs. Crenshaw by now. I'm on my honeymoon." Proud of the steady control she'd kept over her voice, she turned a defiant look toward Luke. "And, yes, I'm alone."

Luke's left eyebrow arched in a manner reminiscent of Aaron's gesture a moment before. As she studied Luke now, she recognized the family resemblance in his chiseled, square jaw, straight nose, and sensual lips. Despite the minor burn scars, which she knew would fade in time, Luke cut a breath-taking image. Her gaze lingered on his lips.

Lips made for kissing. Again her pulse spiked.

"You came on your honeymoon alone?"

Aaron's question served as a welcome distraction, and she faced him. Rather than the titillated curiosity she expected to find, Aaron's expression reflected an admiration she knew she didn't deserve.

"The tickets were non-refundable, and I needed to get away. I'm trying not to think about the fact that this was supposed to be our honeymoon. I'm here to put things in perspective, make a clean start."

"You've got guts, lady. Not many people would have the balls... uh, the *gumption* to do that." Aaron's sheepish grin apologized for his language.

"So what happened to your boyfriend?"

Abby turned a startled glance toward Luke.

"Oh, that's smooth, Dummy!" Aaron grunted and scowled at his brother.

"Same question you were dying to ask."

"But I had enough manners not to."

"Bite me."

She followed the exchange like a tennis match, her gaze shifting from one brother to the other as they swapped jibes.

"Don't you have something else to do besides offending our customers?" Aaron asked his brother.

"Her name was Cindy." Abby's comment won inquisitive looks from both men. "That's what happened to my boyfriend. Another woman."

Luke had the courtesy to look contrite.

Aaron winced. "Ouch."

"She had big breasts, long legs, and a bad attitude. And I caught them in bed." Abby bit her lip, uncertain where the confession came from, other than finding it the handiest way to stop the brothers' sniping.

"Double ouch." Aaron gave her a sympathetic grimace.

"Big boobs, huh?" Luke asked, and Aaron shot him a mortified look.

Still… she didn't detect the same hostility between the brothers now. The anxiety in her chest eased a little.

Willing to take his bait in good humor, Abby demonstrated Cindy's chest size with her hands. Teasing about the incident for a change felt good. Aaron rewarded her efforts with a chuckle.

A devilish spark lit Luke's good eye, and he scoffed. "Implants, no doubt."

Luke's dismissal of Cindy's fake breasts stirred an unexpected sense of vindication in Abby, easing the raw ache that gnawed deep inside her. Seizing the lighter mood, she faced Aaron and lifted her chin. "Now, before I decide that the two of you are jerks like Steve, what are you going to do about the snorkeling trip I should have taken at two?"

He propped a hip against the counter, and she read an unspoken appreciation in his smile. "Tell you what. If you give us a chance to honor our commitment—say tomorrow at ten when we have another group scheduled to go out—then it'll be on the house to make up for your wait today."

She bit a fingernail as if considering his offer, though the decision was easy. "Well, okay."

With a wink, Aaron angled the appointment book to write in it. When he finished penciling in Abby's name, he tossed the notebook on the cluttered shelf behind him.

"Um, I think that's supposed to go under the register," Abby said with a glance toward Luke. The corner of Luke's lips twitched with the hint of a grin, and a tingle skittered over her skin. She could easily imagine when he allowed himself to smile fully, his face would light with the same engaging warmth as Aaron's did.

"So, Abby," Aaron said as he moved the notebook to its proper place. "What kind of plans do you have for tonight?"

Luke's grin faded, his expression clouding. When he shifted his gaze to Aaron, Luke's face hardened with resentment. She barely registered Aaron's question as she puzzled over the abrupt change in Luke's mood.

The glimpse of Luke's good humor had tantalized her, and its disappearance produced a poignant regret. "I, uh…"

Luke rose from the stool with a grunt, his expression black, and he stormed out through the back door. She stared at the empty seat, a sense of loss skirting the edges of her thoughts.

Attributing her melancholy to the earlier discussion of Steve's misdeed, she turned her gaze back to Aaron and shook her head. "I'm sorry. What?"

"I said what are your plans for tonight?" His tone matched the Cheshire cat grin he wore.

A bit startled by his question and what it implied, she only gaped at him for a moment. This man was gorgeous. Surely she wasn't the type of woman he'd typically notice. She deemed her face nothing more than average looking. And her body? Well, hadn't Steve sought a ravishing blond to take her place? "I… I don't know. Nothing much."

"Good. How about dinner, then?"

Her first impulse was to tell him no. Her instincts warned her that Aaron had honed his winning smile and charm on numerous other women. She wagered he was a smooth operator, a womanizer, and, therefore, not the type of man she had any business dating. Steve had proven the risk of involvement with anyone other than a one-woman man. Besides, she simply wasn't ready to start dating again. Her wounds were too fresh, too raw.

Then it dawned on her. He was offering a pity date. He'd made her wait for half an hour, his brother had been blatantly rude, and she'd broadcast the fact that she was alone on her honeymoon. Obviously, he'd felt he should take pity on her and offer her his company.

She glanced down at the merchandise in the glass display and shrugged. "Uh, it's nice of you to ask, but I don't—"

"Are you turning me down?" When Abby glanced up at him, he gave her a comically heartbroken look.

"You don't really mean—"

"I'll pick you up at six. Where are you staying?"

Abby opened her mouth to protest. She'd never been one to let herself be bullied or coerced into doing something she didn't want to do. Yet after she gawked at him for a moment, she heard herself answer, "Sandestin Resort."

"Okay. I'll meet you at the front door to the lobby."

"B-but—"

"I'll see you at six." He winked at her, and before she could voice an objection, he turned his attention to another customer who'd slipped into the office without her noticing.

Stunned by the turn of events, she watched him converse with a man who'd come in to buy a wetsuit. Her limbs felt a little numb, and her mind whirled.

She could back out of the date, of course. He couldn't force her to go out to dinner. Although when she considered it, she could think of a lot of worse things than being kidnapped for an evening out by a gorgeous man like Aaron.

As she walked to the door, she cast a glance over her shoulder letting it all sink in.

Dinner. With a gorgeous man.

One date wouldn't hurt anything, would it? After all, she had come to Destin to put her life in perspective and move beyond the lingering hurt of Steve's infidelity. What better way to soothe the sting of rejection than the attention of another man?

# Chapter 2

AT PRECISELY SIX O'CLOCK, ABBY ARRIVED AT THE front door of the hotel and watched a red, recent-model Mustang wheel in from the highway and speed up the driveway. Even before Aaron stepped out, she knew the sports car had to belong to her date. After all, Aaron was the sports car model among men. If only recent events hadn't left her feeling like an Edsel.

As he walked around to open the door for her, he appraised her with a sweeping glance. Arching an eyebrow, he flashed her a bright smile. "Wow, you look great, Abby."

The compliment shocked her. She'd spent longer than usual fixing her hair and make up, wanting to impress him, but didn't feel the results of her efforts warranted the enthusiasm in his voice. She gave him an appreciative grin just the same.

Aaron sported a pair of pleated khaki pants and a bright orange golf shirt. She couldn't imagine Steve ever wearing such a loud shirt, yet it suited Aaron. Like the gold stud in his earlobe, he pulled it off with panache. But then, Aaron could probably wear a striped polyester suit and make it look good. Whereas Steve—

She stopped herself and shook off the thought. She couldn't spend the night comparing Aaron to Steve. Forget Steve and move on.

"Hope you're hungry. The place we're going has great food."

She nodded. "Starved."

"Great." Aaron zoomed down the driveway and darted into traffic.

Abby clutched her seat as Aaron wove through the other cars. She tugged her seat belt tighter after he narrowly missed scraping a van that pulled onto the highway in front of them. She didn't draw an easy breath until he turned into the crowded parking lot of a restaurant resembling a wharf.

She read the sign out front aloud in amusement. "Fudpucker's?" She cast a sideways glance at him. "Is it just me or does that name sound a little… suggestive?"

"Definitely suggestive," he said, laughing. "But don't let it worry you. You're safe with me."

The devilish glint in his eyes made her doubt the sincerity of his assurance, and her stomach quivered. Aaron escorted her inside with his hand at the small of her back. The gesture seemed awfully intimate to Abby for a first date, yet his possessive touch also made her feel feminine and desirable, a balm to her bruised ego. Steve may have preferred Cindy in his bed, but at least for tonight, Aaron wanted to be near her, wanted to touch her. That thought gave her inordinate pleasure.

The restaurant proved to be a trendy, loud place where patrons were encouraged to leave graffiti on the walls and tables. Everything from birdcages to antique bicycles and inflatable beach toys decorated the interior. The corrugated tin ceiling, exposed pipes, and wood plank floors created the ambiance of dining in a warehouse. Abby smiled, realizing the personality of the restaurant matched what she knew of her date. Both were invitingly casual, stylishly eclectic, and charmingly captivating.

As they were shown to their table, Aaron greeted several of the hostesses and female servers by name. A few of the women eyed Abby with a cool disdain akin to jealousy, confirming her suspicion that Aaron made the rounds of the women in town. Whatever pleasure she'd received from his intimate touch withered. This was a pity date, she reminded herself, and tomorrow Aaron would move on to his next conquest.

*You obviously can't satisfy him the way I do.* Cindy's taunt snuck up from the dark corners of her memory to bite her again. She swallowed hard to squelch the bitter taste rising in her throat.

"So where are you from, Abby?" Aaron gave the wine list a cursory glance before pushing it aside.

She opened her menu and pretended to study it while she regained control over her voice. "Dallas."

"Yeah? Love the Cowboys."

"I presume you mean the football team?"

He flashed a sultry grin. "Actually I prefer the cheer-leaders, but the football team's all right, too."

Abby resisted the urge to roll her eyes. Steve was a rabid Cowboys fan, and his enthusiasm had rubbed off on her. Abby's thoughts flashed to the many Sunday afternoons they'd spent curled up together on her sofa, eating popcorn or chicken wings and watching the Cowboys play. More than the football, Abby had enjoyed the time alone with Steve. They'd had precious little time alone together in the last year as they each built their fledgling careers.

She shook off the memory as Aaron told her about the professional football quarterback who hailed from the area and joked about the group of old men he'd taken fishing that day. His easy banter soon turned to laughter and teasing, and even before the food arrived, Abby was glad she'd come. Aaron had kept her from dwelling on Steve for a full twenty minutes.

With Aaron, smiling came easily, and she hadn't had a good reason to smile in… too long. For that reason alone, she owed her date a debt of thanks.

Once their meals arrived, Abby broached the subject that had plagued her all afternoon. "Tell me about your brother."

"My brother?" Aaron clapped a hand over his heart and winced. "Ouch. Should I be jealous that you'd rather talk about my brother than me?"

She raised a hand and shook her head. "I don't mean it like that. I… What's the story with him?"

"The story?" For the first time that night, Aaron's grin faltered. "Meaning what?"

For a moment, she thought about changing the subject in deference to the jovial mood that had slipped away.

"I just mean he seemed awfully…" She searched for a word that would describe Luke's surliness without offending his brother.

"Pissed at the world?" Aaron supplied when she hesitated.

"All right. But remember that's your term, not mine."

They both quieted as the waitress approached their table. "Can I bring you folks anything else from the bar tonight? Happy hour is almost over."

After Abby ordered a second glass of white wine, Aaron gave the waitress a bright smile and ordered another beer. Abby noticed, to her consternation, that Aaron's eyes raked over their server's curves as she walked away. She cleared her throat loudly, drawing his attention.

"Hm?"

"You were saying that Luke is mad at the world. Why?"

"Well, that's not quite what I said, but…" His smile faded, and he stared at the table for a minute. "There was an accident this spring. A bad one."

He explained how a fuel leak had contributed to an explosion that injured Luke, and her stomach twisted.

When he looked up at her, Aaron's tortured expression mirrored the one he'd worn that afternoon during his argument with his brother. Her heart went out to him, both for his suffering and his brother's. She'd seen plenty of anguish in other people through her job, had been trained to deal with it. Yet given her own recent upheaval, she felt a special connection to Aaron. To Luke. A shared pain.

"You know," she started hesitantly, weighing the wisdom of offering her unsolicited opinion, "Luke's moodiness is understandable, considering the changes in his life. The physical pain alone is enough to make someone grumpy, but he's got a lot of other things to sort out, too. A trauma like the one he survived shakes a person's whole outlook on life."

"I guess." Aaron pasted on a smile for the waitress as she brought their drinks.

Abby wondered how much of her experience and advice on the subject she dared to give. More than anything, she wanted to help ease Aaron's pain. Her innate desire to help people had driven her choice of careers. Occupational therapy served as an outlet for her need to care for people, and the strenuous demands of the job appealed to her athletic nature.

While she sipped her new glass of wine, deciding whether or not to give Aaron any suggestions for helping Luke, she glanced at her date. She found his gaze fixed on the ample bust of their waitress. His audacity aroused her ire, chafed the still raw wound of Steve's infidelity. She kicked his shin under the table.

"Ouch!" He winced and reached down to rub his offended leg.

She ignored the quizzical look he gave her as if she had no idea what had happened. "Can I ask you a personal question?"

"I thought you already had." His lopsided grin told her he didn't mind.

Never one to shy from a challenge, Abby dived into deep waters with him without waiting for his permission. "You blame yourself for Luke's accident, don't you?"

She focused a concerned look on him, and he shifted in his chair like a guilty schoolboy. "You're pretty perceptive."

"Thank you."

Aaron hesitated, then sighed. "Yeah. It's my fault." The grief shadowing his blue eyes broke her heart. "I was supposed to have fixed the fuel leak that caused the explosion." He paused. "Luke blames me, too. I know he does. He yells at everyone and gripes all the time. But I catch the worst of it. He hates me now."

She flattened her palm on the cool varnished tabletop and chose her words carefully. "Try to understand where he's coming from. His life's been turned upside down, and his body's been torn apart and disfigured. It's really not uncommon for a person suffering from a recent trauma or loss to look for someone to blame. But that doesn't make it your fault."

He lifted his gaze, tilting his head and eyeing her with new interest. "You sound like you're speaking from experience."

She smiled. "More experience than you probably think. Besides recently being dumped by my fiancé, I happen to be an occupational therapist. I work with people whose lives have been altered by accidents like your brother's all the time. So most of what you're describing to me isn't news. It's very common." She paused. "Including the guilt you're feeling."

He seemed startled by her assessment.

"It's written all over your face, Aaron."

"I'm that transparent?"

She chuckled. "Not transparent. Human."

Aaron's expression softened as if relieved to have his feelings validated.

"I know you hate seeing the pain your brother is in. Anyone would. It's normal to feel a little bad that you weren't the one who was hurt instead. It's called survivor guilt."

He rubbed the back of his neck, his expression meditative.

After a moment, a smile spread across his face, and he met Abby's gaze, his blue eyes bright and alive. For several seconds, he simply grinned at her. Having his full attention, having his smile shining at her alone, warmed her inside even as she told herself it wouldn't last.

There'd been a time early in her relationship with Steve when she'd commanded his whole attention, been his sole focus. But work, and family, and outside commitments intervened, and his attention became more sporadic. She'd dismissed the changes as inevitable in any relationship, but had there been more to his growing distance?

"You are something else." Aaron's voice called her out of her musing. "You took off by yourself on your honeymoon. You held your own with my brother's foul mood." He gestured with his hands as he spoke, turning up his palms. "And tonight, in ten minutes, you've helped me feel better about what happened to Luke than I could with all my rationalizing for the past month."

She dismissed his compliment with a shrug. "That's because you consider me an unbiased third party. I'm saying the same things you've been thinking and feeling, which gives them more credence and allows your conscience to—"

"Whoa, slow down! That's a little more analytical than I generally like to get on a first date." He chuckled and leaned toward her, his voice dipping to an intimate murmur. "So tell me, Abby. Did you have someone you considered an unbiased third party to talk to after the fiancé and Ms. Big Breasts"—he paused to make the same hand gesture in front of his chest that Abby had that afternoon—"turned your life upside down?"

She forced a grin. Would she ever be able to think about that night without wanting to throw up? Calming the riot of emotions inside her with a deep breath, she tucked her hands under her chin and propped her elbows on the table.

"A couple of good friends gave me their shoulders to cry on. I hated to say too much to them about my problems with Steve, though, because my friends had known both of us since before we started dating. In fact, our mutual friends introduced us, so... it was awkward all around. But…" She felt her throat tighten and stopped. "I don't want to talk about Steve. After all, I'm out with you tonight, right?"

"Damn straight!" Aaron gave her a confident nod and raised his drink to her. She clinked her glass to his and managed to laugh at the devilish smirk and wink he gave her. Just that easily, Aaron restored the light-hearted mood that carried through the rest of their meal.

Her date's charm and humor proved a better medicine for her wounded spirit than she could have imagined. When the waitress took her plate away, Abby was surprised to realize how much dinner she'd eaten. Aaron had managed to distract her from her own troubles long enough to eat a full meal. Steve's betrayal had killed her appetite, among other things. Yet tonight, in one sitting, she'd eaten more than she had in the weeks since she broke her engagement. That was progress.

After dinner, Aaron drove them back to the beach house where she'd met him and Luke that afternoon.

"You have a beautiful home, Aaron. Your snorkeling business is obviously doing well."

He glanced at her as he cut the ignition. "It does okay. Started out more as a hobby for my dad, but it grew. The snorkeling company isn't our main income, though, if that's what you're thinking."

"Oh?"

"In the off-season—that'd be October through March or April, roughly—I work for a construction crew, building the new hotels and such that are flooding into the area."

"As in, the really tall hotel they're framing down the road? Isn't that dangerous, working that high up?"

He grinned. "Yeah. I love it. The higher the better. Besides, we wear safety equipment. Then one year I worked repairing boats in dry dock. Whatever strikes my mood in the fall."

"And Luke?"

"Luke again." He scowled. "My brother designs web pages and helps new businesses set up computer systems. Freelance. Gives him a lot of flexibility, since he's his own boss."

"I guess so. Must be nice."

Aaron opened his door. "So, like to come in for a little while? There's someone I want you to meet."

"If you mean your brother, I already met him, and he didn't like me very much."

"Are you kidding? He loved you."

She guffawed. "How do you figure that?"

"Because I saw the grin he gave you after the exchange about your fiancé." Aaron aimed his car key at her as he spoke, and his expression grew serious. "You're the only person in weeks who's gotten more than a frown out of him. And the fact that he hung out in the store while you were there says something. He hasn't set foot in there since the accident. And crude as it may have been, he was trying to be funny with his implants comment. Trust me. Something you said or did today got through to him."

"Well, I'm flattered, but—"

"But," Aaron interrupted, holding up a finger, "that's not who I had in mind for you to meet." He climbed out of the car before she could ask any more questions and came around to her door to help her out.

"You've given me an idea with all your therapist talk at dinner. I want you to meet Bart."

She sent him a puzzled look. "Bart? Another brother?"

He shook his head. "My dad. Bart teaches business finance and economics at a local college during the school year—only because he loves it and would be bored if he didn't do something. He's built a small fortune off his investments. Bart's a genius with the stock market and has helped Luke and me invest some, too. Ol' Bart could live off his investments alone."

Abby made no comment on the fact that Aaron called his father by his first name, though it told her a great deal about his family. In her family, calling her career military father anything other than Dad or Sir was unthinkable, disrespectful. She also noticed he hadn't mentioned meeting his mother and wondered if Mom was still in the picture.

She followed him inside a split-level, luxuriously decorated—though definitely masculine—beach house. He led her up a short flight of stairs to the living room where large picture windows overlooking the gulf and pier comprised the better part of two walls. A stand lamp at the end of the sofa provided a golden glow in the room and created a homey warmth.

"Have a seat and make yourself at home," Aaron said, gesturing to a long leather sofa under one window. Across from it were two recliners, positioned at angles to a coffee table spread with financial and news magazines. He dropped his keys on the coffee table. "I'll be right back."

Remembering how he'd searched for the appointment book, she grinned, picturing Aaron scouring the house later trying to recall where he'd tossed his keys.

Abby strolled to the wide window and gazed out at the night-darkened beach. She couldn't see much of the view because a bright fluorescent light behind her created a glare on the window.

And captured Luke's reflection.

A long breakfast bar with three stools separated an airy, white-tiled kitchen from the living room. Luke stood in the adjoining kitchen, silently watching her with an intense and heated stare that sent a tremor through her. With a fortifying breath, she pivoted on her toe to face him.

"Hi, Luke." She flashed him a friendly smile.

He'd forsaken the blue cap, and she could better see the thick, dark-blond hair he wore just shy of shoulder-length and tucked behind his ears. His black eye-patch gave him a rakish, dangerous appearance that roused a quiver deep inside her. He still wore the long-sleeved T-shirt and sweat pants he'd worn earlier, but she glimpsed a compression vest peeking out from the T-shirt's neckline, evidence of the burns still healing on his broad and muscular torso.

"I didn't see you when I came in," she said by means of apology for not speaking to him sooner. But then, he hadn't made his presence known either. "I'm Abby. From this afternoon…"

"I remember." The heat in his gaze turned icy.

Despite his chilly reception, Abby headed to the breakfast bar and sat down on the first stool.

Luke turned his back and resumed whatever task she'd apparently interrupted when she came in. Leaning to see around him, she spotted the bread and jars he worked with, clumsily using his left hand and his bandaged and gloved right hand. She considered offering to help him, but she knew from experience that she'd be flatly and rudely turned down.

Besides, he needed to learn to do things for himself, and each task that he completed in the next few weeks, no matter how simple, would help rebuild his confidence and improve his mood.

"What kind of sandwich are you making?"

He sent her a quelling look as he screwed the lid back on the peanut butter and returned it to the cabinet above his head.

"Tuna." His tone dripped sarcasm.

"Mmm," Abby teased, "peanut butter and tuna. Sounds delicious."

His sneer told her he didn't find her amusing.

To her surprise, he took a seat next to her at the breakfast bar and launched into the first of two sandwiches with a large bite. He ate in silence for a minute while she studied his profile. Then, eyeing him carefully for his reaction, she walked her fingers across the bar toward his other sandwich and poised her hand ready to pinch off a bite.

He cast a curious glance her direction.

"May I?"

He set his face with a surly frown. "Didn't my brother feed you on your hot date tonight?"

"Yeah, but... I'm curious what kind of cook you are."

"Cook?" He snorted. "It's a crummy peanut butter and jelly sandwich!"

"Jelly?" She tried to sound shocked and disappointed. "You said it had tuna!" Taking his answering silence as consent, she pinched off a corner of the second sandwich and popped it into her mouth. "Mm, not bad. Just enough peanut butter and plenty of jelly. Just the way I like 'em."

"Get your own," he growled.

When Abby chuckled, he paused in the motion of bringing his sandwich to his mouth. He cut another sideways glance at her, and she saw the flicker of reluctant amusement in the blue eye that peered over at her. She smiled at him and watched his mouth for a hint of a reciprocal grin.

His full, sensuous mouth. The unbidden thought made her breath catch in her throat. Oh, yes, he certainly had lips made for kissing.

The corner of his mouth moved the slightest bit, barely dimpling his cheek, but it was close enough to a smile for her. While he took another bite of his sandwich, she looked for a topic of conversation. "So I hear you're a computer geek."

His startled glance hardened to a glare. "Yeah, that's me. A real Poindexter. A laptop, a joystick, and a hard drive. My idea of heaven."

The way he held her gaze, something smoky and smoldering in his eye, told her they weren't talking about computers anymore. Her breath backed up in her lungs.

Finally he turned away, and she drew a restorative breath. Steve had never stolen her breath with just a look.

"Stop it," she scolded under her breath.

"Hm?"

"I said… Aaron told me about your accident. I'm sorry."

Luke's face became rigid and cold again, and he tossed his sandwich on his plate with a huff. "Oh, did he?" The question held a bitter edge. He turned an icy stare on her. "What exactly did he say?"

"Just that a boat engine exploded, and you were injured." Her gaze flickered to the red scars on his neck.

Luke scowled, then got up abruptly and stormed back into the kitchen. Opening the refrigerator, he snatched out a beer.

"I guess he conveniently left out the fact that if he'd done his job right, the accident might never have happened." Anger vibrated from him, his tone dark.

"No, he didn't leave that out," she returned calmly. "And he feels terrible about it. I could see that in his face even before he said anything."

Luke's stony expression said he didn't believe her. He took a long drink of his beer, then walked over to the counter in front of the bar, where he fumbled to open a medicine bottle. He shook a pill onto the counter. After setting the bottle down, he used the same hand to pick up the tablet and put it in his mouth. His awkwardness plucked at her compassion.

Luke washed the drug down with a swig of beer.

Abby read the prescription label and frowned. "You really shouldn't drink alcohol while you're taking painkillers."

"You really should mind your own business."

"You know, you can ask the pharmacist not to use the child-proof caps and that would make it easier for you to—"

"I said mind your own business!"

The resentment in his tone stung. She'd only wanted to help.

"Where is Aaron, anyway? And why'd he leave you in here?" Luke stormed over to the leather sofa and flopped down hard.

Abby saw him wince, an indication of the pain his angry movement had cost him. Her heart ached for him and his obvious suffering, both physical and emotional.

"So what happened with the boyfriend to make him go to the hot blond?"

She had experience with her patients lashing out. Clearly Luke was retaliating with his bluntness for her probing in his business. Maybe even trying to alleviate his own pain by shifting the focus to her misfortune. Yet even knowing his intent, his jibe hit its mark. Her doubts and insecurities that maybe Steve had strayed because she was somehow lacking sliced through her with razor claws.

*Don't be silly,* her best friend Brooke had told her more than once. *This is Steve's doing. Not yours. You are beautiful, Abby, inside and out.*

Right. What else would Brooke say?

Squaring her shoulders, she tried to hide the raw emotions swirling inside her. "I'd rather not talk about Steve."

Luke scoffed. "So you can talk about what happened to me, what I should or shouldn't drink, how my brother feels about me… but *your* life is taboo? Kinda hypocritical, don't you think, *Abby?*" He said her name as if it were a curse.

She met his angry glare silently. His unpatched blue eye bore into her, as if he could see into her soul. For a moment they just stared at each other. Two wounded spirits. Two shattered lives. And something inside her stirred. She wanted to reach out to him, wanted to tell him he wasn't alone. She wanted to tell him she understood what he was suffering.

"Touché," she said at last.

He seemed startled by her concession and turned his gaze away to take another long drink of his beer.

"I don't know what happened, what changed…" She whispered the admission, but her voice seemed obscenely loud in the quiet room. "I've asked myself the same question a hundred times in the past weeks, but I have no answer."

He studied her again, and his expression reflected a hint of remorse for having brought up a clearly painful subject. "If you ask me—"

"I didn't."

His expression hardened. "If you ask me, the guy was a jerk and unworthy of you."

Despite his gruff delivery, her heart lurched at the unexpected compliment. "Thank you."

"Abby." Aaron's voice came from behind her, and she turned. "This is my father, Bart Morgan. Bart, this is the woman I was telling you about, Abby Stanford."

"You've been talking about me behind my back?" She flashed Aaron a teasing grin.

Aaron's gaze flicked briefly to Luke. "What do you say we go on the deck to talk? It's a pretty night. Good breeze."

Clearly he didn't want to talk in front of Luke. Which probably meant they wanted to talk *about* Luke. If that much was obvious to her, she was sure it was equally obvious to Luke. Her chest tightened in sympathy for him and what he was sure to view as a slight against him.

She followed Aaron and his father out to the deck at the back of the house.

Bart Morgan had to be in his mid-fifties in order to have fathered two boys in their late twenties, yet he looked more like an older brother. He had the same tight, muscled build and blond good looks. His gray eyes reflected a friendly warmth when he smiled at her and motioned for her to sit at an umbrella table on the deck.

"Miss Stanford, Aaron tells me you're an occupational therapist." Bart started the discussion without a lot of preamble. She liked that about him. His desire to get to the business at hand and not keep her wondering was courteous, in her view. She always preferred that people be straight with her and not skirt around issues to spare her feelings.

"That's right." Her gaze flicked to Aaron briefly, then back to Bart.

"I know this may sound rather rash to you, and perhaps even a bit crazy. But please understand, we are desperate to do anything that will help Luke."

"I thought this might have something to do with him." She shifted uneasily in her chair.

"Aaron had the idea—and I agreed—that you might be just what Luke needs to help him through this rough spot. Adjusting to what happened to him has been hard for him, and he's—"

"Pissed at the world," Aaron put in, and Abby smiled knowingly at him.

"Again, your term, not mine."

"What I'm trying to ask, though not very well it seems, is—" Bart leaned forward, an earnest appeal in his eyes. "Would you consider extending your stay in Destin and coming to work for us?"

# Chapter 3

ABBY COULDN'T BELIEVE HER EARS. "WORK FOR YOU?"

"As Luke's private therapist." Now Aaron leaned toward her with an eagerness and expectancy that unsettled her.

She divided her stunned glance between the two men, blinking her disbelief. With a deep breath, she flattened her palms against the cool metal table, searching for a logical response to their outlandish proposal. Their hopeful expressions told her how desperately they wanted her to agree, and she hated the idea of quashing their expectations.

"I'm not the person for this job. Luke's injuries aren't within my area of specialty. I work with patients who have spinal cord injuries. I teach them to walk again, when that's possible, and help them with exercises to regain lower body strength." Abby paused and chewed her lower lip. "An occupational therapist trained in hand rehabilitation and burn injuries would be better equipped to help him. That and maybe a few sessions with a counselor—"

"But he responds to you, Abby," Aaron interrupted. "He's refused to go to a shrink, and we don't know how to help him with what he's going through. Because of your experience with accident victims, you understand what's happening to him and what's going on in his head."

"I never said I knew what was in his head," she countered, holding up a hand in denial.

Bart reached across the table and closed his hand around hers. "Please, Miss Stanford, if what Aaron says is true—and I have no reason to doubt it is—you've already accomplished more with Luke than we have in almost a month."

Coupled with his grip on her hand, his appeal fell just short of begging, and the desperation and love for Luke she saw in his eyes broke her heart.

Shaking her head, she searched for a tactful way to refuse their pleas. Her innate desire to help and heal battled her practical nature, twisting inside her and pulling her in two directions. She could research hand therapy, maybe consult her colleagues in Texas who knew that field…

"I'm prepared to pay you well," Bart said.

"Money isn't the issue." Abby gave Bart a mournful look, wishing she could make him understand her position without hurting him. The fact that he so urgently wanted help for Luke endeared him to her. "And as I said, Luke doesn't need the kind of therapy I—"

"Then call yourself an unbiased third party who just wants to help him get through a rough time."

She swung her gaze to Aaron, startled to hear her own words being tossed back at her. But was she as unbiased as she needed to be to accept this job and remain professional? How could she be, when she'd already allowed herself to identify with Luke's pain? She understood his doubts and fears after having the world he knew and trusted shift under him. She empathized with his desire for isolation, for time to lick his wounds. Wasn't that what she was doing here in Florida?

"I'm not licensed to work in Florida," she said, trying another angle.

"Does that have to be a problem?" Bart sighed. "What if I sign something saying I understand this is not a professional job but more of a... personal favor for friends? We can keep it on the down low, arrange the terms however you need to feel comfortable with it."

"I don't know..."

"I know what we've proposed is unorthodox." Bart released her hand and dragged his palms over his haggard face. "I would do whatever it took to help my son, Miss Stanford." His grave tone mirrored his darkening expression, as if he sensed her inevitable rejection of their offer. But when his concern for his son was so great, how could she turn them down?

"Why me? Surely there is someone in town who could do the job better than I could."

"Abby, he smiled for you today. If you knew the mood he'd been in, if you knew how stubborn my brother can be, if you had any idea how significant that smile was—" Aaron hesitated, raking his fingers through his hair as he searched for the words to explain his point.

A stab of regret spiraled through her chest. But how could she possibly accept such a crazy offer? If Luke's injuries were within her specialty, if she lived in town, if she thought she could really make a difference, maybe...

"You reached him today like no one else has. I don't know why. I don't care why, as long as you can help Luke." Aaron's frustration vibrated in the evening air as he flopped back in his chair and sighed.

"He's refused every other attempt we've made," Bart continued when Aaron finished. "We've tried to get him physical therapy, tried to lift his spirits, tried to encourage him. I can afford to get the best medical and psychological help available, but he refuses the help he needs. He's shut us out. He won't budge."

When Bart paused for a breath, pain filled his eyes. "I'm afraid I'm losing him, Miss Stanford," he added, his voice cracking.

Abby closed her eyes and turned away, unable to bear the guilt and remorse for having to let these men down. She felt their pain to her marrow but was at a loss how she could possibly help them. She could barely handle her own grief without taking on their problems as well.

"I already have a job in Texas. I'm only here on vacation." She spoke her thoughts, her rationalizations, aloud without meaning to. Turning back to them, she tipped her head in query. "How would you explain to him the reason why I—someone he knows is a tourist—was suddenly hanging around the house all the time? Don't you think that any influence I may have over him now would disappear if he knew you'd hired me to help him?"

Bart and Aaron exchanged worried glances.

"We'd think up something to tell him," Aaron said, shrugging.

"You'd lie to him?" The idea of deceiving Luke appalled her, and she shook her head.

"Then how do you feel about helping out in the snorkeling office?" Bart asked. "You could help customers and take reservations a few hours each day, and if you just happened to spend some time talking with Luke, helping him with the exercises his last OT prescribed…"

Aaron's face brightened, and he nodded his approval of the idea.

"I don't know. There's still my job in Texas…"

"Can't you take a leave of absence or something?" Aaron winced as soon as he made the request, as if he realized how selfish his suggestion sounded.

Yet his idea of a leave of absence rolled through her mind, tantalizing her with its possibilities. The rehabilitation hospital where she worked offered limited personal leave without pay as one of her benefits. She'd already considered taking an extended trip to visit her parents in Virginia, to regroup and to nurse her broken heart.

Sometimes helping others in need helped put her own troubles in perspective. Her pulse thumped in her ears. Could she heal herself and help Luke at the same time? If she shifted her focus to healing Luke's spirit, would that same healing energy soothe her own tumult?

Helping Luke would require her to spend lots of time with him, with his piercing gaze and his distracting lips. Remembering Luke's fierce stare brought a prickly heat to her skin, and she fidgeted, uncomfortable with the prospect of spending any length of time with his keen, one-eyed scrutiny. His gaze saw too much, left her feeling raw and exposed. Vulnerable.

"Please, Abby."

The sound of Aaron's voice brought her back to the proposition at hand.

"Oh, Aaron, I don't know. You've given me a lot to think about." She rubbed her temple and frowned.

Rehabilitate Luke? The challenge tempted her. The prospect of helping this family appealed to her. But the idea of spending so much time in Luke's presence struck fear in her heart. She couldn't shake the feeling that Luke posed a vague, unidentified threat.

Something in that intense gaze of his rattled her to the core.

Scoffing to herself, she dismissed the idea as absurd. She'd grown up with two brothers who teased her mercilessly. She handled belligerent patients on a daily basis and held her own with the men at work when they harassed her. She could handle Luke.

Abby realized her hands were shaking, and she clutched them in her lap to stop their trembling.

"Please, Miss Stanford, I don't know what else to do for Luke. If you could have known him before the accident... He was so full of life and good humor. Seeing him like this is the hardest thing I've ever had to endure." Bart hung his head and sighed.

"I need more time to think about it. If I did agree, it would have to be strictly informal, unofficial. And even then you'd have to be clear that I'm not a psychologist or a hand therapist. All I could contribute to Luke's recovery is my personal perspective and the same kind of assistance with his therapy exercises that any family member could do."

Bart lifted his head again, and his expression brightened. "But you will think about it?"

Abby gave him a reassuring smile and nodded. How could she help but think about it? Already her mind raced, considering the challenge for her and the potential for real progress and healing for this family.

Hope blossomed inside her. She could give Luke the tools—or at least a starting place—to put his life back on track. "I'll give you my answer tomorrow, once I sleep on it."

"Cool." Aaron flashed her a devastating grin. Turning to Bart, he arched a golden eyebrow, his cocky self-assurance back in place. "You can eat dinner with us tomorrow night. We'll work out the details and run it by Luke then."

She hesitated, remembering how Aaron had railroaded her into their date. "All right. But I'm not promising anything. I haven't said yes."

"Yet. But you will." Aaron's eyes lit with mischief and seduction. "I have practice getting pretty women to tell me yes."

Abby studied the gleam in her date's eyes, and her sense of being in dangerous, deep waters returned with a vengeance.

Luke watched through the living room window as Aaron and Bart huddled with Abby. He couldn't see well enough to read their expressions, but he didn't have to be a genius to know they weren't discussing the weather or the "good breeze," as Aaron so lamely put it. He knew with an unsettling certainty that they were talking about him. Abby had already admitted that Aaron had talked about him and the accident on their cozy little dinner date.

Humiliation and anger gnawed his stomach. Knowing that his family dared to go behind his back this way, discussing him with a stranger, made him ill.

Aaron's callous indiscretion was bad enough, but now Bart had joined the discussion, throwing in his opinion on his son's miserable condition. Damn them! He clenched his teeth so hard his jaw hurt.

Luke downed the rest of his beer, then rolled the bottle in the fingers of his left hand.

*You really shouldn't drink alcohol when you're taking painkillers.* Abby's warning echoed in his mind. He knew she was right, but he stubbornly shoved aside the nagging truth. Who did the nosy chick think she was, telling him what to do? She'd shut her bossy little mouth fast enough when he turned the tables on her. He'd shown her how it felt to have painful details of your personal life dissected.

With a prick of conscience, he recalled how sad her green eyes had become, how quiet her voice had gotten when he'd put her in her place.

Quiet and sexy. God help him, he'd nearly gotten a hard-on listening to that soft, feminine voice. Seeing her big eyes look so vulnerable made him want to tuck her small body into his arms and hold her, protect her. He'd ached to kiss her sassy mouth when she frowned her displeasure with him. He'd longed to see her eyes light with the kind of fire that told him she wanted him as much as he wanted her.

Luke's grip on the beer bottle tightened until his knuckles blanched, and his gut wound in knots. Who was he kidding? He'd never see that look again in any woman's eyes. His disfigurement doomed him to a life of celibacy.

Luke threw the beer bottle against the wall with a frustrated grunt, and it shattered noisily. Instead of making him feel better, his loss of temper only made matters worse. He was out of control. He'd lost control over his life the minute that damned engine had exploded in his face. Now he only wanted to regain some sense of power over his future. But so much had changed for him, he didn't know where to start. Since the accident, he didn't even have the stars, the constant and ageless night sky, which had been his source of solace when his parents divorced. Because of his distorted vision, all he saw was a blur of faint lights instead of the constellations that had been his solace in years past.

"Luke?"

He glared at his father. Apparently the conference had broken up. Bart surveyed the broken glass, then raised his gaze to Luke's. God, he hated the pity that Bart wore like a banner whenever he looked at him.

"Are you all right, son?"

"Yeah. Just peachy," Luke snarled.

Bart sighed wearily. "I'll get the broom."

"Don't bother."

Bart headed to the pantry. "It's no bother."

"Leave it, Bart!" Luke jumped to his feet, the speed of his movement sending lightning pain streaking through him. The pain sharpened his frustration, and he let a string of scorching obscenities fly, lashing out at the easiest target. "Damn it, Bart! Stop treating me like a fucking invalid!"

His father stopped and stood motionless in the center of the kitchen floor. Bart's stillness told Luke that his bitter tone, or more likely his foul language, tested his father's patience. Bart hated hearing his sons stoop to gutter talk. Under normal circumstances, he'd give Luke a stern look and voice his disappointment.

Instead, Bart moved to the pantry and quietly took out the broom. His father's silent surrender ate away another piece of Luke's soul. Nothing was the same any more.

When Luke turned his attention back to what was happening outside, he discovered Aaron was putting his moves on Abby. The poor girl probably didn't realize she was simply the flavor of the day. Luke's gut bunched with a strange uneasiness when his brother tipped Abby's chin up and kissed her mouth. Her sassy, pouting mouth.

Luke thought of the sparkle in Abby's eyes when she'd stolen the corner of his sandwich, and his irritation grew. He hated that he no longer had what it took to compete with Aaron for the attentions of women like Abby. Aaron still had his health and perfect body. His brother could still charm chicks out of their panties in a flash.

Considering he'd given up one-night stands months ago, Luke wondered why that disparity bothered him so much now. He had only to imagine Aaron charming this particular chick out of her panties to have his answer.

He wanted Abby for himself.

And not just because she was a hottie, though she was that. Her sense of humor, her spunk, her core of strength spoke to him.

Somehow, Abby gave him hope.

# Chapter 4

Abby phoned her best friend in Texas the minute she got back to her hotel room. She and Brooke had barely exchanged hellos before her perceptive friend zeroed in on the excitement and anxiety that had prompted her call.

"Is everything all right, Abby? Your voice sounds strange."

Abby smiled her satisfaction, picturing Brooke's lovely face creased with concern. Nothing ever changed with Brooke, her best friend since they'd roomed together in college. Her warmth and unflagging support provided Abby a pillar of strength through even the roughest times. Brooke had been a rock for Abby since her breakup with Steve. The classic mother hen, Brooke always knew how to comfort, how to bolster, how to listen.

"My trip has taken an unexpected turn." Abby settled back on the bed, propping pillows behind her.

"Did the airline lose your luggage? Do you need me to send money?"

"No, nothing like that." She twisted the phone cord around her finger and wondered where to begin. "I had a date tonight."

"A date? Th-that's great!" Clearly the news stunned Brooke. Abby heard her friend chuckle. "You don't let the moss grow, do you?"

The subtle reminder of Steve stirred a too-familiar ache. Dear God, would she ever be able to think of him without feeling herself splintering inside?

"It was completely unexpected and… and there's more."

"Go on." She heard the wary uncertainty in Brooke's tone. Brooke hated surprises, discord, anything that ruffled her made-to-order life. Blissfully married to her high school sweetheart, she'd just delivered a healthy baby boy four months earlier. She had recently confided to Abby that she feared something had to go wrong eventually. Her life was simply too good to be true. But instead of Brooke, Abby had received the rude wake-up call. Disillusionment raked through her like icy shards.

Drawing a deep breath, Abby pushed aside the distracting thoughts of Steve and plunged in. "I've been offered a job here. I think I might take it, too."

"A job! What kind of job? How… Abby, I—"

"Calm down. It wouldn't be a permanent transfer. I'm not even sure I'll take it. I'm tempted, but…" Abby leaned her head against the wall and closed her eyes. Immediately Luke's face materialized in her mind.

"Abby?" Brooke prompted after Abby had been silent for several seconds.

"Aaron, the guy I went out with tonight, wants to hire me to rehabilitate his brother. I can't help wondering if I'm not letting my decision be influenced by the fact that he's gorgeous. Dangerously, drop-dead gorgeous, Brooke."

"Who? Aaron or his brother?"

Abby paused. Who did she mean exactly?

She'd thought she meant Aaron, yet the image of Luke's face hovered behind her closed eyes.

Luke. Not Aaron. Not Steve. The oddity didn't escape her notice. She blinked the image away, her pulse fluttering.

"Either. Both. God, I don't know. I'm confused. Getting involved with another man now is the last thing I need." Frustration tied her in knots, and she rubbed the pounding spot at her temple. Her whole life had been tossed into upheaval after her breakup. Even simple decisions confounded her at times.

"Abby," Brooke said in her most maternal, pragmatic tone. "Who said you had to get involved with him in order to take the job? If the job is something you want to do, do it."

"I know. You're right." Abby shook her head while her thoughts raced with dizzying speed.

"Do you want this job? Are you sure it is what's right for you?"

She'd asked herself the same question a hundred times while Aaron drove her back to the motel. Abby sighed her consternation. "I can't be certain of anything these days. How can I know if I'm making the right move when my judgment was so bad with Steve?"

The weight of her new doubts bore down on her, and she struggled to clear her mind. She knew how fear could paralyze someone into inaction. The last thing she wanted was to miss an opportunity due to fear and indecision.

"Don't keep beating yourself up over what happened with Steve. He made the choice to cheat, not you. I say, if the job feels right, then it is. Go with what your heart tells you."

"It's saying I should give the job a shot. But—"

"But what? Abby, what aren't you telling me?" Brooke's tone dipped, full of suspicion.

"It's Luke. He—"

"Oh, rats!" Brooke interrupted.

In the background, Abby heard a baby's wail and Matt's deep voice shouting for his wife.

"Hang on, Abby. I'm sorry."

While she waited patiently for Brooke to return to the phone, her thoughts ran the gamut of options over and over again. Every time her circular deliberations came around to Luke's piercing gaze, the tiny smile she'd earned from him, the heartbreaking way he'd fumbled to make his sandwich and open his bottle of pills.

He needed her.

No, he just needed *someone*. Anyone could do this job. Yet Aaron and Bart were convinced only she could do it.

"Sorry about that." A breathless Brooke came back on the line. "Chad threw up all over Matt, and he needed an extra hand."

"How is the new daddy, by the way?"

"He's fine. He fell asleep on the sofa with Chad on his chest tonight. It was so sweet."

Abby grinned, picturing Brooke's handsome husband, the former high school football star, covered in baby barf.

A bittersweet pang twisted in her chest. As happy as she was for Brooke, her friend's domestic bliss served as another reminder of what she'd imagined having one day with Steve. A loyal husband, a precious baby. A love that stood the test of time.

*Right dream, wrong man*, Brooke had told her. *You'll have it all someday, Abby. I know you will.*

Her best friend's confidence bolstered Abby's faith. Someday.

Brooke cleared her throat and continued in a more business-like voice. "Now what bothers you about the job? Is it Aaron?"

Abby refocused her thoughts. The Morgans' job offer. Her reservations. "Not Aaron—Luke. The brother."

"You've lost me."

"Forget it. It's silly."

"Come on, Abby. Talk to me."

She hesitated, trying to put into words the odd sensation that quivered in the pit of her stomach when Luke stared at her. "There's just something about him that… well, scares me. Not like he'd hurt me or anything… I can't describe it. He's intimidating."

"You? Intimidated?" Disbelief filled Brooke's voice with humor. "Never."

"I know I could handle him. I grew up with two brothers, remember, and I deal daily with the stuff my clients dish out. But I can't shake the feeling he's manipulating me on some level. I'm through with deceitful men, Brooke."

"Hm."

Abby could picture Brooke knitting her brow and biting a fingernail as she thought out the situation.

"But you have the advantage of forewarning this time. You can watch your back, because you've already seen the signs. Just stay one step ahead of Duke."

"Luke."

"Whatever."

Abby swung her feet to the floor and pushed her bangs from her forehead, scoffing at herself. "I told you it was silly."

"It's not silly, Ab. You've been through a nightmare, and you have every right to be wary. You still have more guts than I would have in your place. That you're even considering the job says a lot."

She shrugged, even though she knew Brooke couldn't see the gesture.

"Call me when you decide for sure. Okay?"

"You know I will. Thanks, Brooke."

When she'd hung up, Abby got ready for bed. But sleep proved elusive. She tossed and turned, considering the proposal Bart and Aaron had put before her.

How could she take the job? She'd come to Destin to deal with her own wounded heart. And now she was thinking of getting mixed up with the Morgans' troubles? She knew she'd never be able to keep herself emotionally detached. Already she sensed a deeper connection to this family than was advisable. She cared too much about them and their current suffering.

Bart's poignant desperation spoke to her own need to nurture. Aaron's deep-seated guilt stirred her compassion and left her feeling raw. And Luke's magnetic gaze seemed to peer into her soul, exposing the deepest reaches of her broken heart. His intensity unsettled her.

But for the same reasons she knew she shouldn't take the job, she also knew that she would.

The next evening, Luke emerged from his bedroom, where he'd spent the afternoon watching cartoon creatures solving crimes and talk show guests acting like animals. Another day down the toilet thanks to his damn injuries.

He climbed the steps slowly, the dim stairwell and his screwed-up, one-eyed depth perception making even the simple task of climbing stairs a challenge. He refused to concede his vulnerability and hold the handrail.

He gritted his teeth. Everything these days took effort. Writing his name, getting dressed, making a lousy peanut butter and jelly sandwich. He remembered how Abby had watched him the night before, and humiliation and resentment clawed at him. He hated appearing so helpless and clumsy in front of her.

But since Aaron had almost certainly had his way with her last night, he figured she'd soon be going back to Georgia or Iowa or wherever the hell she came from. He'd never have to see her again. So why did he care what she thought of his sorry ability to make a sandwich?

Denial didn't ease the irritation. He did care what she thought, and realizing that only made him madder.

The spicy aroma of oregano and Parmesan greeted him when he reached the living room. Bart's spaghetti sauce. His stomach growled at the thought of food, and he strolled toward the kitchen.

Taking a seat on one of the bar stools, he watched Bart stir a large pot.

"What's the occasion? You haven't cooked spaghetti in months."

"Reason enough right there." Bart sent a quick grin over his shoulder and went to the refrigerator, where he took out a green pepper.

"Somehow I doubt that." He glanced at the table and saw his father had taken out their real dishes, not the paper plates they most often used. Four places were set. "Expecting company, Bart?"

"Mm-hm. Abby Stanford, Aaron's date from last night, is joining us."

He couldn't deny the unexpected thrill that spiraled through him at the thought of seeing Abby again.

Then suspicion settled in. "What the hell's she comin' here for?"

"She was invited."

He snorted at his father's asinine, vague response, the same kind he'd gotten good at tossing at Bart lately.

"In that case, I'll eat in my room."

"Suit yourself, but we'll be discussing company business, making decisions about hiring extra help, that kind of thing. If you want a vote, you should eat with us." His father gave him a cursory glance, obviously trying to act casual. But something in Bart's manner set off alarms.

Leery, Luke narrowed his gaze on Bart. "Why is this the first I've been told about it? And why does she have any part of our business decisions?"

Bart shrugged. "We just wanted to spare you the details until we were ready to go ahead. And Abby is who we want to hire. She'd be a consultant of sorts."

Luke voiced his doubt with a terse, earthy obscenity.

The profanity won Bart's full attention. He faced Luke, frowning. "I'll expect you to mind your manners tonight. Understand?"

He tensed and glared back at his father. "I'm not some kid you can call down anymore, Bart."

"Then stop acting like one."

The retort startled Luke. The truth behind it pricked. He couldn't deny his behavior of late qualified as childish. It scared him to realize the bitter man he'd become, yet his anger and frustration over the accident squelched the voice of reason whispering inside him. The resentment had taken a life of its own and ruled his actions. He didn't know how to control it, so he gave in to it time and time again.

God help him, he was losing it. Losing control of himself. His body. His life.

Bart opened his mouth as if to say something more, then checked his response. Stiffly, he turned back to the stove. Bart's silence lay between them like an intruding stranger until Luke wanted to scream.

He needed his father's support, his strength and guidance, now more than ever. Instead, Bart treated him with kid gloves. Luke couldn't even shock him into responding.

This wasn't the first time Bart had failed to give his son the direction and stability Luke craved. Yet his father hadn't always been so passive, which made the change in Bart harder to accept. Frustration twisted the kink in his gut tighter.

He heard the front door open, and Aaron's voice followed. Luke groaned. He could head back to his room and avoid Abby, but what good would that do? Bart had said he intended to hire her. If he stayed and ate at the table, perhaps he could put a stop to that plan.

"Hello, Bart, Luke."

He turned and greeted Abby with a sullen stare as she preceded Aaron into the living room. Her gaze connected with his, and an uneasy smile flickered at the corner of her mouth.

Good. He made her nervous.

With every intention of using that fact to his advantage, he raked a cool, deliberate gaze over her. With slow precision, he appraised her dainty white sandals, appreciated her sleek legs, and admired the proud lift of her chin. Her short skirt looked like she'd wrapped a scarf around her slim hips and knotted it at the waist, and her T-shirt clung to the subtle swell of her small breasts. Heat flashed in his groin when he imagined cupping those breasts and fitting them in his hands to his liking.

With a wary expression, Abby crossed her arms over her chest as if she sensed where his thoughts had wandered, and he tugged up the corner of his mouth, sending her a satisfied look. She turned away with a jerk, facing Bart with an over-bright smile.

"Something smells delicious. I hope you didn't go to too much trouble." She sauntered past Luke into the kitchen, where she peeked under the lid of a steaming pot. "Can I help with anything?"

"No, I think we're ready to eat."

They gathered around the table, Aaron claiming the chair next to Abby, which left Luke the seat across from her. While they served their plates, Luke kept a cool gaze leveled on their guest. Though she chatted politely with Bart and flirted with Aaron, she avoided eye contact with Luke.

Either his tactic of staring at her with open suspicion rattled her as he intended, or she couldn't stomach seeing his injuries while she ate.

Whichever the case, his unflinching attention clearly set Abby on edge. As the meal progressed, her laughter sounded increasingly forced, her hands began to tremble, and she ate less and less of her food. She tucked her short-cropped hair behind her ear eight times in the span of five minutes.

Luke took satisfaction in knowing he wasn't the only one uncomfortable with the lame dinner party. He wondered if Bart's excuse of needing to discuss business held water and, growing impatient with the banal conversation thus far, decided to put his father to the test.

"Bart says you're some kind of consultant."

Her gaze darted up from her plate to meet his. She drew her small frame erect and took a deep breath as she returned his stare with a composure that contradicted her previous signs of unease.

"He says he wants to hire you to work for us."

Abby hesitated, and Bart jumped in to fill the brief silence.

"That's right. I thought she could stay in the extra bedroom, help out in the office, give us pointers on where to improve customer relations." Bart sounded overly enthusiastic and uncertain at the same time. He gave a nod toward Abby and glanced at Aaron.

"Sounds good to me. Especially the part where she moves in with us." Aaron wiggled his eyebrows at Abby, and she sputtered.

"I... I, uh, don't remember that being part of the arrangement." She sent Bart a hard gaze under a furrowed brow.

Luke followed the unfolding events with interest. He smelled a rat.

"But surely you agree that having you live on the premises with us makes sense. I could include room and board in your salary."

"It's just... I—"

"I think you could get a better understanding of... our situation, if you're living here."

Luke tried to read between the lines of Bart's carefully chosen words while keeping a watchful eye on Abby's apparent reluctance.

"I can see your point, Bart, but I—"

"I agree with Bart. I like the idea," Aaron interrupted, nodding with enthusiasm.

"So you've said," Luke groused. "Personally, I think the idea sucks." He pinned another hostile gaze on Abby. "Bart built this business without any damn consultant. He knows more about money and finances than most of the people on Wall Street. And while Aaron may be clueless when it comes to running the office—"

His brother's head snapped up, and he grunted in protest.

"—he can fix anything with an engine and can have customers eating from his hand. As you know."

Her sea-green eyes flashed her affront at his implied insult, and she squared her shoulders.

Luke cast a meaningful glance at his father before continuing. "I may have lost my eye and my thumb, but I still have a brain. We don't need any damn consultant."

Abby sent Aaron an anxious look. A stab of petty envy prompted Luke to add, "Despite what my brother may have promised you under the sheets last night."

"Hey!" Aaron barked.

"Luke—" Bart started, his tone grave.

Abby raised a hand to cut his father off. In the tense silence that followed, Abby set her fork down and narrowed a challenging gaze on him. "You're probably right. The business has obviously thrived without outside help before now. It's quite possible that I'll have nothing new to offer. Nothing is settled. We're merely exploring alternatives right now."

She propped her elbows on the table and leaned forward. "And I spent last night under my own sheets, thank you, though I find your interest in where I slept very… interesting." Her lips curved in a sassy smile, as if she thought she'd bested him at his own game.

He mirrored her posture, bracing his arms on the table and leaning toward her. "I don't give a rat's ass where you slept or who you're giving it to. Just stay away from me and my family's business, and take your cocky attitude somewhere else."

"Damn, Luke, what's your problem?" Aaron said. "Abby's only trying to help."

He turned a scathing look on his brother. "I don't need her help or anyone else's."

Aaron gave him a dirty look, a muscle in his jaw twitching, but he turned away without replying.

His brother's lack of response irked Luke. A month ago, Aaron gave as good as he got. Now his brother walked on eggshells around him. Frustration wrenched Luke's gut.

"All right," Bart said evenly. "We have one vote against and two in favor. It looks like the decision is now yours, Miss Stanford. If you're willing to accept the terms laid out earlier, the position is yours."

Luke turned toward his father, anger roiling inside him. "Wait a minute! My 'no' vote should count for something! We don't need any damn consultant." He aimed a finger and a narrow gaze on Bart. "You can't do this without me."

"I think we just did," Aaron muttered under his breath.

"Listen here, you sonofa—"

"Stop!" Abby's cry reverberated with the same anguish darkening her face, confirming his suspicion that more was at stake than a consultant for the business. She slid her chair back and stood, her petite body trembling.

Guilt brought a hard knot to his chest. The longing to tuck her in his arms and soothe her distress swelled within him, a yearning so sudden and so strong that his own body shuddered. Her eyes riveted on him, and he felt himself sinking in their turbulent, green depths.

"I... I don't want to be the source of more problems for you." She rubbed her hands on her arms as if cold then hugged herself.

She looked small and defenseless. And beautiful. A protective instinct flared in him, battling with a hunger to possess her. In all his years of meaningless one-night stands, he had never wanted a woman the way he wanted this feisty, tempting brunette.

But what good were his urges, his cravings, when his new deformities practically guaranteed he was the last man she would want touching her?

Knowing his interest in her would be unwelcome caused a sharp ache to slice his heart. He fought to suppress the razor-like pain, burying it under a shroud of icy hostility. Better that she should hate him for his monstrous behavior than risk her rejection for reasons beyond his control. He'd already lost so much control over his life.

And now it seemed he was losing his influence in the family business. He couldn't stand another loss.

"Perhaps I could start on a trial basis."

Abby's voice sounded confident now, and her quick recovery slapped him with another dose of reality. She didn't need his protection or comfort. Somehow her show of strength felt like a rejection of his unspoken desire to console her.

"Maybe once Luke and I have a chance to get better acquainted…"

He tensed.

"Forget it," he growled.

The last thing he needed was to have her around, reminding him of what was now out of his reach, taunting him with those fathomless eyes and irritating him with her perky disposition. "I don't want to 'get acquainted.' I don't want you prying in our business, and I sure as hell don't want you living in my house."

"It's Bart's house," Aaron mumbled.

Luke glared at his brother.

"I think a trial run would be a good idea." Bart gave Abby a weak smile.

They were going to do this regardless of his feelings. The bitterness of betrayal and abandonment washed through him. His claim on one-third of the business was all he had left since the explosion, and now his father and brother were trying to steal that from him as well.

Anger and grief constricted his chest, squeezing his breath from him.

"Why don't you come down to the office tomorrow morning, and we'll get you started… show you how we operate," Bart suggested.

Abby nodded and returned a smile. She turned her gaze toward Luke, and her eyes searched his. She seemed to be looking for some sign of a truce, for some acceptance from him. He clenched his teeth and glowered at her instead.

Shoving away from the table, he sent his brother and father a dark scowl. "I won't forget this."

# Chapter 5

As arranged the night before, Abby met Aaron at the snorkeling office early the next morning. He walked her through the shop, showing her the merchandise and the gear for rent. She took mental notes, wondering how she'd ended up in this position.

She still harbored a deep reluctance to follow through on Bart's plan, though their need for her guidance through this emotional minefield grew increasingly obvious. But Luke's brutal opposition to her employment had plagued her through the night, his stormy gaze haunting her dreams. The lie they'd presented to Luke, and her participation in the deception, nettled her conscience. Bart's unexpected suggestion that she live in their spare bedroom made her palms sweat. Even a few minutes in close proximity to Luke unnerved her. Under his trenchant scrutiny, she felt naked, exposed—a sensation she'd never known.

How could she risk the undefined, emotional jeopardy she sensed around Luke? Yet here she was, listening to Aaron explain the office procedures, all under the pretense of being something she wasn't.

*I must be crazy.*

"We take a snorkeling trip out every morning at ten and another at four." Aaron showed her their promotional brochure, which listed the basic information she needed.

Though she tried to concentrate, her thoughts wandered to Luke. What would she say to him this morning? How did she go about breaking down the walls he'd erected?

"If we have at least two fishermen signed up, I'll take a boat out deep sea fishing from one to three, any day. Here's the office phone number if someone comes into the office and wants to call in a reservation later. The reservation book is... um—" Aaron glanced around him.

"Under the register," Abby supplied, not bothering to hide her amusement.

"Huh? Oh, yeah." He gave her a quizzical glance. "How'd you know?"

"That's where it was when I came in about my reservation."

"Oh, yeah. Good memory." Aaron's eyes shone with the same admiration as his gentle smile. He patted the pockets of his shorts. "Well, if you don't have any questions, then I've got to take the ten o'clock... Have you seen my—?"

"Keys?" Abby finished for him, reaching around him to pluck his key ring out from under some papers on the counter.

Aaron flashed her a sheepish grin. "Thanks, Abby. I can see you don't need my help, so I'm gone." He headed out the front door of the shop. "If you do run into any problems, Luke's in the house. He can answer your questions."

She nodded. "Got it."

He winked as he headed out the door, and she watched him saunter down the pier. Aaron left a fuzzy sort of warmth in his wake, which wrapped around her like a familiar, old quilt. It was the same sort of safe, contented feeling she'd had with Steve before—

With a deep breath, Abby cut the thought off without finishing it. Instead, she compared the benign sensation she experienced with Steve and Aaron to the disturbing heat and restlessness she experienced in Luke's presence, and a quiver raced through her.

"Well, look who's been turned loose with the store."

As if conjured by her thoughts of him, Luke's deep voice invaded her reverie. She turned to face him, steeling herself for a confrontation.

"Good morning, Luke." She kept her tone bright, prepared for his sour mood and willing to meet his opposition head on. She began straightening the shelves behind the counter, sorting the piles of papers into stacks of receipts, old contracts, and customer-signed liability waivers. "Organization is not one of your brother's strong suits, is it?"

He answered with a cool stare. "Neither is acting."

"Acting?" She wrinkled her brow to reflect her confusion.

"That whole charade you put on last night for my benefit. I don't buy for a minute that you're a business consultant. And any pimple-faced kid looking for a summer job could have been hired to help in the office if we really needed it." Luke carefully crossed his arms over his chest and leaned against the door frame. His hard stare spoke his challenge.

She turned away and continued sorting forms without commenting. In contrast to the calm detachment she hoped to present, her stomach fluttered uneasily. Lying was anathema to her, and she feared Luke would read her duplicity in her expression.

The phone rang, jangling her already taut nerves, and before she could answer it, Luke snatched up the receiver.

"What?" he barked.

Abby jerked the phone away from him, scowling her disapproval of his gruff tone. "Gulfside Snorkeling," she said brightly. "May I help you?"

The muscles in Luke's jaw flexed. His hot gaze bore down on her, distracting her from the woman on the phone. She barely registered the question the lady asked.

"Yes, ma'am. Hold on for just a moment, and I'll check." She put her hand over the mouthpiece and met his glare. "How much do we charge for a child under twelve to snorkel?"

He lifted one eyebrow in cynical amusement. "We? How much do *we* charge?"

She returned an even gaze for several tense seconds, struggling to hold on to her patience. She remembered her first meeting with Luke and his aggravating habit of making her drag information from him. "The woman is waiting for an answer, Luke."

He sighed and sent her an annoyed look. "Half price."

Abby relayed the information to the woman on the phone, and after hanging up, she pivoted on her heel to face Luke again. He still glared at her, his jaw set in a rigid line and his lips drawn tight with tension. If she hoped to make a difference with his recovery, somehow she had to earn his trust.

"Who are you?" he asked evenly.

"You already know I—"

"The truth." His tone was as hard and uncompromising as his stony expression.

She worked to keep the guilt that flared inside from showing on her face. Turning back to the papers, she avoided looking at him as she fumbled for an answer that qualified as the truth without betraying Bart's plan. "I'm just someone Aaron and your father thought could help give your family some insights—"

"Give me a little credit, Abby."

A little credit. He deserved more than a little credit. She raised her eyes to him, drawing a deep breath for courage. She saw his keen intelligence in his searching gaze, heard his frustration vibrating in his voice. And she had sensed his pain last night when his family had voted against him, ignoring his vehement protests. Whatever argument she'd constructed to assuage her conscience when she agreed to lie about her employment crumbled under Luke's incisive stare.

"You're right, Luke. I'm not a business consultant. It was an insult to your intelligence to pretend otherwise, and I'm sorry."

Luke arched an eyebrow and moved away from the door to loom over her. Her pulse picked up its rhythm as he moved toward her. He stood nearly a foot taller than her and clearly meant to intimidate her with his superior size. She tipped her head back to meet his gaze, unwilling to let him daunt her. Or at least not show him that she did.

"So what are you doing here?" he growled.

"I'm an occupational therapist, and your father has hired me to help you with—"

Luke's snort of derision cut her off. He balled his left fist and turned his simmering gaze away. Abby studied the twitch of the muscle in his cheek as he gritted his teeth.

"Your father is worried about you, Luke, and he—"

"Don't give me that crock!" He pinned her with another chilling glare, but this time she saw myriad conflicting emotions swimming in his unpatched blue eye. "My father pities me and treats me like an invalid!"

More than anger, despair resounded in his voice. She'd heard enough patients' self-doubt to recognize the subtle difference in Luke's tone. That small difference reached out to her from the bleakness that haunted his expression and wrapped itself around her heart. His pain was a deeply imbedded thorn, and behind his roaring, she heard the voice of need and a longing she couldn't ignore. Compassion twisted a knot in her chest and tightened her throat. "If I stay and work for you, I plan to point out to your father how his treatment of you is counter-productive. I want to help your whole family to accept the changes—"

"Accept?" he interrupted again, and she drew a slow, patient breath. "I will never accept what happened to me! It was totally unfair!"

His voice boomed in the office, and she tried not to show the discomfort his yelling caused her ears.

"No one ever said life was fair, Luke."

He gave her a short, humorless laugh. "That's pretty unoriginal. Can't you do better than that?"

Stepping closer, he braced his hands on his hips, and his shirt pulled taut over his broad chest. Heat from his body shimmered around her, and her skin tingled in response. Standing this close to him, she smelled his soap and Old Spice. And energy, like the ion-charged air following a violent storm. The heady scent of him made her blood run thick and her bones feel weak.

She tried to block out her overwhelming awareness of him as she angled her chin up another notch. "I can help you, Luke."

"Well, I didn't ask for your help. So you can pack your bags and haul your sassy little butt back to wherever you came from!"

"Texas."

"What?"

"I came here from Texas. Dallas."

Luke's face contorted with an ugly snarl. "I don't give a damn where you came from. Just stay out of my life and my business."

She twitched her lips in amusement. "Aaron said you'd try to fire me."

The grim line of his mouth told her he didn't see the same humor in Aaron's prediction that she did.

"But you can't get rid of me that easily, Luke. Your father hired me and only he can fire me." She made sure she kept her tone even and not haughty.

He narrowed his gaze and leaned down to put his nose in her face. "Then I'll make your life such hell that you'll be dying to leave."

She had no doubt he could make good on that promise.

"My fiancé already made my life hell. That's why I came to Florida." The words slipped out before she thought about what she was saying. But just standing this close to Luke spun her world off its axis, muddled her thoughts.

His cerulean gaze flickered with a tenderness that reached deep inside her. A connection. Compassion. Empathy.

Then the cool challenge returned, leaving her longing for the warmth she'd glimpsed.

"I'm not a quitter, Luke, and you can't intimidate me."

He glanced away, huffing his frustration. She watched an expression of sheer determination set his square jaw. Then, stepping back, he raked a slow, deliberate gaze over her. Abby stood motionless, unyielding, while her heart did a jittery dance. He had a power and vitality about him that eclipsed everything else in his presence.

She straightened her spine, making the most of her petite frame. His piercing scrutiny seemed to cut clear to her soul. With effort, she focused on the task of matching his bluster with calm assurance. His expression softened unexpectedly, and smug satisfaction tugged his lips to one side.

"You're not wearing a bra, are you?" he asked in a quiet, seductive tone.

Her composure cracked. She hadn't been prepared for that tactic. "What?"

"What's more," he said smoothly, his grin becoming more cocky, "I think arguing with me turns you on, sweetcakes. Your nipples are hard as rocks right now."

She fought the urge to cover her breasts with her arms. That would only show him he'd shaken her with his ploy. The fact that he could tell she'd not worn a bra this morning disconcerted her. As small as she was in the breast department, she'd believed the heavy fabric of her loose shirt would hide her omission of a bra. Now she fumbled for a way to recover the upper hand.

"You're very funny, Luke. Don't change the subject. I have a job to do, and I fully intend to do it, with or without your cooperation."

Until she heard herself say the words, she hadn't realized the decision she'd made.

She couldn't walk away.

Not when she believed she could help Luke. If he would let her in, she could make sense of the confusion, the turmoil surrounding him. The real problem would be how to avoid entangling herself in his web in the process. Even now she found herself drawn to the hypnotic look in his eye as he locked gazes with her.

He stepped close again and, involuntarily, she stepped backward. Her back came up against the shelving, trapping her, and she straightened her spine in defiance.

Mistake.

His gaze dropped to her chest and her prominent nipples. The pupil of his good eye grew large like that of a cat preparing to pounce. Her heart hammered against her rib cage. "Luke—"

Her tone warned him away, but he reached for her with his left hand, catching her side just under her arm. His touch burned her skin even through her shirt. Abby's breath stilled in her lungs, and her mouth went dry. With his thumb, he rubbed her nipple, circling and teasing it. Arousal streaked like lightning through her, puddling moist heat at the seat of her womb. She bit her lip, swallowing a moan.

"You are turned on, aren't you, Abby?" His voice was thick and enticing, self-assured, but it snapped her from her shock-induced paralysis. She slapped his hand away.

"Keep your hands off me!"

His lips twisted in a sly grin, and he braced an arm on the shelf behind her, pinning her with his body. She lowered her eyes and sucked in a calming breath.

"Do I make you nervous?" His tone was rife with his enjoyment of her discomfort.

"Back off," she warned.

"I do, don't I?" He moved his hand to her cheek and continued to caress her intimately. His hand possessed a gentleness that contradicted the boorishness of his behavior.

"Back off… or I'll have to hurt you."

Luke chuckled his disbelief. "You're going to hurt me?" He shook his head. "Not possible. You're… what? Ninety, hundred pounds maybe. Five foot three tops."

"I know self-defense."

"Self-defense?" he scoffed. "What do you think I'm going to do, Abby?"

With a swift jerk, she raised her knee toward his groin. But he anticipated her move and blocked her leg with his own. When she grabbed for his uninjured arm, he turned the move against her, spinning her 180 degrees and pulling her up against his chest. He held her securely, her arms pinned by his.

The feel of his hard body wrapped around hers caused a dizzying surge of blood to whoosh to her head. Her heartbeat pounded in her ears as she struggled for control of her traitorous body.

"I know a few moves, too." She heard amusement lacing his voice.

"Now you tell me."

Luke chuckled, and she felt the vibration from his hard chest.

While his guard was down, she lifted both her feet from the floor, shifting her body weight to his unsuspecting arms. When he stumbled off balance, she kicked his kneecap with her heel.

"Ouch!" he yelled, releasing her. She spun away from him and put a safe distance between her and the angry glare he leveled on her.

"I told you I'd hurt you if you didn't back off," she gloated. "What's more, defensive moves or not, I could have you flat on the floor in a matter of seconds if I wanted to."

"Never." The light in his blue gaze dared her to try.

But she didn't get the chance. As she plotted her strategy, the bell over the door alerted her to the entrance of a customer.

Luke stalked through the door into the family's residence.

With a deep breath to recover her wits, she faced the customer with a smile she didn't feel.

At noon, when Aaron returned and relieved her of her duty in the office, Abby trudged upstairs to the kitchen to find herself some lunch.

Luke sat at the breakfast bar eating, and at the place next to him, she spotted a second plate with a sandwich.

She pointed to the plate. "This belong to anyone?"

"You, if you want it," he mumbled without looking at her. Abby's heart warmed. Though it was a simple gesture, she guessed the sandwich was his apology for his behavior. She also knew he'd never admit as much.

"Thank you," she murmured, taking the stool next to his.

"So why'd you crack? What made you tell me the truth?"

"I don't like to lie. It goes against my nature. Besides, you deserved the truth. I'd expect as much from you if the tables were turned, and I want you to trust me."

When he didn't respond, she took a large bite of her sandwich.

And gagged.

Her eyes darted to Luke, who turned his head slowly to face her, his expression carefully blank.

She chewed and forced herself to swallow. "This is peanut butter and tuna, isn't it?"

"Yes, it is." He gave her the same triumphant, lopsided grin he'd had before he manhandled her in the office.

"That's disgusting!" She dropped the sandwich onto the plate and frowned at him. So much for her belief that he wanted to apologize.

"The other night you told me it sounded delicious. Don't tell me you were lying… again?"

"I—"

Luke's expression brightened. A spark of mischief flickered in his eye, and a chuckle bubbled up from inside her.

"Smart aleck," she said under her breath.

Taking one of the sandwiches off his plate, he handed it to her.

She eyed it warily, the corner of her mouth twitching with amusement. "What's this one, jelly and mayonnaise?"

"Something like that." He turned away from her, his features more relaxed than she'd ever seen them. As she studied his profile, she ate the peanut butter and jelly sandwich, savoring every bite. Gourmet cuisine it was not.

But it was a beginning.

❖ ❖ ❖

"In the beginning, Luke cooperated with everything his doctor said and went faithfully to his occupational therapy appointments." Bart rocked back in his desk chair, lacing his hands behind his head, and sighed. "Then after only a couple of OT appointments, he quit. Flat out wouldn't budge. He became surly and withdrawn, really negative about his prospects of recovery."

Leaning over the opposite side of Bart's desk that afternoon, Abby scribbled notes as Luke's father recounted the accident and aftermath. "So what happened? Why the change?"

"No tellin.' He won't talk to me about it."

"Do you have the name of the occupational therapist he was seeing? I'd like to talk to them about our plan and Luke's treatment."

Bart spun his chair toward a filing cabinet. "Sure. I have all the contact information here. Her name was Joyce Harris."

While Bart dug for the file, Abby tapped her pen restlessly. "I want the person he started with to remain the therapist of record. Luke should stay with whatever regimen Ms. Harris prescribed. My role will be to see that Luke follows through, just like a concerned friend or family member would do. I'll have the advantage of my OT training behind me, but I'll encourage him, guide him, cajole and harass him if needed. I intend to report my progress to his OT, get instructions from her how to proceed, and eventually get Luke to go back for official treatment sessions." She bit the tip of the pen and sighed. "But like we agreed, this is not an official therapy job for me. It can't be. I'm just helping Luke do what he won't do on his own. Okay?"

Bart nodded. "Understood. We're paying you to help in the snorkeling office and inspire Luke to complete his therapy and shake out of his current funk, by whatever means you see fit."

Abby took the file Bart slid across the desk to her and flipped the cover open. "I, uh, have a confession."

"Oh?"

"I told him the truth this morning. He cornered me in the office, and I didn't feel right lying."

Bart raised his blond eyebrows. "Oh."

"He took the news pretty well… all things considered. But he's upset with you and Aaron."

"Naturally. I suppose he has a right to be." Bart dragged a hand down his haggard face.

Abby closed the file and scooped it off the desk. "May I keep this for a while? I plan to call Ms. Harris this afternoon and get started with Luke right after."

Bart waved a hand in agreement. "Absolutely. As far as I'm concerned, the sooner you start the better."

# Chapter 6

"READY TO BEGIN?"

Luke turned from the living room window to face Abby when she spoke. She had disappeared with Bart after lunch, and Luke could only guess what kind of scheme they'd dreamed up now.

Did Bart really think some cute little chick was the trick to interesting him in rehab? If so, Bart was wrong.

He'd get better on his own terms and on his own schedule. He didn't need the humiliation of someone hovering over him while he struggled like an incompetent klutz. And he especially didn't need to make a fool of himself in front of a sexy woman like Abby.

By now she'd no doubt reported to Bart how he'd hassled her into admitting her real reason for being here. Though he didn't want to admire Abby for her belated honesty, it seemed she was the only one leveling with him lately.

Now, as she crossed the room toward the sofa where he sat, he studied the strange collection of items she carried: pencils, a small ball, a rock, a seashell, scraps of cloth, and a stuffed animal. When she sat down next to him, he eyed her with suspicion. "What's all that for?"

"Your rehab. I called your occupational therapist a little while ago, and she filled me in on the exercises she showed you the last time you went—what, three weeks ago?" She paused and gave him an admonishing look.

"She also suggested a little test that will help her know where things stand with your sensory discrimination."

"No."

"I'll stay in touch with your OT and help you do the daily exercises she thinks you need," Abby continued without blinking. "I'm sort of your dad's assistant—helping with the snorkelers as needed but also making sure you stay on track with your rehab."

"The snorkelers might need your help. I don't."

She shrugged one shoulder. "Just the same. I'm here. You're here. Why not give it a try?"

Her perky voice and blithe attitude grated on his nerves. "Go away."

"Not until we do some status checks that Ms. Harris suggested. Give me your right hand." She wiggled her own extended hand, encouraging him to comply.

"Get lost," he grumbled and turned back to the window.

Trying the silly exercise didn't bother him nearly as much as knowing he might not be able to pass her simple little test. He hadn't wanted to do the tests at the OT's office, so why would he do them now? The idea that his abilities were now limited yanked a knot of frustration and grief in his chest. Before the accident, he'd never doubted himself—never had a reason to.

He watched a large pelican swoop down to perch on a post along the pier. The regal bird, standing alone against the vast backdrop of the gulf, created a haunting image, one with which Luke identified all too well. Never in his life had he felt so alone against such imposing odds. He wanted to get out of this rut, but the hurdles seemed insurmountable. Especially with so many unknowns…

Abby still sat beside him on the sofa, and he sensed her gaze on him. Damn, she was stubborn! He thought about the way she'd stood up to his intimidation tactics that morning and had to admit he respected her grit.

"Come on, Luke. Ms. Harris wants me to assess your range of motion, your sensory discrimination, that sort of thing. It's normal to—"

"Normal?" He jerked his gaze around again, narrowing a glare on her. "My life will never be normal again thanks to that damn explosion!"

"Oh, maybe not your old normal, but I can help you deal with your new normal, and—"

"My new normal? What kind of psychobabble shit is that?"

Despite his sharp tone, she remained calm. Her unwavering composure, when his snapped so easily these days, irritated him all the more. She shook her head, giving him a withering look. In return, he regarded her with cool detachment and took a magazine from the coffee table.

Abby sighed and propped a hand on her hip. "Do you want to get better, Luke? Or would you rather struggle and be miserable for the rest of your life?"

"I'd rather you shut up and left me alone."

"To sulk?"

He slapped the magazine back down and shot a hard look at her. "What difference does it make to you?"

"It makes all the difference, Luke."

The compassion and gentleness in her green eyes twisted him inside. He remembered the flash of apprehension he'd seen in those same eyes when he'd reached for her that morning in the office. She'd trembled when he'd stroked her breast, yet the desire he'd stirred in her had been unmistakable… and reciprocal. Her muffled moan had made him hard.

But if she'd enjoyed his touch, why had she fought her pleasure? His first thought was she'd been repulsed by his injuries, even though electricity crackled between them. Resentment for this rejection seethed inside him. The shadows of a memory, long ago pushed to the recesses of his mind, taunted him, stirring a hollow ache. Another rejection, many years old.

As he'd practiced in recent weeks, he buried the rising pain under defensiveness and anger, disturbed that Abby had somehow summoned the ancient hurt. Unable to meet her sympathetic gaze any longer, he stood up and stormed toward the kitchen.

She pursued him. "I have a patient at home who was paralyzed from the waist down when a drunk driver hit his car."

Though he didn't answer her, he sent her a querulous look meant to silence her. It didn't work.

"You could learn something from him." She wagged a finger at him. "Terrence will never walk again, but he's glad to be alive and thankful for the chance to see his daughter graduate from high school later this month. You are lucky to have—"

"Lucky?" He smacked his good hand on the kitchen counter and pinned her with a scowl. "Just how the hell do you figure I'm lucky, lady? Was I lucky when that engine blew up? Was I lucky to lose an eye and all practical use of one hand? Was I lucky when you and my family ganged up on me and lied to me?"

She didn't answer, and he stepped closer to her, yelling. "Well, was I? Am I lucky, Abby? I don't think so!"

His outburst reverberated in the tiled kitchen, but she didn't so much as flinch. Rather than feeling he'd scored any ground, her disapproving frown ate away another piece of his self-respect. Who was this ogre he'd become?

With a slow deep breath, she kept a maddeningly patient gaze on him. "Yes, you are very lucky, Luke. You have a father who would do anything for you. You have a brother who loves you so much that your pain is tearing him up inside. You have a heart that is still beating, two legs that work, a successful family business, a beautiful home, and… me."

She stepped closer and fixed an earnest, tender gaze on him. "I'm here to help you, Luke. I know you're confused and frightened right now."

He opened his mouth to deny her assessment, but she put her hand over his lips. The gesture stunned him, silenced him. The cool gentleness of her fingers sent a sharp stab of longing and loneliness to his heart. He pulled away from her touch, glowering at her.

"Luke, let's get one thing straight from the start." She aimed a finger at him, and her voice stayed even but firm. "Life is about choices. I can't make you do anything you don't choose to do. You have to want it.

"I'll help you if you want my help. And I'll badger you if you don't want my help, because your dad is counting on me to get through to you. But, ultimately, you have to make a choice. You can remain bitter, or you can get better."

He backed away from her. He couldn't think, couldn't breathe with her so close. Her eyes were deep pools of green, pulling at him like a riptide and sucking him into their depths. The walls seemed to close in on him. His thoughts whirled, tangling with the powerful desire she'd aroused in him with a simple touch.

She'd managed to get under his skin despite his need to thwart her, to keep her at bay. Because she had penetrated his defenses, whether she knew it or not, she posed an even greater risk to his search for peace of mind. She made him want more than his self-imposed isolation, made him hunger for things he knew he couldn't achieve. He forced himself to harden his heart to the pleading and understanding in her eyes.

"It's not that simple, and you know it," he said tightly, then stalked across the kitchen to the refrigerator. He opened it and aimlessly stared inside.

She shadowed him.

"It can be that simple. I'm not going to give up on you. You can yell or pout or insult me, but I will not give up on you. Can you say the same thing? Are you giving up on you?"

Her question kicked him in the gut. The wily woman had turned things around on him, in essence daring him to prove he wasn't a quitter.

Before the accident, he would have pounced on such a blatant challenge. Before the accident, he had thrived on competition. Before the accident... he had believed he couldn't fail.

But the accident had proven he wasn't infallible. Now he was painfully aware of his limitations and reluctant to test himself. All it took was a few sessions at the OT's clinic to see failure looming like a great black demon. That vulnerability and certain defeat scared the hell out of him. He'd rather do nothing than try and fall on his ass.

His new cowardice filled him with self-loathing. His head started to throb. Taking a bottle of water from the top shelf, he slammed the refrigerator door shut and crossed the kitchen again. Abby stayed close behind.

Grabbing his pain pills from the counter by the sink, he fumbled to open the lid, hating the display of incompetence in front of Abby.

"Do you really still need those?"

"I really still need these." His resentment of her doggedness darkened his tone.

"Look, I don't want to fight with you, Luke." Abby sat on a stool by the breakfast bar and leaned on an elbow.

"Good, then scram. You're giving me a headache."

"Likewise, mister. Your pouting is wearing mighty thin."

He gave her a menacing glare. "I'm not pouting."

She lifted a thin eyebrow. "Then what would you call it?"

Luke huffed impatiently. "I'm not in the mood for word games, Abby. I just want you to leave me the hell alone. Got that? I didn't hire you. I don't want you here. I can't say it any plainer than that. Now go away."

She hesitated a beat. "Maybe. If you ask me nicely."

He clenched his teeth. "God, you are irritating."

"That's not what I had in mind."

Her saucy grin infuriated him. And tantalized him. He wondered how her spunky attitude translated in bed. His body ached to find out. Before she could wreak any more havoc on his faltering control, he plastered a tight, insincere smile on his face. "Go away."

"Please."

Luke growled his frustration. "Please." He nearly choked on the word, but she seemed satisfied.

"See how easy that was?" Her smile brightened, and she climbed down from the stool. "If you change your mind about doing that exercise, let me know. I'll be in my room unpacking."

"Don't hold your breath."

He watched her saunter across the room, wishing her hips didn't have such a provocative sway when she moved. She paused at the entrance to the living room.

"Have it your way. Remember, the amount of progress you make is your choice. I'm only here to help if you choose to get better." With that parting shot, she disappeared up the stairs.

Luke grunted in disgust. If he chose to get better? What a crock! His freedom of choice had been taken from him when that engine exploded.

Given a choice, he'd not have a pesky little brunette meddling in his life, living in his house and keeping him awake at night with visions of her sweet body beneath his.

Storming back to the sofa, he dropped down on the cushions to stew. He hated to be manipulated. He wanted to learn to deal with his injuries on his own terms and when he was ready.

But Bart hadn't respected his wishes about his recovery. He'd brought in another occupational therapist, when all Luke wanted was peace.

He'd show them. By the end of Abby's "trial period," Luke intended to have her so frustrated and offended that she'd run back to Texas with her tail tucked between her shapely little legs.

But...

Doubt crept over him like the stealthy morning fog, clouding his mind. If she left, where would he be? What if he did need her help?

Luke tried to curl the fingers on his right hand and the pull of healing tissue shot pain up his arm. He gritted his teeth and tried again, cursing at the fiery throbbing. Frustration sawed inside him. He could bend his fingers further a month ago when he'd left the hospital. Without regular OT sessions or the stretching exercises Joyce Harris had prescribed, the healing burns on his finger and wrist joints were tightening up.

Just like the doctors and therapist had warned him they would.

But damn it, it hurt like hell to stretch his fingers the way his OT had, and he'd prayed that in time, once the burns healed more, the pain would subside. Instead he'd allowed his hand to get stiff, tight, nearly nonfunctional.

His emotions tugged him in too many directions at once, tearing him apart inside. He was tired of feeling so lost, so helpless, so uncertain.

He turned sideways to stare out the window at the gulf waters that he loved. He missed the water, longed to get out on the waves again, itched to get back to work. But his blind eye meant he couldn't pilot the boat. His sensitive, burned skin kept him out of the hot sun, and he felt shut out of the family business since the explosion. Despair washed over him, dragged him deeper into the pit of hopelessness from which it seemed impossible to climb out. Abby's parting words came back to him.

*The amount of progress you make is your choice. I'm only here to help if you choose to get better.*

If he chose to get better.

Was it possible she was right? He wanted to believe her. But was it worth the risk that she could be wrong? Failure was not an option.

Yet the alternative, staying in this rut, wasting the rest of his life on regret and wondering what could have been, sucked even more.

Luke sighed and dragged a hand down his cheek and chin. Working with Abby would mean trusting her, and trust didn't come easily for him. Not since…

He shook his head, pushing away the intruding memory.

Before he would rely on Abby, he needed certain assurances that she wouldn't betray his faith in her, that she truly was an ally and understood his needs as she claimed she did. Then, and only then, would he risk himself, even for the brighter future she promised.

The next morning, Abby made two phone calls. The first she made to Joyce Harris to report her false start with Luke and get more information about the hand exercises she had recommended.

"My main concern, if he's not doing his exercises, is contracture. As his burns heal and form new skin, the tissues pull tight, and he'll lose flexibility and range of motion in his joints," Joyce said.

She elaborated on the passive stretching techniques that Luke should be practicing daily, giving Abby a detailed description of how all the joints in Luke's injured hand and arm needed to be flexed and extended repeatedly to keep the tissue supple. "Once you have him in a routine of stretching exercises, he'll need hand massages, either with your fingers or some tools that I can order for you, to increase the blood flow in the healing skin. Make sure he continues to wear the compression garments I fitted him with. Is someone still changing his occlusive dressing each night?"

"I don't know, but I can sure find out." Abby made a mental note to ask Luke about this, then go to Bart if Mr. Stubborn gave her guff. Keeping the healing tissue healthy was paramount.

"Until the doctor gives his okay to stop wearing bandages on the burns, his skin still needs the elastomer gel strips to reduce scarring," Joyce Harris said, echoing Abby's thoughts. "You can have him squeeze a little rubber ball for strengthening, and as soon as you can, I'd like an update on his sensitivity."

Abby made copious notes as Luke's OT continued.

"Some patients will become hypersensitive to certain stimulus, and if that is the case with Luke, I'll give you some methods of desensitization."

Abby bit the cap of her pen and reviewed her notes. "Anything else?"

"That's an awful lot already. Let's start with that and see how it goes. Call me if you have more questions or if any problems arise."

"Thanks, Ms. Harris." Abby hung up, chomping at the bit to put some of her new knowledge into practice. Her personal goal, in addition to the therapy goals Ms. Harris outlined, was to make enough progress with Luke's attitude that eventually he'd go back to his therapy appointments with Joyce, and Abby's role in Luke's treatment could be restricted even further.

Next, she called Brooke to let her know she'd be staying on indefinitely in Destin.

"I hope I didn't wake you," she said, hearing her best friend's groggy voice answer.

"No, Chad took care of that at about 4 a.m. He's been up ever since, going great guns, while I'm ready to drop!" Brooke yawned. "So what did you decide about the job down there?"

"That's why I'm calling. I took the position. Will you go by my place and water my fern for me? Or better yet, just take it home with you and keep it alive until I get back?"

"When do you figure that will be?" Brooke sounded more alert now.

"No telling. I'm playing it by ear for the time being."

Brooke's resigned sigh filtered through the line. "I'll get your fern, but no promises what condition it'll be in when you get back. You know my black thumb."

Abby grumbled, "Yeah, I remember."

"You'll stay in touch, right? Gosh, I miss you already!"

Abby heard another disgruntled sigh at Brooke's end, and she chuckled. "Of course, I'll call. Kiss that sweet boy for me. I gotta run now."

Abby hung up and, belting her bathrobe, made her way down to the kitchen. A lonely pang settled in her chest that she attributed to a touch of homesickness. Though, if she were honest, she had to admit she envied her friend's domestic bliss. She'd believed she would have that kind of happiness with Steve.

*You obviously can't satisfy him like I do.*

The pang sharpened, and by sheer will, Abby forced the depressing thoughts aside as she padded barefooted into the kitchen for breakfast. Bart sat in the living room in one of the recliners, reading the *Wall Street Journal*. The mellow scent of fresh coffee greeted her, and she breathed deeply of the welcoming smell.

"Mm, how nice. I like a man who can fix coffee."

Bart folded down the corner of his paper and peered at her. "Morning, Abby. Sleep well?"

"Wonderfully. In fact, I'm taking that mattress with me when I leave. Just thought I should warn you." She grinned at Bart, then headed to the coffeepot.

He chuckled and raised his paper again. "I think I should warn you, the Morgan men like their coffee strong."

"Not a problem. I'm of a similar mindset."

A family of flirts. She poured herself a mug of coffee and took a sip. And coughed. "Wow, you weren't kidding! That'll put hair on your chest."

While she debated whether to dilute the potent brew with water or make do without, Aaron strolled into the kitchen.

Even with sleep-rumpled hair and his cheeks shadowed with yesterday's beard, he looked sexy. Like the day she had met him, he wore only a pair of swimming trunks. Abby's pulse fluttered at the sight of so much raw masculinity.

Aaron yawned and raised a hand in greeting.

"Mm. Who made the coffee, you or Bart?" his voice rumbled, gravelly with sleep.

"Bart."

He grunted, though Abby couldn't be sure how his caveman-like response should be interpreted. Aaron pulled the filter out of the coffee maker and grimaced. "Geez, Bart! Did you even measure?"

"Measuring is for sissies," Bart returned from behind the screen of newspaper. "Not afraid of a little caffeine, are you, son?"

Aaron chortled as he threw the grounds-laden filter in the trash. "Maybe you should let one of us make the java from now on, Bart. We have Abby to consider now, you know."

Bart continued reading without comment. With his newspaper, Bart kept himself isolated.

She took mental note of the morning routine as it unfolded, learning more about the men she'd been hired to help than just simple habits. Their interaction, their playful banter told her about the family dynamic.

"Join me in some Froot Loops, Abby?" Aaron took a box of cereal from the cabinet and the milk jug from the refrigerator and sat at the bar.

She scoffed. "Between Bart's caffeine and your sugar, I'd be bouncing off the walls all morning."

Playfully, she demonstrated the jitters, making her whole body convulse. Aaron chuckled, a sound as rich and potent as the coffee Bart had brewed. Abby raised her mug to drink, and as she peered over the rim, Luke walked through the living room door.

He was naked.

Well… except for the compression vest and glove he wore over his burns.

"Oh, my God," she muttered, a little louder than she intended. Luke obviously heard and met her stunned gaze with a smug smile.

In response to her mumbled oath, Aaron turned, and Bart lowered his paper.

"Luke!" Bart barked.

Aaron swung back around, clearly fighting the laughter that threatened to erupt.

Stunned by Luke's immodesty, her gaze drifted over the well-formed example of male beauty, and her heart pounded.

*Don't look. Don't react. You'll be playing into his hands.*

But she couldn't look away. She stared in fascination, her gaze roaming from his broad shoulders to his flat stomach, lean hips, and long, muscled legs. And, of course, that part of his anatomy that was purely male. And unscathed by the explosion. And breath-taking. And... good Lord!

Her mouth became arid, and her hands trembled in earnest now.

While Aaron's appeal had caused her pulse to flutter, Luke left her body quaking, her heart racing, her knees weak.

Her coffee mug thumped as she set it down, sloshing the contents on the counter, and she grabbed the edge of the sink to steady herself.

"Mornin', little brother." Aaron's greeting rang with amusement.

"Good morning." Luke sauntered into the kitchen, casually poured himself a cup of coffee, and took a sip. "Don't tell me. Bart made the coffee."

"Yep," Aaron replied, then ducked his head, covering a laugh, as Bart whizzed past the bar and into the kitchen.

"What the hell do you think you're doing?" Bart snapped.

"Drinking some damn strong coffee at the moment." Luke's glib response won another chuckle from Aaron.

"Go to your room and put on some clothes!"

"That tone hasn't worked on me since I was twelve, Bart."

Abby reached for the faucet and turned on the water for no other reason than to have something to do. Filling her lungs, she struggled to rein in the chaos in her body. Shock warred with desire. Apprehension tensed her muscles while lust turned her bones to mush. Hot, languid blood heated her cheeks, yet she shivered from a prickly chill that slithered down her spine.

She'd come to Destin seeking tranquility and healing. But Luke left her in a state of perpetual turmoil and searching for control over her visceral attraction to him. Three weeks ago, she'd been certain she would never want anyone but Steve. Yet Steve had never stirred the powerful, sensual longings inside her that Luke evoked with just a look.

She shouldn't have taken this job, yet she had followed her soft heart instead of her head. Mistake number one. So now she found herself in the untenable position of dealing on a daily basis with this man who riled and enticed her. She must be insane.

She'd play it by ear, do her best to fulfill her obligations to Bart, Aaron, and, most important, Luke. But how?

"Luke," Bart growled. "We're not amused by this stunt."

"What stunt?" Luke moved to the living room… and back into her line of vision.

Bart pursued his son, the father radiating a palpable frustration and ire. Abby gripped the edge of the sink tighter and followed the argument with quick glances from one man to the other.

"Get some clothes on!"

"Why? This is my house, too! If I choose to be naked, why can't I?"

Abby didn't miss the emphasis on the word "choose," and her stomach clenched. If she'd had any doubt that this charade was for her benefit, she didn't now.

"You know damn well why!"

"Oh, yeah. The house guest." Luke snapped his fingers as if it had just occurred to him. "So, let me get this straight… because of your house guest, I'm no longer free to make choices in my own home about what I want to do?"

"Luke, you are way out of line." Bart balled his fists at his sides. "Get your butt to your room or—"

"Or what, Bart?" Luke's scowl returned. "This is still my house too, and I'll do what I choose!"

"Good!" Abby surprised herself with her bravado. "I want you to feel comfortable in your own home. If you choose to have breakfast in the buff, please don't let me deter you."

Bart looked at Abby like she'd lost her mind. Aaron raised a stunned, but amused, gaze.

"By the way, Luke," Abby continued, squelching the butterflies in her stomach to meet his gaze without faltering, "you have a cute butt. Nice buns!"

Luke arched a golden eyebrow, propping his hands on his hips. He exchanged a lingering look with Abby, and her heart thudded from the blue flame lighting his unmasked eye. "Thanks."

He turned away abruptly and faced his father. "Well, that settles it, doesn't it?"

Bart tensed his jaw but said nothing.

"By the way, I have a doctor's appointment today," Luke added. "Any volunteers to drive me or should I call a cab?"

"I'll clear my schedule," Bart said, tight-lipped.

"No, I'll take you."

Bart and Luke both looked to Abby when she spoke. She cast an apologetic glance at Bart, hoping he would be patient with her strategy. "Of course, I'll need to borrow a car."

"That's not necessary. I can—"

"We'll need to leave at 10:15. You can drive my Wrangler," Luke interrupted Bart. Without further discussion, Luke turned and headed out of the living room.

Abby shut off the water that had been running pointlessly for the entire episode. "Bart, I apologize if I stepped on your toes. But you were giving him just the reaction he was angling for. He was proving a point and testing the parameters of this new situation."

"Always the spoiled brat," Aaron said around a mouthful of Froot Loops.

"I don't see how your acceptance of what he was pulling solved anything." Bart furrowed his brow, giving Abby a concerned look.

"He was rebelling against the constrictions of having a house guest imposed upon him against his will."

"Obviously." Bart raised a hand, conceding the point.

"So arguing with him, trying to impose your will on him, even if it was a legitimate request, exacerbates the notion that he's had his rights taken away." She paused and sighed. "He was also conveying a message to me with his little speech about choices and what he chose to do. I had to support his choice or I'd be a hypocrite. I'd lose credibility with him."

"So now we have to put up with him strutting around here in the raw?" Aaron asked, clearly disgruntled by the idea.

Abby shook her head. "He won't try it again. He's proved his point. But... I think you should make a point of including Luke in decisions over the next few weeks, even if he seems uninterested in being bothered. Especially regarding the business. I know you've tried to shelter him from reminders of the accident and, therefore, business questions. But I sense that he feels left out and, therefore, useless. He needs to know he still has purpose and importance in the family and with the business."

"He knows he's important to us!" Bart argued.

"Deep down, probably. But remember, this accident has shaken his whole belief system. He believed he was invincible, and a boat engine proved him wrong. He's questioning everything, testing everyone, trying to find his footing again."

Bart sighed. "In other words, I blew it."

"No!" Abby stepped from behind the counter to walk toward Bart. "You're all making adjustments. There is no black and white. You reacted like any normal parent would to his outlandish behavior. But what he needs is patience. Lots of it." Abby turned to Aaron and jabbed his shoulder with a finger. "And no ridicule."

"I hear you," Aaron said without looking up.

Bart sank down in the recliner again, and Abby walked over to kneel beside him. Putting a comforting hand on Bart's arm, Abby tipped her head to give Bart a reassuring smile. "Luke is strong and resilient. I can see it in him. He'll pull through this just fine. You all will. Give him time. And give yourself time to get used to the changes. In the meantime, I'm not going anywhere until I've finished the job you're paying me to do."

Bart's cheek twitched, but his eyes remained shadowed with worry. "Thank you, Abby. At least I know I was right to hire you."

"I'll give Luke back to you, Bart. I promise."

# Chapter 7

AT 10:15 SHARP, ABBY APPEARED IN THE LIVING ROOM as she'd promised. Secretly, Luke had hoped she'd be late. So far, he'd found little about Abby to dislike.

He figured she was as near to perfection as humanly possible. Hell, she wasn't even tardy. If he could find something wrong with her, some glaring flaw, he could justify resenting her.

Instead, he found more and more to admire. She'd proven a sucker for honesty and had the guts not to skirt around touchy issues with him. Her willingness to tackle a challenge and her determination to succeed were impressive. Her ability to hold her own with the Morgan men and their teasing gave him a badly needed reason to smile.

She'd gotten under his skin, leaving him off balance, uncertain how to proceed with her—or if he even should. He needed to find a way to regain control in their relationship, to stay one step ahead of her.

He hated that she'd found a way to lower his guard, hated that she couldn't be intimidated by his scathing temper, hated the way her green eyes seemed to read his mind. His injuries and new physical limitations were enough without Miss Green Eyes blindsiding him.

From Bart's recliner, where he sat comfortably slumped, Luke raked his gaze over her. She'd applied a shimmering lipstick to those perfectly bowed lips of hers, and her skin glowed as though it had just been scrubbed. But then, her lightly freckled complexion always looked dewy soft and clean, and he ached to feel its satiny softness beneath his hands. Abby wore a pair of khaki shorts that showed a generous amount of leg, a short-sleeved blue sweater that molded to her small breasts, and leather sandals from which her toes peeked out. She'd painted her toenails blue.

Blue toenails?

Luke battled a surge of lust when an image of himself sucking those toes, with their in-your-face nail polish, flashed in his mind.

Damn! Wanting her like this would be the death of him. His body already suffered a sweet agony in her presence without conjuring fantasies about her toes.

"Ready to go?" she asked, tipping her head toward the door.

"Ready as I'll ever be," Luke grumbled as sourly as he could to hide both his arousal around her and his apprehension about his doctor's appointment.

He levered out of the recliner and brushed past her on his way to the carport, where he'd parked his white Jeep Wrangler the last time he'd driven it. Before the explosion.

After sweeping CDs from the passenger seat, he climbed in. Until he learned to compensate for the blind spot his lost eye created, he couldn't drive. That injustice brought a scowl to his face as he handed Abby the keys. "Try not to scratch it."

"I'm an excellent driver," Abby replied in a quirky voice.

"Rainman," he replied, identifying the movie from which she'd stolen the line.

She grinned. "Very good."

When she turned the key, the engine whined, and Abby pumped the gas pedal. Her second try had similar results, and his frown deepened.

"Not so much gas. You'll flood it. Geez, you're going to wear out the starter!"

"Are you going to breathe down my neck the whole way?"

Luke fixed a hard gaze on her. "Maybe I should just ask Bart to take me."

"Sit tight and chill out. I won't hurt your precious Jeep." When Abby tried a third time, the engine roared to life. "Now, which way?"

"Head west on 98." Luke buckled his seat belt.

"That's the main road through all the tourist stuff and hotels, right?" Abby glanced over her shoulder as she backed out of the driveway.

"Yep."

"Then what?"

"I'll let you know when you need to know."

She chuckled. "You sound like my father. 'Information only on a need-to-know basis.'"

"Yeah? Your father in the military or just an ornery bastard?"

"Lifetime military. I'm an Army brat."

"No kidding? And here I was thinking you were just a civilian brat." He turned a cool gaze in her direction to gauge her reaction to his jibe.

Rather than being put off, she laughed. "I'll be lucky if you're not calling me worse by the time I'm finished with you."

He arched an eyebrow. "Why is that? Planning to break out the whips and chains?"

"You'd like that, wouldn't you?" Her expression turned sultry, and a sensation like hot syrup in his veins sluiced through him.

"Only if I get to take my turn using them on you." He'd intended his reply to be gruff, but a husky quality crept into his voice, giving away his interest in the tantalizing scenario she evoked.

Heat suffused his body, envisioning what he'd really like to do with her. But the vision had no instruments for pain. Sex for him was about pleasure—sweet, hot, and satisfying. But recreational sex only went so far in satiating a man's needs. His needs went beyond the physical. With the right woman, Luke imagined sex could be an earth-shaking experience.

On the heels of that thought, as if she read his mind, Abby cast him a sideways glance, and their gazes locked.

Could Abby be that woman? She'd already shaken his closed, post-explosion life, and he certainly felt more powerfully drawn to her than any woman in his past. He knew she sensed the sparks that crackled between them just as he did. Desire glittered in her eyes in moments like this one. Desire and anxiety.

Why the anxiety? The most obvious answer to the question needled him, squeezed him inside. Though they might connect on some internal level, she couldn't get past his monstrous appearance. Why would she want to get it on with a freak when she could have her pick of healthy men… like Aaron? Jealousy made the prick of her aversion even sharper.

When she tore her gaze away and reached for the radio knob, her hand shook. Except for the rock music on the radio, they rode in silence until necessity demanded that he give her directions or have them wind up in Alabama.

"Turn right up here." He directed her the rest of the way to the office complex where he had his appointment, and she pulled the car into a parallel parking space.

She gave him a smile that said she knew her driving skills were, in fact, excellent. "How'd I do?"

"Acceptable," he said blandly, stubbornly refusing to give the compliment she deserved.

Once inside, Abby took a seat in the waiting room while Luke signed in at the receptionist's desk, awkwardly scrawling his name on the appointment pad with his left hand.

"Please fill out these forms, and the doctor will be with you in a minute." The woman behind the desk handed him a clipboard and pen with a cursory smile.

"Sure." His gut twisted with dread. He could barely write his name, and now the chick wanted him to fill out a whole form?

He took a seat beside Abby and tapped the pen nervously on the edge of the clipboard. He hated the idea of bumbling with the form in front of Abby. Why did such a stupid, mundane task have to be so hard? Blowing out a deep breath, he started with the easy part, checking the boxes by a list of ailments and conditions under the heading "medical history."

When he'd finished that section and the "reason for today's visit" column, he slanted a glance at Abby. She raised her eyes from the magazine she read as if she felt his gaze. Her sights dropped to the mostly blank form, and her expression softened.

"It would go against everything I believe if I offered to fill in that form for you. You have to learn to do things for yourself despite the effort it takes right now. It's the only way you'll learn to cope." She blinked her beautiful eyes at him, and his pulse soared.

"Did I ask for your help?" he snapped. "Or your pity?" Luke turned back to the form and started writing his name. Damn, he hated having her see him struggle.

"I don't pity you. Get that through your head now and remember it. I don't plan to say it again." Abby used her gentle, persuasive tone—the soothing, you-can-trust-me tone that made him want to believe her. He steeled himself against the lulling quality of her voice. *Keep your guard up.*

After he'd taken an excruciating amount of time writing his name legibly, she held out her hand. "Give it to me."

He cut a sideways glance at her. "What happened to 'it would go against everything I believe'?"

"Some rules were made to be broken. Especially if we want to leave here before lunchtime. Besides, I'll give you plenty of practice writing later. You're not completely off the hook."

"I can do it myself. I'm not an idiot."

"No one said you were an idiot. All right-handed people have trouble using their left hand at first. We can include some transfer training in your daily regimen, and eventually something like this will be a breeze."

He hesitated. "Say please."

Her expression said he'd surprised her. Ha! Score one for him.

"Please."

Giving her a testy glare, he handed the clipboard to her.

Abby scanned the page. "Birth date?"

"July ninth."

"Hey, that's just around the corner!" Her voice rang with genuine enthusiasm.

"Whee." Luke slumped lower in his chair.

"Grouch." She scowled at him, then glanced back at the form. "Social security number?"

He huffed, then reached in the back pocket of his jeans and pulled out his wallet.

"There," he said, tossing the whole thing in her lap. "Everything you should need to know is in there somewhere." He got up and stalked over to a tank of colorful fish to watch the lazy movement of the guppies.

When she finished the form, Abby took it to the receptionist and joined Luke by the fish tank. "May I ask what this appointment is for?"

"You can ask."

She studied his face, obviously waiting for him to explain, but he said nothing. Finally she sighed and walked back to her chair.

Guilt for his unnecessary obstinacy nettled him. He realized that because of his trying, churlish behavior, the picture of him she was getting was most unfavorable. That had originally been his intention—to keep her at a distance, to ensure that if she did reject him it would be on his terms. Yet now he wondered what might be possible between them if he weren't so crude and abrasive.

If he had to work with her—rather, if he *chose* to work with her—wouldn't it serve him better to have her as an ally? He needed to have her trust, needed to trust her. Taking a deep breath, he faced her.

"I'm supposed to get the bandages off today. If everything's healed enough." His tone was non-confrontational for the first time in months. It felt good. His defensiveness really wore him down, physically and mentally.

She lifted a startled, hopeful expression that turned his insides to Jell-O.

"That's great! You must be healing really well to get your bandages off."

He shrugged.

"What's wrong? Why aren't you happy about it?"

He angled his face away from her deep, probing gaze.

"Luke Morgan." When the nurse called him, he headed back to the exam room without addressing Abby's question.

Why *wasn't* he happy about it? He should be ecstatic, but instead, he dreaded having the bandages gone, no longer hiding the damage left by the burns. Of course, he'd still have to wear his compression garments. He'd have those unsightly fashion items for a year or more, his OT had said. And wasn't that a cheery thought? A year of wearing a girdle-like vest that looked like a grandma's hand-me-down and one glove, à la Michael frickin' Jackson.

Luke gritted his teeth as the doctor manipulated his hand through the exam and probed the tender new skin. The doctor complimented Luke's progress and the speed with which his skin had healed, but Luke's focus remained on the unsightly scarring and pink growth of new skin on his chest, right arm, and hand.

"Will the scars always look like that?" he asked tentatively.

"Most of the redness will fade in time, but I doubt your natural color will come back," the doctor explained as he unwrapped the bandages around Luke's chest. "The compression garments will continue to minimize the appearance of the scars as they finish healing. But you'll never look the way you did before the burns, if that's what you're asking. More than appearances right now, I'd be concerned with regaining use of my hand. I noticed your fingers are rather stiff. Have you been going to your occupational therapist as I instructed?"

"My OT," Luke grunted.

"You have an occupational therapist, don't you? We discussed the need for one at the hospital."

"Uh, yeah. I have one." *And now her pesky minion enforcer, too.*

"Good." The doctor gave him a stern look. "Do your exercises or you'll lose use of your hand."

Luke stared down for the first time at the stub that used to be his thumb, and his heart wrenched. When he winced, the doctor asked, "Does it still hurt?"

"Yeah, some." *Especially when I do the dumb stretches you and the OT want.*

Luke was about to downplay the significance of the pain when the doctor took out his prescription pad.

"I'll only write this prescription for one order. No refills. A milder pain reliever from over-the-counter should be your first line of defense against pain by now."

"Sure." Luke stuffed the prescription for the narcotic in his pocket. "Is that all?"

"Unless you have questions?"

Luke shook his head.

"Well, then, have a nice afternoon, Mr. Morgan."

Sliding off the examining table, Luke retrieved his shirt and headed out to pay his bill. When he reappeared in the waiting room, Abby looked up from her magazine.

"That didn't take long. What did the doctor say?"

"He asked me who I thought would win the Stanley Cup this year."

A patient grin flickered at the corner of her mouth. "And you said?"

"That I don't follow hockey. I'm a baseball man."

"Mmm. What about your burns?"

"They like football better."

Abby faked a riotous laugh. "What a comedian!"

He scowled at her and finished his business at the front desk. Then, shoving his hands deep in his pockets, he turned to leave. Abby trailed after him.

"Luke?"

He didn't slow his pace.

"Luke?" Her sandals pattered a quick cadence on the pavement behind him as she hurried to catch up.

He climbed in the passenger side of his Jeep and tried to close the door, but Abby stepped in the way.

"Luke, please, talk to me. What's bothering you?"

He answered with glowering silence.

"Luke?"

Why did she have to say his name that way? Like an intimate whisper between lovers? Her voice washed over him like the warm waves from the gulf, seducing him, lulling him.

"Can we go, please?"

"Don't shut me out, Luke."

Her plea sent a sharp ache spiraling through him. He couldn't let her in, couldn't forget the lingering pain from the last time he'd poured out his soul to a woman.

Stubbornly he stared out the windshield to avoid her insightful gaze. "Get in the car, would you?"

She put a hand on his arm and, even through the fabric of his long sleeve, her touch felt warm. "Please, Luke, let me see."

Clenching his teeth, he braced himself against her gentleness. "Trust me. You don't want to see it. I look like a side-show freak."

Abby sighed softly. "No."

"Don't patronize me!" he snapped, turning a hard glare on her. Abby's eyes met his, and he found them brimming with tears and understanding. His heart lurched.

He turned away, refusing her with his brooding silence. A knot in his chest made breathing difficult.

"Are you going to keep your hand in your pocket for the rest of your life?"

"Damn it, would you give it up?" Luke narrowed his gaze and pressed his lips into a thin line.

Abby didn't relent. She pulled gently on his arm, and finally, with an exaggerated sigh of disgust, Luke took out his hand to show her. She was right. He couldn't hide it forever, much as he'd like to.

After gently tugging the compression glove off, she laid his palm on top of hers while her other hand caressed the burn-damaged, thumbless hand with tender strokes. He carefully monitored her expression for any sign of repulsion. But like the day she'd met him on his front porch, she showed no visible rejection of his appearance—not even when she turned his hand to brush her fingers over the stub of his thumb.

He winced.

"Does it hurt?" Her feminine voice soothed some of his anxiety.

"No, doctor."

Her eyes flickered up to his face briefly, and her lips curved. "Can you wiggle your fingers?"

Gut clenching in dread, he gave her an impatient frown but demonstrated that he could wiggle his fingers. Barely.

"Do you remember Ms. Harris talking to you about contracture of the skin as it heals?"

"Are you gonna lecture me now for letting my stretching exercises slide?"

"No. But I am going to insist you do them from now on. At least twice a day."

He ground his teeth together imagining the agony. "Stretching my hand still hurts like hell," he growled.

"And it will only get worse if you don't start loosening the skin in your joints. No one said the road back wouldn't hurt. But the results will be worth it. I promise."

He sent her a dark glare. "Whatever."

"It's a good hand, Luke. Certainly nothing to be ashamed of." She folded her hands around his injured one.

When he met her gaze, his snide retort stuck in his throat. Sincerity and compassion lit her emerald eyes. Abby laced her fingers with his and brought his hand up to her lips to press a gentle kiss to his knuckles.

Luke's breath stilled. Fiery bolts shot through him and kicked his libido into overdrive. He battled the urge to grab her and kiss her senseless. Need clawed at him—the need to slake the hunger she created in him, the need to have her softness pressed close to him, the need to fill himself with the sweet oblivion he saw in her eyes.

But a more powerful force, something dark and strange to him, held him back.

Doubt. Fear. *A memory.*

Inside him, the black hole yawned wider.

When she raised his hand to her cheek, he snatched his arm back. Her startled gaze questioned him.

"Don't overdo it," he said testily. "You'll lose credibility." Planting his hand on her chest, he moved her away from his car door and slammed it shut.

While she circled the back end of his Jeep, he sucked in deep, calming breaths. Damn her! Why did she have this effect on him? She'd managed to lull him into a false sense of well-being with her soft, sexy voice. She'd made him believe for the span of a reckless heartbeat that she didn't see his deformity and could even care about him. He berated himself for falling prey to her manipulations. She was just doing her job, doing what Bart paid her to do, and he resented her attempt to make her duties appear to be more.

Her gentle touch and her teary eyes had almost fooled him. But he'd not be so gullible again. It took more than a pretty face and some sweet lies to win his trust. He knew her game now, and he'd be ready the next time she tried to lower his guard.

And he'd have a few surprises for her, too.

# Chapter 8

AFTER REMOVING THE STEM FROM A HEAD OF LETTUCE, Abby poked her thumbs into the hole and pulled the leaves apart. She separated the halves, then stared down at the lettuce in her hands. How simple the action had been for her. She took her thumbs for granted, much the way Luke probably had before he lost one of his. Setting one half aside, she started chopping the other into salad for dinner.

Luke had avoided her most of the afternoon. When she had literally run into him on the stairs, he'd barked at her about watching where she was going, then stomped off. Now, as she thought about the brief encounter, it occurred to her how difficult those dark stairs must be for Luke to negotiate with his diminished vision. Depth perception problems could make steps tricky at best.

Her thoughts wandered to Luke's dark mood at the doctor's office. No doubt the sight of his injured hand had reminded him of his new limitations—limitations which she'd reinforced by filling out the form for him.

With a grunt of self-reproach, Abby gave the lettuce a vicious whack. She'd known better when she offered her help with the form, yet her compassionate side had overruled her sensible side. Not something she could do if she wanted to make a difference with Luke.

She remembered, too, the glimpse of vulnerability and tenderness that had flickered across Luke's face when she'd kissed his injured hand, and a lump swelled in her throat. Her demonstration of support had obviously caught him off guard, and the emotions she'd seen him battling had reached deep into her soul and stirred something elemental in her heart.

Her hands stilled, resting idly on the chopping board and half-finished salad. If she could just get through that protective shell of Luke's, the defensive wall of anger and despair he'd built around himself, she knew she'd find a wealth of character and a gentle spirit. That much was evident from the brief glimpses he'd shown her of himself when he'd momentarily lowered his defenses.

Through the large picture window in the living room, she caught sight of Aaron on the back deck. Maybe he had some ideas how to lift Luke's spirits, some insights into how she could befriend his brother. Pushing the salad aside, she headed out to the deck to pick Aaron's brain.

She stepped quietly onto the weathered wooden deck, trying not to startle Aaron, who had his head down and his eye pressed to the eyepiece of a telescope. She wondered for a moment what he could be studying so intently through a telescope during daylight hours.

He re-aimed the telescope without lifting his head and mumbled, "Well, well, well, what have we here?"

Her curiosity got the best of her. "Mind if I look?"

Aaron jerked to an upright position and swung his gaze toward her. "Abby… uh, hi. I didn't see you come out. I, um…"

She nudged him out of the way, highly suspicious now because of his nervous fumbling. She had no doubt he was ogling some unsuspecting female in a bikini. "Spying on the neighbors, Aaron?"

"Wh—No! I'm not a Peeping Tom. The telescope's not even mine. It's Luke's."

She scoffed her disbelief.

"I swear!"

Great, so Luke was the pervert. One more reason not to get involved with him.

"I suppose you were gonna tell me you were watching the dolphins?"

"Actually, you can use this thing to see them, and it's pretty cool. But, no. I was checking out the ship way out there on the horizon." He moved out of the way and swept a hand toward the telescope inviting her to look. "See."

She stepped closer and pressed her eye to the viewfinder. A large gray ship came into focus. "Okay, you're off the hook—this time."

Aaron chuckled. "Give me a little credit. Sheesh."

*Give me a little credit.* The phrase rang familiar, reminding her of her reason for tracking him down.

"Hey, I need your help with something."

"Sure. Shoot." He slipped a protective plastic cover over the telescope, which was screwed firmly onto the railing of the deck, making the device a permanent fixture.

"It's Luke. He got his bandages off today."

"Oh, yeah? Cool." Aaron motioned with a nod for her to follow him inside.

"Not cool to him. It's put him in a foul mood and—"

"How can you tell?" Aaron interrupted. He opened the door and held it for her. "He's been in a foul mood for weeks."

"I'm serious. If you could have seen his face, Aaron. It was heartbreaking." Abby headed back to the kitchen and the salad she'd abandoned. She walked over to the cabinet to retrieve a bowl, then scooped the chopped lettuce into it.

"Do you think we could lift his mood any if we took him out somewhere tonight? You know, try to get him back into the swing of his old lifestyle." Aaron crossed his arms over his chest as he leaned one hip on the edge of the counter.

"What did you have in mind?" Abby asked with a suspicious lift of her eyebrow.

"I don't know. It was just an off-the-cuff idea. Luke and I used to go out partying together all of the time." His expression grew pensive. "I miss it."

"You miss him, not the partying. You could go out anytime you wanted."

"Isn't that what I said?" He stepped closer and slipped his arms around her waist to pull her closer.

She tipped her head back to see Aaron's face, a little uneasy with the familiarity of his embrace. Shaking off the discomfiture, she focused her thoughts on helping Luke. "It's worth a try. Think he'll go for it?"

"We won't give him a choice."

Aaron gently caressed her back, and the intimacy of his touch made her pause. Did Aaron still intend to pursue a relationship with her? Pleasant though his roving hands were, she pulled away and busied herself with her salad preparations again. A date was one thing; entangling herself with a man whose home she was sharing was quite another.

Shaking her head to dismiss his idea, she cleared her throat. "No, we can't force him to do anything. He has to make the decision to go on his own, or he'll only build up more resentment."

"I'll leave convincing him to you then. You seem to be good at persuasion." Aaron leaned in to kiss her just as Luke walked in. Abby ducked away from Aaron's lips and spun out of his reach, moving to the refrigerator to get the last vegetables for the salad.

She glanced at Luke and saw the disapproving scowl he'd fixed on his brother.

Aaron seemed oblivious to the daggers shooting at him from Luke's direction as he stole a piece of lettuce from the bowl. "Hey, Dummy. I hear you got your bandages off today. What do you say we three go out tonight and celebrate?"

"What's to celebrate?" Luke took a seat at the bar and watched Abby slice a tomato.

"Aren't you glad to be rid of the bandages?" Aaron asked.

"Couldn't care less."

"Bull," Aaron challenged.

Abby looked up at Luke. "I understand you are quite the party animal, stud. What do you say? Show the new girl in town a good time?"

"Thought Aaron had already done that."

"Yeah, we went out. But he tells me the real party is when the Morgan brothers hit the town together. He's been kind enough to say I could tag along."

"Seems to me I'd be the third wheel. No thanks." Luke drummed his fingers on the counter, frowning.

"A tricycle works best with three wheels." Abby cast a casual glance at Luke as she tossed the tomato onto the lettuce. "Say you'll go, Luke."

"Forget it."

"Come on, bro, don't be stubborn."

"Please?" Abby begged. "It would do you good to get out and have some fun."

"No."

"Please?" Abby repeated as dinner was being served.

"No!" Luke said for at least the fiftieth time that night.

As persuasion tactics went, she knew irritating repetition and begging lacked grace and finesse. At best, the strategy was juvenile. But it was straightforward, and Luke couldn't say she'd manipulated him. Annoyed him, yes. Schemed, no. She hoped he'd find some levity in her persistence.

After dinner, she followed him down the stairs to his bedroom repeating, "Please, please, please."

"Go away, you damn pest!"

"Please!" Abby wrapped her arms around him in a careful hug from behind, propping her chin on his shoulder and batting her eyelashes. "Please?"

"Oh, that's subtle," Aaron laughed.

"Please, please!" Abby met his gaze in their reflection from his dresser mirror as she peered over his shoulder. She flashed him a mischievous grin. "Please?"

He grimaced then shook his head in defeat. "If I go, will you shut up and leave me alone?"

Aaron laughed.

"Uh-huh." She bobbed her head and held her breath, hope filling her with a glad warmth.

He heaved a deep sigh. "All right." Though the words held a hard edge, a spark of humor glinted in his good eye. "But only if you say please."

"Thank you." She rewarded him with a peck on the cheek, and when she met his gaze in the mirror again, something more intense than humor heated his blue eye.

She became acutely aware of the press of her body, her breasts against his broad, muscular back. His hair brushed her cheek like a lover's caress. A tremble shimmied through her and her skin tingled.

What she'd intended as a playful prank suddenly swamped her with seductive undercurrents. The warm, musky scents of his cologne and his masculinity made her head swim. Her pulse raced, sending a whooshing sound to her ears. The dizzying sensations crashed over her with an overwhelming speed. The possessive, predatory hunger reflected in his gaze unsettled her.

She wasn't ready, wasn't prepared for the volatile attraction sizzling between them. How could she be so drawn to a man so soon after another man had broken her heart?

And yet she hadn't given Steve more than a cursory thought all day. The realization stunned her. She'd been too involved with Luke, too centered on his needs—and on controlling the sensual urges he awoke in her.

Stiffly, she pushed away from Luke's back, averting her gaze. While Abby the friend wanted to celebrate Luke's capitulation and the opportunity to boost his mood, Abby the woman with the recently broken heart shivered with apprehension. She'd just committed herself to spending an entire evening in his presence.

Aaron pulled his Mustang into the parking lot of a nightclub advertising Karaoke night, and Abby groaned.

"You can't be serious." She fixed a look of disbelief on Aaron. "This is your idea of a great time? Listening to people sing off-tune?"

"For once, I'm in agreement with the lady." Luke crossed his arms over his chest and settled deeper into the back seat. His body language said he wasn't about to budge. He had to sit sideways to accommodate his long legs, but he'd insisted Abby take the front seat.

She chuckled and turned to Luke with an imploring tilt to her head. "I will if you will. What do you say? Give it a try?"

Luke's expression remained impassive. "Have fun. Maybe you could send a beer out to the car for me?"

"God, you're bullheaded!" She grabbed his knee and jostled him. "Come on. It might be fun. What if we promise not to make you sing?"

Luke snorted. "I'd say you must have been smoking crack if you thought I was gonna sing. The answer is no. But you two run along and have a nice time." He said the last with a fake, sappy smile on his face.

Aaron drew a slow careful breath and turned to face his brother. "What if I promised that *I* would sing?"

Luke's blond eyebrow shot up, and his lips curved in a wicked grin. "You'll sing?"

"If you'll get off your butt and lose the attitude…" Aaron hesitated, grimacing.

Clearly, singing for the crowd was not part of Aaron's original plan and didn't appeal to him. That he'd make the effort for his brother's sake told Abby plenty about the affection the brothers shared, despite the verbal sparring she'd witnessed over the past few days.

"… Yeah, I'll get up there."

A low, sinister-sounding chuckle rumbled from Luke's chest, then he zeroed in on Abby. "Both of you have to sing."

She held up a hand and chortled. "Now you're getting greedy. Not a chance."

"Okay." Luke stacked his hands behind his head and leaned back against the seat as if settling in for a long wait.

Aaron gave her a commiserative shrug.

She knew when she'd been beaten. Luke had consented to come with them. Aaron had agreed to sing despite his reluctance. Could she do any less?

Growling playfully at Aaron, she narrowed her eyes to slits in mock ire. "All right, but I'll get you for this!"

"It's a deal?" Surprise and amusement colored Luke's tone.

Abby and Aaron glanced at each other.

"Deal," they groaned. She buried her face in her hands as Aaron got out and flipped the seat forward for Luke to climb from the back.

As they entered the nightclub, she wagged a finger at Luke. "You are incorrigible."

He arched an eyebrow. "Incorrigible?"

"It means you're a pain in the butt," Aaron muttered.

"I know what it means," Luke tossed back. "But I'm surprised you do."

"Heh, heh, heh." With a sarcastic smirk, Aaron jabbed his brother in the left arm.

She accompanied the brothers into the noisy nightclub, where a thin veil of cigarette smoke hung in the air and couples writhed on the dance floor in a sea of color and motion. The music reverberated so loudly that she felt the thumping bass vibrate in her body.

Aaron wound his way through the crowd to an empty table near the center of the room. As Abby took her seat, she noticed the way Luke tugged his baseball cap lower and hunched his shoulders as he cast a nervous glance around the room. He slumped in his chair and kept his gaze down as if trying to make himself as unnoticeable as possible. His obvious self-conscious discomfort stirred a bittersweet ache in her chest.

Other patients had told her that the first time they'd gone into public with a new handicap, they'd felt as if everyone stared at them. She inched her chair closer to Luke's and placed a hand on his forearm to show her support.

Luke looked at her hand then raised his gaze to hers. She gave him what she hoped he'd interpret as an encouraging smile, but he glared at her and pulled away from her touch.

"I'll buy the first round," Aaron offered. "What'll you have, Abby?"

"Beer's fine. You pick the brand." She turned to Luke. "How about you?"

He shrugged. "Whatever."

Every trace of the good-natured teasing they'd shared in the car had fled Luke's rigid features, and her heart sank.

"Please, Luke." She leaned closer and touched his arm again, despite his earlier reaction to the same gesture. "Try to have fun. Aaron's got your best interests at heart, and he's trying to—"

"Who asked him? As I recall, I got dragged along on this little farce against my will."

"Why shouldn't you have a little fun? God knows I could use a few laughs. It helps you forget, if you'll just—"

"All the laughing and beer in the world won't change this." He aimed a finger at his eye patch.

"No," Abby said tightly, returning his cool stare with an uncompromising one of her own. "But it would go a long way to improving your attitude!"

"Don't start about my attitude. I've heard that lecture."

"Fine. Spend the rest of your life with a chip on your shoulder and the people who love you at arms' length."

Luke snatched his arm from her grip again. "It's my right."

Abby shook her head slowly and frowned at him. "Yes, it is, but it's also your anchor. It's holding you back."

His lips pressed in a thin tight line. "Save it for your patients, Miss Sunshine."

He turned his back to her as Aaron returned from the bar, and she tried to shake off the dark mood her discussion with Luke had created. Disappointment and defeat weighted her chest, and a grain of the truths she'd been tossing at Luke chafed her like sand in an oyster.

Was she approaching the changes in her life with the right attitude? Was she dwelling on her losses or looking to the future with pragmatism and hope? The truth hurt, and she resolved to do better. She could do no less than what she asked of Luke.

Aaron set three bottles of beer on the table, saying, "Drink fast. Happy hour's over in twenty minutes."

"So—" Abby flashed Aaron a smile and helped herself to one of the drinks. "Ready to win us all over with your lovely singing?"

Aaron choked on his beer and swiped at his mouth as he set his bottle down, chortling. "Lovely? Boy, are you in for a shock. And no, I won't be singing until I get good and numb first." He raised his bottle to her and took another long swig. "How about you?"

"I'll sing right after you do!" She raised her own bottle.

"Chicken!" His eyes lit with good humor.

"Darn right!" She laughed as she studied Aaron's broad grin, determined that she would have fun, even if Luke wouldn't.

She'd come to Destin with her own heartache to shake. When the deejay opened the microphone to the floor, Abby's stomach flip-flopped. But she'd promised to sing, for Luke's sake, and she would keep her word if she died of embarrassment in the process.

When Luke left the table and headed to the bar to replace his drink, she leaned over to Aaron. "This isn't working. He's determined to be miserable."

Aaron cast a glance toward the bar and sighed. "Forget him. You and I will have fun without him. He's always been as stubborn as the day is long."

"If I may ask, why in the world did you pick a place like this?" Abby shouted to be heard over the crowd that was growing increasingly rowdy.

"Don't let him fool you. We've been here together plenty of times. When neither of us had a date, we'd come down here to get a beer and heckle the people with the guts to sing. I never imagined I'd be one of the idiots doin' it."

Abby nodded her head in Luke's direction. "From the looks of it, he's well on his way to getting drunk tonight."

His gaze drifted across the room to the bar where Luke waited for a drink. Aaron's eyes found hers then, and he shrugged. "We can't live his life for him. He's an adult. If he wants to mess his life up, that's his problem."

"You don't mean that. You don't want to see Luke hurt himself any more than I do."

"No, but I'm tired of talking about my brother."

Abby started to protest, and he silenced her with his lips. His kiss startled her, and she forgot her argument. His warm mouth moved against hers with precision and skill, and she waited for the zing of heat and excitement such a kiss should, by all rights, elicit. Instead, she experienced only the nervous twinge of knowing Luke could see them.

Why should it matter to her if Luke saw her kiss his brother? She wasn't looking for anything lasting from Aaron and certainly didn't expect it. And his attention, no matter how fleeting, boosted her bruised ego. So why not?

Despite her attempts to justify her actions, she couldn't shake a nagging disquiet, a disturbing guilt that centered around Luke. When Aaron raised his mouth, he gave her a devilish grin then headed up to the stage. As Luke returned to the table, Aaron's voice boomed over the speakers, loud and strong.

"This should be good," Luke said dryly.

Aaron fumbled a little until he got a feel for what he was doing. When he belted out the refrain, a bright smile spread across his face. Abby couldn't help but laugh. She laughed, that is, until she remembered her promise, and her stomach clenched.

She was next.

# Chapter 9

Luke watched his brother sing to Abby, and the beaming expression she returned yanked a knot in Luke's chest. Telling himself he should get used to having women choose Aaron over him didn't make the ache any less bitter. Luke took another swig of beer to soothe the bite of acid his despair created.

Aaron walked down from the stage and grabbed Abby's hand, leading her back to the stage with him. Abby looked terrified.

The music and shouting pounded in Luke's head, and he winced in pain. Digging in his pocket, he pulled out the small pill he'd brought with him. He washed the painkiller down with his beer. When the song ended, he glanced up at the stage in time to see Aaron pull Abby close and capture her mouth with a long kiss. The crowd cheered and applauded.

Luke's heartbeat slowed. Why Abby? Aaron could have his pick of women. Why the one woman he—?

Without finishing the thought, he yanked his gaze away and fought to suppress the taste of bile rising in his throat. He shoved away from the table and headed back to the bar for something harder than beer to drown the jealousy ripping through him. He'd known coming with them would be a mistake.

Mistake? Hell, it was torture.

Not that he could blame Abby for picking his brother.

Mr. Perfect-face, killer-charm, call-for-a-good-time. Abby deserved a good time. She'd just come through hell with the unfaithful jerk in Texas. But despite her tough-as-nails posturing and sharp wit, he sensed that a fragile soul lay beneath the layers of bravado and grit. Aaron was just clueless enough about relationships with women to miss the vulnerability that shadowed Abby's eyes, the hesitance when she smiled. Where Abby was concerned, Aaron was a disaster waiting to happen.

Luke gritted his teeth. He shouldn't care what happened between Abby and his brother, but, damn it, he did. He couldn't suppress the instinct burgeoning in him to protect Abby. At the same time, he knew his concern for her could backfire, and he would be the one to get burned. He'd do better to keep his distance, ignore his nagging worries.

Another song started playing, and Luke glanced back at the stage. It was Abby's turn to sing. He could read her jitters in the way she flexed her fingers and rubbed her hands on her legs. Luke experienced a prick of guilt for having put her up to something she so obviously dreaded. Yet she'd consented—to appease his fiendish, stubborn pride.

He watched her straighten her posture as if she had a steel rod in her back. That was Abby. Five-foot-three and one hundred pounds of sheer will, conquering another challenge, letting nothing hold her down. Certainly not fear.

Deep in the center of his chest, a warmth grew. Admiration for Abby's guts and tenacity filled him, pushing aside some of the bitterness he'd harbored against her. She hadn't let her broken engagement ruin her life. She'd chosen to move on, make the best of her situation.

*Life is about choices.*

"She's pretty good, huh?"

Luke glanced up at Aaron as he returned to the table. He shrugged one shoulder. "She's all right."

Aaron shook his head in disgust and turned to watch Abby. He sent her a smile, and it seemed Aaron's unspoken encouragement gave Abby inspiration. She kept her eyes trained on Aaron while she sang, and a smile blossomed on her face. As she gained courage, she sang with more conviction and won more support from the crowd. Pride tugged at Luke's heart as she stepped off the stage and headed back to their table. But his pride quickly soured when she went straight into Aaron's waiting embrace.

His brother wrapped her in a bear hug and kissed her forehead. "You were great!"

"I was terrified! Look, I'm still shaking!" She held out her trembling hand as proof.

"God, am I glad that's behind us!" He released her and pulled out her chair. Flashing Aaron another beautiful smile, she took a seat and scooted up to the table. She looked to Luke then, her gaze clearly seeking his approval.

His breath caught, but he maintained an even stare. When he refused her the approval she sought, disappointment flickered in her eyes, and regret squeezed his chest. Luke emptied the shot of tequila he'd gotten from the bar earlier, and the slow burn of liquor eased the tension inside him.

"Aaron!"

Abby's gaze left Luke's when the woman's voice intruded on the dearth of conversation at their table. He followed Abby's gaze to the tall, shapely brunette who grabbed Aaron's arm.

"How've you been? I saw you sing. You're pretty good!" the brunette gushed.

"Hey, Ashley!" Aaron's face lit with a smile for the beauty. He pulled her into a hug similar to the one he'd just given Abby. Abby's face fell.

Luke leaned close to Abby to murmur in her ear. "Do yourself a favor."

Abby raised her eyes to his again.

"Don' fall 'n love with 'im." He heard the slur of his speech. How much had he had to drink? He couldn't remember.

Abby drew her eyebrows together. "What's that supposed to mean?"

"Jus' what I said. If you're smart, you won' fall for him. Consider yourself warned." He pushed his chair back, intending to get another drink.

Abby caught his arm to stop him. "Do yourself a favor. Switch to coffee for the rest of the night."

Snatching his arm from her grasp, he sent her a dark glare. "I've done jus' fine without a mother since I was eight years old. I don't need you to be one now."

"Say, Abby," Aaron's voice interrupted any retort from her. He dropped his car keys on the table. "Do you think you two can get home by yourselves? You can drive a stick shift, can't you?"

"Where are you going?" The shock and hurt in her expression spoke for themselves.

"I have some catching up to do with an old friend."

Abby's eyes shifted to the woman hanging on Aaron's arm.

"I'll see ya'll later." Aaron had the nerve to wink at Abby as he left with the other woman. Abby stared helplessly at his retreating back while her emotions played over her face like a home movie.

Silently, Luke called his brother a selection of choice names. He clenched his teeth in frustration and disgust with Aaron's heartless behavior.

When Abby glanced up at him, she clearly mistook the rigid set of his jaw for an "I told you so."

Before he could deny her assumption, she shot to her feet.

"I'm ready to leave." She snatched her purse off the back of her chair and tossed the strap over her shoulder.

"Good. I've been ready t' get outta here since thirty seconds after we 'rrived." He tried to stand, but his knees buckled, and he landed back in his chair.

Abby watched Luke sway and drop back into his chair. "You're drunk!"

"Corre'tion." He tried again to get to his feet. "I'm barely buzzed."

Abby gritted her teeth. Her resentment toward Aaron for his callus abandonment boiled over into impatience with Luke's inebriation. The night had taken an ironic twist in the last five minutes, but Abby wasn't laughing. Old wounds seeped fresh blood inside her, raw, stinging reminders of being forsaken for another woman by another man. She was angry with herself for caring enough about Aaron to feel hurt by his leaving. And she'd love to throttle the lothario for being so rude.

Instead she was left to deal with his drunken brother. She sighed, and her body sagged with defeat. Tears of frustration and outrage stung her eyes, and she looked away, refusing to let Luke see how Aaron had hurt her.

Had she really thought anything had changed because Aaron had paid a little attention to her? When all was said and done, she was still the woman whose fiancé had gone elsewhere for sex. She was still a flat-chested plain Jane. She couldn't compete with beautiful women like Cindy. Like Ashley.

She chewed her lip for a moment, then squared her shoulders, pushing away the self-defeating thoughts. Stomping around the table, she gave Luke her shoulder to lean on. Without the real target of her anger and discouragement around to chastise, she focused her wrath and hurt on Luke. His self-destructive mode bothered her almost as much as Aaron's desertion.

"And how many painkillers have you taken tonight?" she asked him as she helped him stagger toward the door.

"Don' know. A couple."

"Are you trying to kill yourself?" Abby shouted over the din in the room.

"Are you tryin' to piss me off? I told you I don' need your lectures."

She growled her frustration. Fine, let the moron flirt with death by mixing alcohol and narcotics. Let him put himself in a coma!

After helping Luke into the car, she climbed into the driver's seat and cranked the engine. Before she backed out of the parking space, she looked around for a post or wall where she could give Aaron's Mustang a good scrape. Luckily for Aaron, none was available, so she pulled into traffic and headed back to the beach house, seething silently.

After about a mile, Luke reached over to the steering wheel and covered her hand with his. Her heart thumped, and a mellow warmth filled her at his tender gesture. Whether as a show of support or comfort or apology for his behavior, she didn't care. He'd made the first conciliatory move. The corner of her mouth twitched as relief spilled through her. Maybe she was getting through to him after all.

"Better pull over."

The gravelly quality of his voice fired warning flares in her mind, and she jerked her head around to look at him.

His complexion was almost gray.

He wasn't comforting her. He was sick. Disillusionment coursed through her like hot lava, singeing a path through her soul.

She steered the car to the side of the road, chiding herself for her foolish optimism, for the giddy thrum in her blood when she'd believed Luke was reaching out to her.

He opened his door even before she'd stopped the car. Squeezing her eyes shut and covering her ears as he retched on the side of the road, she rested her head on the steering wheel and groaned. When he flopped back on his seat with a moan, she mumbled, "You finished?"

"For now. But don' drive so fast, and be ready t' pull over 'gain in a minute."

"Dang it!" She slapped the dash with her palm. "I could have told you this—"

"Spare me, Abby." Luke leaned his seat all the way back and moaned again in misery.

"It would serve your brother right if I let you barf in his bucket seats."

Luke peered at her from his one hooded eye. "If I didn' feel like hell, that'd be pretty funny."

"I'm not laughing." With a glance over her shoulder to check traffic, she eased back onto the road.

Luke had her pull over twice more before she got him home. Sometime between the karaoke bar and the Morgans' beach house, Abby's anger and frustration gave way to deep concern for Luke's health.

He'd grown eerily still, and his head lolled to one side. If he had, in fact, taken the potent painkillers on top of the alcohol, Luke's life could be in real danger.

# Chapter 10

DON'T PANIC. ABBY TOOK A DEEP BREATH AND SORTED through her options. Should she take Luke to the emergency room? Wake Bart? Wait it out and hope for the best?

She didn't want to be an alarmist, and Luke would resent her dragging Bart into things unnecessarily. His throwing up was a good thing, she figured. He was getting the stuff out of his body on his own. Sighing, she decided to hold off on any drastic action. She would stay with him, monitor his condition, and if he gave any signs of worsening, then…

"Come on, slugger." She looped Luke's left arm around her neck and helped him climb out of the car, no small task given the differences in their size and weight. Luke was over six feet tall and all arms and legs.

Slowly but surely, they staggered together into the house and down the steps to his bedroom, where she dumped him unceremoniously onto his bed. After she tugged off his shoes, he rolled onto the floor with a groan and crawled to the adjoining bathroom to be sick again.

When Luke didn't return, Abby walked to the bathroom and found him lying on the floor in front of the toilet. Under normal circumstances, the sight wouldn't have affected Abby. A grown man stupid enough to get sick-drunk deserved to sleep on the cold floor.

But circumstances weren't normal. Luke wasn't just any man. He was confused and suffering over the tragedy that had befallen him. Her compassion for his anguish swelled in her chest with a dull ache. She knelt beside him and dragged him to a seated position. Propping him to sit with his back against the wall, she grabbed a washrag from the towel bar by the sink and soaked it in cold water. She cleaned his face, then rinsed the rag out and refolded it to dab on his forehead, cheeks, and neck.

His unmasked eye opened a crack, and he regarded her through the slit.

"Am I gonna die, Abby?" His voice sounded thin, laden with remorse. And fear.

Her hand stilled with the damp cloth on his cheek. She drew a shaky breath. "No. I won't let that happen."

She met his gaze, and he stared at her with the guile-less tenderness of a child and the grief-stricken agony of a man in turmoil.

Abby's heart slammed against her rib cage. "I won't leave you, Luke. I promise."

His body tensed, and an emotion, akin to hope, yet shrouded with sadness, flickered over his face. He studied her with a shrewd, dubious look for several tense seconds but seemed satisfied by what he found in her returned gaze.

As if comforted by her vow, his body and face relaxed, and his eye closed. She thought he'd drifted to sleep until he spoke again.

"I wanted to die... before... in the hospital. The burns hurt... so much."

"I know."

"It would have been better... than living like this."

Abby caught her lower lip in her teeth as her chest tightened. "Then stop living like this. Let me help you,

Luke. I know what has happened is hard to understand, hard to accept, but I want to help you get through this rough time."

"I'm… scared." He whispered the confession so quietly she wasn't sure she'd heard him correctly. Squeezing his eye more tightly shut, he turned his face away from her. "I don't like feeling scared."

She absorbed the pain that filled his voice, making it her own, feeling it sink its claws into her heart. The threat of tears seized her throat. "I know, Luke. I know."

Boy, did she know. The fear and uncertainty of her future had been one of the hardest parts of Steve's betrayal to swallow. *Now what do I do?* she'd thought more than once. Her answer had been Destin. Moving on. Leaving the past in the dust and starting over. It was hard, but she refused to accept defeat. Her military father had drilled that into her.

Never give up.

That was what she had to give Luke. The will to fight back. Despite the fear.

She smoothed Luke's sand-colored hair back from his eyes, and her heart turned over. Caring this deeply for Luke was dangerous and could only lead to sorrow for her later. According to Aaron, Luke had been as much of a ladies' man as Aaron before his accident. Losing her heart to him would be foolish. Even knowing this, she didn't fight the emotions pulling her in, binding her closer to Luke. Tonight, Luke mattered most.

"What kind of man am I? Bein' scared like this?"

"The human kind. Being scared is normal. It's okay. Quitting is not okay. Fight the fear and work with me."

When he made no response, she assumed he hadn't heard her. In truth, she doubted by morning he'd remember much of anything said between them. She was getting a rare, albeit alcohol-induced, glimpse of what Luke harbored in his heart, in his head. Still, the confirmation that his hostility masked his confusion and pain fired her resolve to break down the walls he'd erected.

She struggled to get Luke from the bathroom and into his bed, under the sheets, not bothering to undress him.

Looking around the room for a chair where she could sit for her vigil, she found a rolling desk chair parked in front of a desk where an elaborate computer sat idle under a clear plastic dust cover. Aaron had mentioned Luke's side business designing web sites and advising businesses on computer systems, and she made a mental note to talk with Luke about his computer work. He needed to get back to the things he loved as quickly as possible.

*A laptop, a joystick, and a hard drive. My idea of heaven.*

Abby's skin prickled remembering the double entendre he'd tossed at her the last time they talked about his computer work.

Opting out of using the desk chair, she turned out the lights and lay down next to Luke. She turned on her side, propping on an elbow and resting her head on her hand while she watched him sleep. With her free hand, she combed her fingers through his dark-blond hair, much the way her mother had calmed her when she'd had nightmares as a child. As she smoothed his hair away from his face, she studied the masculine lines of his cheeks and jaw.

The pink, new skin on his chin, where his less serious burns had healed, stood out against his tanned skin and the stubbled shadow of beard. He'd probably have a little scarring on his chin when all was said and done, she realized. Yet not even scars could detract from his handsome face.

Deciding Luke had more rugged appeal than his GQ-worthy brother, Abby wondered how many women he'd seduced with his good looks and heated gaze. His hot, piercing stare had left her weak and trembling several times, and, remembering that, she shifted uncomfortably on the bed. She didn't want to be a statistic where Luke was concerned. She wanted…

With a huff of disgust, she pushed the incomplete thought aside. What she wanted didn't matter. Common sense wouldn't allow her to pursue any involvement with him regardless of what she wanted. A ladies-man like Luke was the last person she needed to fall for. Aaron's desertion tonight proved that point in spades.

Even knowing Aaron wasn't looking for a relationship with her, knowing she didn't feel more than a superficial attraction to him, having him abandon her for another woman still hurt. More than she wanted to admit. She'd thought she'd come farther in the healing process after Steve's betrayal. But she'd thought wrong.

As she drew her hand along the side of Luke's face, he turned his cheek into her palm and rubbed gently against her hand. The tender, unconscious gesture crumbled any residual anger she had toward Luke.

"Abby?" He raised a hand to her face, groping blindly. "Is that you?"

"It's me. I promised you I wouldn't leave."

His fingers caressed her cheek with a gentleness that weakened her defenses. As much as she wanted to protect herself from more groundless hope and the pain of disillusionment, at that moment, she couldn't have pushed him away for all the world.

His tender touch hinted at the loving soul buried under his hostility and dour mood. He traced the curves of her face with his fingertips, and a honeyed warmth seeped through her veins, weighting her eyelids and relaxing her guard. Some last vestige of reason warned her to break free from the hypnotic web he wove. His intensity was infinitely dangerous to her heart.

"I never thought I'd have a woman in bed with me again," he whispered. His deep, sexy voice roused her from her thoughts.

"Why wouldn't you?"

Luke sighed heavily. He pulled his hand back and turned his face away from her. "Women don't want damaged goods."

"The right woman would. And you're not damaged goods, Luke."

His soft huff told her he didn't agree. Conversation ceased for several minutes, and in the ensuing silence, her mind whirled with questions that the events of the evening raised.

"Why did you tell me not to fall in love with Aaron?" The words slipped out before she could catch herself, and, once spoken, they hovered in the darkness between them. Silence answered her for so long that, when Luke did speak, his voice startled her.

"Because I don't want to see you get your heart broken again. Your boyfriend did a good enough job of that."

"And you think Aaron would break my heart?"

"Not on purpose." Luke yawned, and his voice grew groggier. "He's a good guy, my brother. Real good. He won't mean to... but he'll hurt you."

She'd decided the same on her own, but Luke's confirmation of her intuition left a strange hollowness in her soul. Still, Aaron's attention and humor had temporarily lifted her spirits.

"Besides," Luke said suddenly, interrupting her private musings, "if you fell for Aaron, where would that leave me?"

Abby's heartbeat stumbled. "What does that mean?"

The deep and steady rise and fall of his chest told her he'd drifted to sleep. He probably hadn't even realized what he said. But Abby couldn't help wondering about the cryptic statement. Was he concerned that her relationship with his brother would interfere with her assistance in his healing process? Or could he have feelings for her himself?

Given the wealth of information he'd revealed, Abby had no trouble staying awake to guard Luke's condition.

*I wanted to die.*

*Women don't want damaged goods.*

*Where would that leave me?*

She'd seen the same fear, uncertainty, and self-doubt that he revealed tonight in her other patients. Yet something about Luke's earlier blustering and stubborn pride had made her ignore the simple truth. She should have recognized the signs. Luke refused therapy, refused to try anything new since his accident, because he knew he could fail. For a young, handsome, cocky man like Luke, his new limitations, the possibility of failing, the uncertainty of his future, undoubtedly struck fear in his heart.

But she'd also seen his competitive streak, especially where Aaron was concerned. Understandable, considering they were brothers. Maybe she could use that sibling rivalry in her favor. Perhaps the key to motivating Luke lay in appealing to his competitiveness. She began plotting her strategy, and a smile tugged the corner of her lips.

Glancing down at Luke, she realized he'd grown terribly still. A frisson of alarm spiraled through her.

"Luke? Are you with me? Let me know you're still with me, slugger." Pressing her ear to his chest, she listened for his heartbeat. "Luke, say something!"

He grunted and rolled his head to one side. "Sumthin'."

With a deep sigh of relief, she chastised herself for panicking. The steady thudding of his heart beneath her ear reminded her that Luke was made of tougher stuff than that. He wouldn't go down without a fight. She allowed herself to linger with her cheek against his hard chest, savoring the life-affirming beat of his heart. After a moment, his hand settled on her head, pulling her closer, curling his fingers into her hair to massage her scalp. She tingled all the way to her toes with a sensation like champagne bubbles on her skin. She nestled closer to the solid warmth of him, inhaling the musky aroma of his aftershave.

*Don't be lulled into a false sense of security,* her head warned as she closed her eyes.

Sunlight from his window woke her the next morning, telling her she'd finally managed to sleep in the early morning hours. Without opening her eyes, she knew Luke was gone. The space beside her felt cold, drafty, empty.

Her pulse quickened. "Luke?"

"What?" The familiar, grumpy voice answered from the bathroom.

"Are you all right?" She swung her feet to the floor, ready to rush to his aid if needed.

"Leave me alone." The groaned response told her the extent of his hangover.

She padded across the soft carpet to the bathroom door. "You decent?"

"Define decent."

His dry humor was intact, so he couldn't be so bad off. She was formulating a glib reply when she heard a clatter and a mumbled oath from behind the closed door. "Luke? What are you doing? Can I help?"

With a quick knock to warn him she was coming in, Abby cracked the door open enough to peek inside.

"Who invited you in here?" Luke stood at the sink, fumbling with shaking hands to open a prescription bottle. His haggard appearance shouldn't have surprised her, but it did. The pale, drawn look of his face spoke for the pain he suffered. His rumpled hair and clothes and the day's growth of beard made him look disreputable and menacing.

"I don't believe you! After the scare you gave me last night, you're going to take more pills?"

His one-eyed glare glittered with anger. "I have a headache!"

"Not surprising," she returned in clipped tones. "Try aspirin!"

"Get lost."

"I will not!" She stomped into the bathroom and snatched the pill bottle from him.

"Give it back!"

"No!"

He winced when her voice reverberated in the tiled bathroom.

"These are narcotics, Luke." She waved the bottle in his face to punctuate her point. "I won't watch you become an addict!"

"Then leave!" He swiped at the bottle, and she jerked her hand behind her back.

"Give me the bottle, Abby!" he snarled through clenched teeth.

"No!"

He grabbed her arm, and his fingers bit into her wrist.

Abby deftly switched the pills to her other hand and held them out of his reach.

Dropping her wrist, Luke snaked his left arm around her waist. With a quick fluid motion, he hauled her body against his, knocking the breath from her lungs and lifting her feet from the floor. While she pushed against his chest, trying to free herself from his restrictive grasp, he grappled for the pills.

She kept them away from him, straightening her arms and wiggling in his vise-like hold. Despite his manhandling as he fought for control of the bottle, she used her thumb to pry off the loosened cap. With a flick of her wrist, she dumped the tablets in the toilet.

"Don't!" he bellowed as she kicked the toilet lever with her toes to flush the pills. Luke lunged for the toilet, dropping her in a heap on the hard floor. She landed with a jarring thud, biting her tongue in the process. The metallic taste of blood filled her mouth, and a buzz rang in her ears.

"Damn you! Why did you—" Luke's tirade ended abruptly, and she glanced up.

He stared at her with a haunted, horrified look as the color drained from his cheeks. "Oh God, Abby! I'm sorry. Are you hurt?"

Abby struggled to her feet, knocking aside the hand he offered to help her. She'd had enough of his childish, selfish behavior and his moping. Burning with outrage, she hardened her heart to his pleas for forgiveness. Damn it, it was time he shaped up and quit taking his frustration out on the people around him!

No more Miss Nice Guy. Today the hard work began.

"I didn't mean to, Abby. I swear!" he rasped.

Ignoring his apology, she stalked to the bedroom where she snatched her shoes off the floor then turned and glared at him. "Thank you, Mr. Morgan, for a lovely evening!"

"Abby!" His voice cracked with regret.

As she left, she slammed the door.


"Damn! You look like hell." Aaron smirked smugly over his bowl of Froot Loops and swiped milk from his mouth with the back of his hand.

Luke pressed the heel of his palm to his throbbing temple and scowled at his brother. "You don't have to yell."

What happened to their unspoken code of hangover courtesy?

"Luke? You okay, pal?" Bart asked from his morning post in his recliner. Luke blatantly ignored the question and the worried look on Bart's face as he stumbled to the coffee pot.

Aaron chuckled. "Nothing he hasn't suffered through before."

"Let him answer for himself, Aaron."

"I'll live." Luke poured himself a cup of coffee and took a seat at the dining table.

"Do you need me to—"

"I said I'll live!" Luke shouted, interrupting his father. He winced as the sound of his voice ricocheted in his head. Damn, but he needed one of those pain pills!

"Well, if you do need me, I'll be in my office." Bart rose from his seat, dropping the *Wall Street Journal* in the chair.

"Do you want me to take the first trip out solo?" Aaron called to Bart.

Luke groaned and pinched the bridge of his nose while his business partners discussed plans as if he weren't there.

"I could get Abby to watch the shop this morning, if you need time to do paperwork."

*Abby.* The mention of her name twisted inside him with a sharp ache of regret. He'd screwed up royally this morning and could only pray she'd forgive him.

"Sounds good. I'll take the afternoon run," Bart said.

"Works for me," Aaron returned.

Longing and frustration gripped him, and Luke swallowed the surge of acid that rose in his throat. If his family missed his participation in the business, they sure hid it well. It irritated him to think he needed his work more than the business needed him. He was bored stiff and itching to get back to work. He couldn't even update the Gulfside Snorkeling web site, because he'd done that just before the accident.

"So, little brother, had a bad night, did you?"

Luke glanced across the table at Aaron and grimaced. He was in no mood for Aaron's ribbing this morning. "Bite me."

"Morning, Abby," Aaron said, and Luke's heart jumped like a nervous cat.

"Good morning, Aaron."

Did the cheer in her voice sound forced to anyone besides him?

Luke raised his gaze to peer at her, but she waltzed past him without a glance. His stomach roiled with guilt. He had no excuse for his rough treatment of her this morning. By hurting her the way he had, he'd sunk to an all-time low. The memory of her anger, blazing like green fire in her eyes, knotted inside him. He'd never forget the sight of her blood darkening the corner of her mouth, and the grimace of pain she'd worn as she struggled to her feet.

Somehow, he swore, he would make it up to her.

After pouring herself a cup of coffee, Abby joined them at the table.

"Say, Abby, can you work for us in the shop for a couple of hours this morning? Bart's got paperwork to do."

"Well, I had planned to work with Luke. His OT assigned some exercises to help him with dexterity, but once I get him started, I can help out."

"Dexterity exercises?" he groused. "Think I'll pass this morning. You go on and work in the office."

Abby raised a scathing glare. "Don't think you can bully your way out of working with me today. I'm in no mood for your stubbornness."

Aaron gave a long low whistle. "Little brother, it looks like you have your hands full."

"I'm not backing out of anything. I'll do the dumb exercises later."

"No, you'll do them this morning. No more stalling."

Luke sighed. "Does the term hangover mean anything to you?"

"Oh, yes, I'm quite familiar with your hangover, remember?" She crossed her arms over her chest, clearly unwilling to be moved on the point. "You'll have to work through the pain. I think you can manage if you try."

"And if I refuse?" Luke challenged.

Abby braced her arms on the table and leaned closer to him. "Then I'll follow you around the house and make as much noise as humanly possible until you cave."

Aaron laughed, then imitated the sound of a cat in a fight. "Rrrrow!" He pushed his chair back and sauntered to the sink with his bowl.

Luke met her uncompromising gaze evenly. Abby's militant opposition struck a humorous chord in him. For a tiny woman, she could sure stand tall when she needed. He respected that, even though her wrath was aimed at him. A grin tugged the corner of his mouth. "You have no mercy, Abby Stanford."

"Thank you." Pushing away from the table, she gave him a satisfied smile that said she knew she'd won that battle. "All my clients say that at one time or another. But I get results."

"I'm not one of your clients."

"True. But I promised Bart results, and I'll use anything in my arsenal to get through that brick wall of yours. Don't go anywhere, I'll be right back."

She left Luke at the table, nursing his hangover and marveling at the tornado of a woman who had blown into his life.

❖ ❖ ❖

Abby carried a ham sandwich and corn chips on a plate to Bart's office and knocked on the door. The time had come to begin filling in the gaps of her knowledge about the family, and especially about Luke. She figured Bart was the best source for that information.

"Excuse me, boss. I was wondering if you had a minute to spare?" Abby advanced into the room holding out the offering of lunch.

"Sure, Abby. Come in. What can I do for you?"

"For starters, tell me you like mustard and mayo on your ham sandwiches, because that's how I fixed this one."

Bart glanced at his watch. "Is it lunchtime already?"

"Yep."

He rolled the kinks from his shoulders then punched a couple of keys on his computer to save his work. Turning to her, he reached for the plate she'd brought him. "Wow, room service. To what do I owe this honor?"

"I need information." She watched Bart shove aside one of the stacks of papers that littered his scarred wooden desk to clear a spot for his plate. The mess reminded her of Aaron's disorganization in the snorkeling office. Like father like son.

"Is this a bribe or something?" He flashed her a playful grin as she took a seat on an old sofa across from his desk.

"Or something."

"Oh? Is Luke giving you trouble?"

Abby waved a hand. "No. No. Nothing like that. At least nothing I can't handle." She paused and chewed her lip.

"Go on."

"Well, I was wondering about the family dynamic. I'd like to hear some history, some tidbits about who Luke is, what he was like before the accident, his interests, his relationship with you and Aaron. That sort of thing."

"Ah." Bart nodded his understanding and steepled his fingers. "Where should I start?"

"Well," Abby said awkwardly, tucking a wisp of hair behind her ear. "Why don't you tell me about Luke's and Aaron's mother and your divorce. Was it acrimonious?"

Sadness flickered across Bart's gray eyes, and he pressed his steepled fingertips against his lips before he spoke. "My wife was a good mother and a warm, compassionate woman. As much as I loved her, I took her for granted and didn't question whether she was happy. I poured my energy into getting this business going and making sure it succeeded. One day she informed me that she'd met someone else, fallen in love with him, and wanted a divorce. I was so out of touch with our marriage, I hadn't seen it coming. I was shocked. By then, it was too late, though. She'd made up her mind, and she could be so stubborn. I'm afraid my boys, especially Luke, inherited their mother's stubbornness."

Abby grinned. "I'm familiar with Luke's stubbornness. Fortunately, for my purposes, I'm an even bigger mule. How did Luke and Aaron react to the news of your divorce?" She leaned forward, eager to absorb any information he offered.

"Not well. Aaron was furious and let everyone know. Luke withdrew. He used to be so open and loving, generous with his affection. But almost overnight he became closed, cautious."

This fact intrigued her. "Why do you think he withdrew?"

He twisted his mouth in an uncertain frown. "When my wife left, rather than fight for custody of the boys, who were eight and ten at the time, she gave them the choice to stay with me if they wanted. I think she truly expected at least Luke to go with her. Luke had always been her pet, the one who was most like her. She was hurt beyond belief when they picked me.

"In all truth, I think Aaron chose to stay with the house and business he knew, his friends, his school... what kid wants their whole life uprooted when given the choice to stay with something familiar?"

"And Luke?"

Bart pinched the bridge of his nose. "Luke broke my heart. He was so torn. He loved his mother and wanted to be with her. But like Aaron, Destin and the status quo held great appeal and security for him. In the end, I think Luke chose to stay here because of Aaron. He's always looked up to him, tried to model himself after his brother. They were inseparable, especially after their mother left. It was like they leaned on each other to get through the divorce. They've been best friends ever since. That was the only good thing that came out of the whole ordeal. I've never seen two brothers grow so close."

He stared past Abby with a melancholy sigh.

"Where did that leave you?"

"On my own. It left me in charge of a struggling business and two rebellious sons who resented me for not holding their family together."

She saw his guilt and regret in the creases that lined his brow. Her heart wrenched in sympathy.

"Aaron rebelled against me and my authority immediately. That's when he started calling me Bart, breaking his curfew, taking risks."

"Risks?"

"Small things at first, like reckless stunts on his skateboard. But as he got older, he moved on to dangerous sports. Bungee jumping, motocross. Bed hopping." He gave her a meaningful look. "He was out of control, and I had no idea how to help him. I wanted desperately to regain Aaron's trust, and rather than striving to be his father, which was what he needed me to be, I tried to be his friend."

Abby winced. She was familiar with the results of that parenting mistake. "And with no boundaries, no parental structure or guidance, Aaron pushed the envelope more and more," she concluded.

"He never did anything illegal, mind you. I never had to worry about drugs or stealing or the like—thank God—but he was a loose cannon in other respects. For instance, his women. It was like a game to him to meet and seduce women, then flaunt it in my face. He knew I didn't like it."

She shifted uncomfortably. They were skirting close to a subject that was a sore spot in her life. Still, one question begged for an answer. "What about Luke? Was he as... casual... about women?"

"Luke wanted to be like Aaron. Aaron was his role model. When his brother took him out cruising, he started womanizing like Aaron. But Luke never flaunted it. I always sensed the appeal to Luke was more in the contest of besting Aaron. Luke has always been very competitive with his brother. I think maybe Luke was searching for something to fill the void that his mother left. Competitiveness and carousing with Aaron worked for a while, then he became more interested in learning the business, and lately—"

Bart shook his head as he thought.

"Lately?" Abby prodded anxiously. She processed not only what Bart told her but his tone of voice and facial expressions. Bart fit the image of a man in quiet agony, beating himself up for his mistakes, and unsure how to proceed.

"Before the accident, for at least a year, I'd say, I sensed that Luke wasn't happy. He was amiable, pleasant, good-natured, content with work and whatnot, but... he seemed restless. The lifestyle Aaron leads isn't really Luke's style, though he tried to make it appear that way."

This bit of information calmed the anxious flutter inside her to an extent. She knew she shouldn't have been so concerned about Luke's womanizing, but she was. Bart continued, and she refocused her attention on what he said.

"Of course, the staid businessman's life I lead was equally unsatisfying to him. So he was searching."

"For what?" Abby leaned so far forward, she nearly fell off the edge of the sofa. What she was learning fascinated her. She didn't pause to question why she took such an interest.

Bart shook his head. "I don't think he even knew. But I'm afraid he thinks that now, because of his condition, his injuries, that he'll never find whatever he was looking for."

Abby flopped back on the sofa, remembering Luke's admission to her the night before. *I should have died. It would be better than living like this.*

"He's lost hope. He's afraid of his future," Abby mumbled to herself more than to Bart.

Bart got up from his chair and took a picture from the shelf of a bookcase behind his computer. "This is the Luke I miss."

He handed the photo to Abby, and she grinned back at the three handsome faces smiling at her, all with the same heart-stopping brilliance. The picture was a recent one of Bart, Aaron, and Luke showing off their catch after a fishing expedition.

She studied Luke's face in particular. She'd never seen Luke without his eye-patch and scarred chin. His face glowed, lit by his smile and by an inner quality that radiated from his sparkling blue eyes. Love for his family, for life, Abby surmised.

Abby stared into those eyes, and her heart turned over. The Luke that smiled at her from that picture was the man she had been hired to find hiding beneath the layers of grief, despair, and fear that he masked with surly discontent. And, Abby discovered, that was the man she longed to meet, wanted to know, wanted...

"I'm afraid I've left you with a rather grim impression of my sons, Abby. Especially Aaron."

She looked up at Bart, whose face was dark with concern. "I want you to understand that they are both good, decent people. Aaron's a daredevil, a party man, sure, but he has a big heart. He cares about people. He's witty and fun-loving, but he can be just as compassionate and sensitive as a situation dictates.

"My wife gave the boys a firm foundation of ethics and decency which, with the exception of their sexual exploits, I'd challenge anyone to find fault with. Luke is… was… is …" Bart sighed as he struggled with his own uncertainty. "Luke is a kind, understanding man. He's intuitive like his mother was, and organized. He's stubborn and, as the baby of the family, a little spoiled, but he's got a lot of character and, if he'd just share it, I know he still has that heart full of love."

Bart's voice cracked. He cleared his throat and turned to switch off his computer. "Well, enough about us. I've been wanting to ask you a few questions, too."

"Me?"

Bart leaned forward, propping his arms on the desk. "I don't mean to be insensitive or rude, but I know this trip was supposed to be your honeymoon." His brow puckered, and warmth filled his eyes. "How are you doing?"

Bart's concern touched Abby, and she mustered a smile. "I'm fine."

He quirked an eyebrow, his expression skeptical. "Really? Don't forget, I had the person I loved leave me for someone else, too. I know what it feels like."

Her chest tightening, she forced a grin. "You mean the feeling that someone has ripped your heart from your chest without the benefit of anesthetics?"

He gave her a sad smile. "That's the one. Trust me, the pain eases with time, and it will get easier to remember the good stuff without second-guessing every memory."

Abby sat straighter. "You did that, too? Wondered if there'd been clues you ignored, opportunities to avoid what happened that you missed?"

Bart rolled his eyes and snorted. "God, yes. For months."

Abby chewed her bottom lip and stared down at her hands in her lap. "Sometimes I wish I could hate him. I think it would be easier to get over Steve if I could work up a good loathing, you know?"

"You don't hate him for what he did?"

She blew out a deep breath. "No. I'm angry as hell, hurt beyond belief. Disappointed. Frustrated. But Steve is a good person—his cheating on me aside. I fell in love with him because he was smart, and civic-minded, and ambitious, and had a good sense of humor. He inspired me to be my best and to try new things." She laughed as a memory of one failed experiment flickered through her mind. "Some with more success than others."

The curious lift of Bart's eyebrow encouraged her to expound. "One time, he made me eat raw oysters with him." She pulled a face and shuddered to reflect her distaste. "Slimy, nasty things, if you ask me."

Bart laughed. "An acquired taste, for sure."

"Anyway, apparently it was a bad batch. We were both violently ill for three days afterward." She shook her head at the memory and chuckled. "Nothing says togetherness like a shared case of food poisoning, huh?"

Bart's smile warmed. "See? You can still laugh about it. That's good. Hold onto those good memories, Abby."

She swung a startled gaze up to meet Bart's incisive gray eyes.

"The good stuff's not negated by how things ended."

She opened her mouth to respond, but no sound came.

"You don't want to hate him, Abby. Bitterness only hurts you and slows your recovery. Take it from one who knows." He shoved to his feet and jammed his hands in his pockets. "Now, if you'll excuse me, I promised Aaron that I'd take the afternoon tour, so..."

"I'll let you go." Abby stood and handed him the picture of the three Morgan men. "Thank you. For your time and for sharing your family with me. And for…" She waved a hand, unable to verbalize what his encouragement regarding Steve meant to her.

"Sure." With a wink, he followed her out of the office, then stopped before heading toward the back to the snorkeling office. "There's nothing more important to me than my sons, Abby. I may have made mistakes in raising them, but I couldn't love them more."

She put a hand on Bart's arm and squeezed. "That much is obvious, and I think they know that, too."

On her way upstairs, she mulled over all she'd learned. A family shattered by divorce, a father struggling with his mistakes, an oldest son living on the edge of danger.

And Luke. Withholding a heart full of love, hurt by his mother's desertion, striving to be like Aaron, searching for fulfillment… a deeply complex and intriguing man.

She had her work cut out for her.

# Chapter 11

"WHAT THE HECK AM I SUPPOSED TO DO WITH THOSE?" Luke scowled at the needle and thread Abby offered him.

"Plant a garden," she quipped with a sarcastic edge. "You're going to sew, of course."

He scoffed. "Like hell I am."

When he tried to stand up from the sofa, she planted a firm hand on his shoulder and shoved him back down. Luke knew he could fight her on the point if he really wanted to. One hundred pounds of woman couldn't stop him from leaving if he were truly determined, but his male pride insisted he put up at least a token resistance to sewing.

Geez, if he didn't owe her big for this morning's debacle, he'd be gone in a heartbeat. Sewing!

He gritted his teeth and sank back into the couch. His hand already hurt from the hour or so of stretching and strengthening exercises she'd put him through.

Abby held out the needle and thread again. "Your OT thinks you need to practice using your left hand to develop that hand's dexterity and fine motor skills." She paused, tipped her head, and regarded him with a certain smug confidence. "Sewing fits the bill, but I guess I could find something simpler if you're not up to the challenge. Even I have trouble threading a needle sometimes."

Ouch! A sucker punch right to his ego. Damn, she was good.

Abby started to turn away.

"Yeah, yeah, all right." He took the sewing things from her and stared at them for a moment. "So what am I supposed to do?"

"For starters, you could practice threading the needle."

Luke arched an eyebrow skeptically but said nothing. Abby knelt in front of him, in the vee of his legs and demonstrated the technique. Then she passed the needle and thread back to Luke. "Now you try."

Pinching the needle between his thumb and index finger of his left hand, he blew out a slow breath. How could he concentrate with Abby between his legs? Her placement gave him far too many ideas of other things he'd like to try with her. Even the goal of poking the thread through the needle's eye called graphic images to mind. To make matters worse, she propped her arm on his leg while he awkwardly gripped the thread between his right index and middle fingers.

As he squinted, hoping to bring the thread into focus, he was keenly aware of her hand on his thigh. The contact rattled his thoughts and kicked up his pulse. If her hand moved just a few inches up… well, he wouldn't be responsible for his actions.

"Come on. Try again. Lick it." She patted the outside of his leg, and his libido went ballistic.

He cocked an eyebrow and sent her a you've-got-to-be-kidding look. *Lick* it? He bit his tongue and swallowed the moan that swelled in his chest. She was determined to taunt him with graphic images, apparently. He closed his eyes to take a deep breath and collect himself. He'd imagined therapy sessions with her would be hell, but this was a torture he hadn't been prepared for.

"If you dampen the thread, it will be easier to maneuver. Like this." She leaned in and slid the thread between her lips.

Luke's pulse kicked, and a strangled groan rumbled from his throat.

Raising the thread he held in his right-hand fingers for another attempt, he fought clumsily to get the tiny string to cooperate with his intentions. After several misses, Luke threw down the needle with a huff. It pinged as it bounced on the coffee table. "This is pointless."

"It's not pointless, it's practice. Be patient. You'll get it." She handed him the needle again, and he took it with a grudging scowl.

"Luke, how is your depth perception since the accident? How well do you estimate stairs, for example?"

He gave her a short bitter laugh. "Don't ask."

"That bad, huh?" Abby chewed her fingernail with a thoughtful wrinkle in her brow. "Okay, try it this way instead."

She moved his hand so that his aim was left to right instead of up and down. If she thought anything of touching him, helping him with the motion, she didn't show it. But the feel of her hands on his reminded him of how she'd laced her fingers with his at the doctor's office parking lot. The sense of connectedness he'd experienced then flooded back, filled him, taunted him with a sweetness that seemed just beyond his reach. He found himself staring at her rather than watching her demonstration with the needle and thread.

Her passion for helping, for healing, radiated from her face and glowed in her eyes, and he wished that just once he could see that same passion in her expression and know that it was meant for him as a man instead of a charity case.

"Okay, your turn." She lifted her gaze until it connected with his. In a heartbeat, her radiant enthusiasm disappeared, replaced by a startled frown. Then just as quickly, a smoky desire filled her eyes, and her sassy lips parted as if waiting to be kissed. A palpable sizzle charged the space between them. The tip of her tongue darted out to wet her lips and left them moist and tempting, asking to be nibbled like a summer peach. Luke groaned and leaned toward her, ready to sample her sweet mouth.

With a gasp, Abby pulled away and sat back on her heels. She covered her lips with a trembling hand.

Frustration sliced through Luke, and he flopped back on the sofa cushions. "Are we finished here? This is getting tedious."

Abby cleared her throat. "Nope. Nowhere near done. Repetition may be tedious, but it's the only way you'll improve. Try the sideways motion." Her tone was all business, a clear attempt to distance herself from him. Erecting an invisible shield, she took back the control she'd lost for a moment.

Luke tamped his irritation. He'd seen the heat, felt the crackling energy zing between them, and knew she had, too. She could deny it all she wanted, but an attraction this hot couldn't be ignored. He, for one, intended to pursue the pull between them to its fullest. With his new objective set, he turned his attention to the exercise she'd given him with a fresh determination to show her what he could do.

❖ ❖ ❖

While she watched Luke work with the needle and thread, Abby drew slow breaths, calming the flustered beat of her heart. How in the world was she supposed to work with him and avoid touching him? The massages he needed on his hand were enough to send her imagination into overdrive. How could she touch him and not drown in the heady sensations that flooded her body from the briefest contact? The potent chemistry between them baffled her, intimidated her. She had so little experience in this area.

Steve had been her only serious relationship, and there'd certainly not been this kind of magnetism with him. Abby shook off that thought. Ever since Aaron had dumped her for the brunette at the bar, the old wounds Steve left had seeped fresh blood. She needed to remember what Bart had said about not letting the ugly end of her relationship with Steve override the good memories. She didn't want to become bitter, didn't want to get stuck in a pattern of self-pity that delayed her healing.

So how did she get Cindy's gloating taunt to stop replaying in her head?

"Forget it. I quit. It's impossible." Luke shoved the needle and thread at her and brought her out of her morose thoughts.

Abby frowned. Maybe a needle and thread had been too ambitious for his first dexterity test. All she'd done was discourage him with another failure. "Maybe we should have tried this with beads and yarn first."

He narrowed a threatening gaze on her that might have frightened a weaker soul. "If you bring out another exercise, I'll—"

"Sit tight. I'll be right back." She scurried upstairs and searched her room for a legitimate substitute for yarn. Her attention landed on her tennis shoes, and she quickly unlaced them and took the two-foot cord downstairs. "We'll use this with the needle threader, minus the needle."

"The what?"

She held up the wire loop used to pull thread through a needle. "A needle threader, courtesy of my granny. It's an antique."

Luke took the coin-sized disc with the one-inch wire loop with a huff of frustration.

"Go ahead. Put the shoelace through the loop." She grinned. "And give me props for my creativity on the fly, dog."

With an amused snort, Luke tried the new task. When he succeeded, she smiled.

"Good. Now do it again"

"For the next hour?" His tone reflected wariness. "Let's not, and say we did."

She rewarded his wisecrack with a lopsided grin. At least he wasn't being so bitterly hostile anymore. She wondered what prompted his change of attitude. Remembering her tactic of playing upon his strong sense of competition, Abby added with a shrug, "If you don't think you're up to the challenge, we could keep doing the same old—"

He cut her off with a growl. "Give me the damn shoestring."

Luke mastered that exercise in short order and made no secret of his boredom. Suppressing a smug grin, she scooped several buttons with larger holes out of her travel sewing kit.

After demonstrating how she wanted him to practice aiming the needle through the buttonhole, she passed the needle to him. Luke sighed and practiced guiding the needle through the fat buttonholes. "Just my luck. Aaron rips the buttons off your shirt in his frenzy to bed you, and I get stuck sewing the dumb things back on."

Her gaze flew up to Luke's disgruntled frown. "Aaron and I haven't—"

She stopped herself. What business was it of Luke's what she and Aaron had or had not done? "Just do the exercise."

He sighed dramatically and started to work. His slow progress obviously frustrated him, but within a few minutes he was hitting his mark with every stab. Pride swelled inside her. She'd known he could do anything he set his mind to.

When she heard footsteps behind her, she turned and saw Aaron enter the living room. He stopped and watched Luke patiently poking the needle through the button.

Luke glanced up at his brother, and Abby saw the flicker of embarrassment that crossed his face. Her gut knotted in dread.

"What's up, Betsy Ross?" Aaron teased, chuckling.

She shot Aaron a quelling look, but his attention was focused on his brother's activity. Aaron's jesting clearly disrupted Luke's concentration, and he jabbed his finger.

"Ow! Damn it!" Luke threw the needle aside with an angry grunt and sucked his offended finger. Aaron laughed harder.

"I'm sorry, Mr. Washington, but the flag won't be ready for a while," Aaron said in a soprano voice as

he strolled into the kitchen and opened the refrigerator.
Luke glared at his brother's back, then stormed out of
the living room. Abby's heart sank.

She climbed to her feet and walked over to the kitchen
where Aaron was still laughing as he poured himself a
soft drink. She slapped the back of his head.

"Hey!" Aaron turned to meet her angry glare. "What
was that for?"

"For being such a thoughtless bonehead! I was
making progress with him. He was finally willing to
try, and you came in and laughed at him! I could gladly
strangle you."

Contrition molded Aaron's face, and he muttered an
obscenity under his breath. "I didn't realize that was something you were doing to... ah, hell. I'm sorry, Abby."

"You should be sorry, and you should apologize to
him, too." She took Aaron's drink from him and took a
sip before handing him back the glass.

"I'm going for a swim at the beach," she announced
as she stalked out of the kitchen. "Call me when dinner
is ready."


Later that evening before bedtime, Abby stood in
the shower and let the warm spray wash over her. As
she soaped her body, her thoughts returned to Luke's
comment that afternoon.

*Aaron rips the buttons off your shirt in his frenzy to
bed you...*

Why hadn't Aaron tried to seduce her? He'd had
the opportunity. Was she undesirable even to a ladies'
man like Aaron? It wasn't that she wanted to sleep with

Aaron. She'd never been that casual about sex—but, darn it, it stung her pride to know he hadn't even tried to get her in bed!

Was she *that* unappealing?

An image of Luke's hot, sensual gaze flickered in her memory. Unsettled by the thought and the prickly heat it caused in her blood, she pushed it aside. Luke was all wrong for her.

Forbidden. Dangerous. Out of her league.

She'd probably only imagined the desire she thought she'd seen in his face. Or, more likely, he'd figured out how to unnerve her and used it to his advantage.

Glancing down at her shapeless body, she sighed. Who was she fooling? She fell far short of being a temptress. And short was the operative word. Her small stature and lack of curves had been a sore spot throughout her childhood and teen years and an easy target for her two brothers' teasing. Their taunts filtered back through her memory. *Short Stack. Little Bit. Tomboy.*

All of her childhood insecurities about her petite size, flat chest, and ordinary appearance returned. She may have graduated cum laude from college, established herself in a rewarding career, and proven herself a match for her toughest patients, but deep inside, she still harbored the scars of her brothers' jests. Her doubts had multiplied when Steve sought out another woman's arms. And breasts. And...

*You obviously can't satisfy him the way I do.*

Cindy's taunt made her stomach churn. If she couldn't turn a guy on, couldn't satisfy her partner in bed, was she doomed to lose any man she cared for to a more voluptuous woman?

She stepped out of the shower, mulling the gloomy possibility, and pulled on her bathrobe. Abby bit her lip and regarded her reflection again in the mirror. Just why hadn't Aaron tried to seduce her? Was there something specific wrong with her, something that turned men off?

The longer she considered that question, the more it bothered her. She had to know.

Without giving herself a chance to chicken out, without stopping to analyze the mistake she could be making, Abby marched out of the bathroom and down the two flights of stairs toward Aaron's bedroom. She wanted answers, needed answers so she could finally understand her part in Steve's betrayal.

Balling her hands and sucking in a deep breath for courage, she knocked on Aaron's door. At his summons to enter, she let herself in and closed the door behind her. Aaron sat on his unmade bed with his legs stretched out in front of him. He wore no shirt or shoes and the sight of his broad, tanned chest sent the first stirrings of doubt through her.

A financial ledger lay open in his lap and receipts littered the bed around him. He took a well-chewed pencil from his teeth to speak. "Can I do something for you, Abby?"

"I… I'm sorry. I didn't realize you were working. Forget it."

"I was just finishing this. What's up?" He closed the ledger and scooped the receipts into a hasty pile.

"Um… I…" She fidgeted with the belt of her robe.

She'd come this far. If she backed out now, would she ever have the answers she craved?

"Tell me what's wrong with me, Aaron. I know I'm not a knockout, but is there something specific that is a turn off?"

His mouth gaped open, but he said nothing. The proverbial deer in the headlights. She supposed her question was loaded at that. Right up there with "Does this make me look fat?"

Still, his silence worried her.

Despite the swarm of bumblebees buzzing around in her stomach, she stood her ground.

"Please, Aaron. I have to know why Steve deserted me for Cindy. Is it 'cause I'm flat? Too skinny?" Tears burned her eyes and leaked onto her cheeks.

"Ah, geez, Abby." Aaron groaned and dragged a hand down his face, still staring at her. "I can't answer that."

She took a deep breath. "Then why haven't you tried to take me to bed? After our date the other night, why didn't you try to seduce me?"

His eyes widened, and color rose in his cheeks. "I… I, uh…

"Why, Aaron?"

"I don't know. I've… I've never turned down a woman before in my life, but I…"

An icy chill raced through her. "Y-you what?"

He sighed heavily and shook his head.

Tears rose in Abby's throat and burned her eyes.

"But you're not like the other women I know. I couldn't do it. I'm sorry, Abby."

Humiliation clawed at her and, without giving him a chance to say more, she spun around and ran for the door. In her haste, her robe snagged on the post at the end of Aaron's bed and pulled loose. Cold air slapped her damp, bare skin.

"Abby, wait! Please, don't leave like this. Let me explain. Abby!"

Grabbing her robe closed as she went, Abby flew through the door.

And straight into the wall of Luke's chest.

Luke took one look at her tear-stained cheeks, her dishabille, and turned a murderous glare toward his brother.

Embarrassment and horror twisted inside her, and she scurried to close her robe. She wanted only to escape to her room and bawl. She'd made a fool of herself and might never live it down.

Spinning away from Luke, she started for the stairs, but he grabbed her arm. She raised a startled glance to him and tugged her arm, trying to free herself from his hold. Rather than releasing her, Luke led her into his own room across the hall.

"Luke, let me go!" Fresh tears filled her eyes.

Closing the door behind them, he pulled her into his embrace and held her close. She trembled with frustration and dismay, shaking as sobs racked her body. "Please, let me go."

Instead, he drew her closer. "Did he hurt you?"

A gentle, caring quality filled Luke's voice. The steady thud of his heart throbbed beneath her cheek, and she clutched his shoulders, savoring the solid strength and comfort he offered.

"Did he hurt you?" he repeated more firmly, plainly struggling to keep his fury with Aaron in check.

"No. This... this was my fault. Aaron did nothing wrong. I—" Her voice cracked, and he hugged her harder, so hard she could barely breathe.

Slowly, as her hysterics calmed, she grew increasingly aware of certain facts. The scent of the ocean breeze and Old Spice clung to him. She felt complete security nestled in his arms. His unshaven chin scraped against her cheek.

With soothing strokes, he rubbed his hand up her spine and down again. Murmured reassurances rumbled from his throat, and his warm, moist breath fanned the hair at her ear. With little effort, she could forget that Luke had a love 'em and leave 'em reputation just as Aaron did. She could forget that this man could turn her insides to mush with his heated gaze, that this man posed a greater threat to her heart than Aaron.

Because Luke made her feel things she'd never before felt. And with a deeper intensity. A ready-made heartache if she let her attraction to him go too far.

Recalled to her senses by the reminder of whose arms held her, Abby pulled away. "I want to leave now. I want to be alone."

He gave her a worried look as she backed from his arms. "Are you sure you're okay? He didn't—"

"I'm sure. I'll be all right. Thank you."

He released her and shoved his hands in his pockets as he stepped back from the door to let her pass.

She studied Luke's face before she left. The muscle in his square jaw flexed, and his expression reflected a deep concern, mirrored in the azure depth of his good eye. His sensuous mouth pressed in a firm, serious line, and it occurred to her how badly she longed to see him smile, really smile, even once before she left. She sensed, too, something deeper from the dark expression he wore. Was it hurt? Sadness? Reserve?

"Good night, Luke," she whispered.

He gave her one quick nod, and she stepped into the hall. Then Abby mounted the stairs in haste, eager to hide in her room and put this night behind her.

Aaron would give anything to put last night behind him.

He stared down at the sick greenish-purple milk his Froot Loops swam in, and his gut twisted with remorse. The wounded expression Abby had worn when she left his room the night before had haunted him through a sleepless night. Abby's expression and a host of nagging questions about why he'd turned down a beautiful, willing woman. His answer had hurt her. That much was clear. Maybe he hadn't worded his response well, but, hell, she'd shocked him with her blunt question. One thing was for damn sure. The jerk in Texas who'd hurt her had been an idiot. Abby had a gorgeous bod. Small, yes. But, sheesh! If he weren't trying to keep things platonic between them because of Luke...

He'd seen her trembling and that had been his first clue something was amiss.

Damn. Why did women have to be so mysterious and hard to figure out? His own motives for staying away from her were difficult enough for him to sort through, but he'd reached a few conclusions early that morning.

On some gut level, he knew making love to Abby would be a mistake, would be wrong. Sure, he'd considered it in the past few days, but every time he played with the idea, he thought of Luke.

Luke had a thing for Abby. That was the whole reason he and Bart had asked her to stay and work for them. Any time Aaron put the moves on Abby, he felt like a thief, stealing something that belonged to his brother, something his brother needed and treasured.

And then there was Abby. His own feelings for her confused him.

He dreaded facing her this morning. He'd never been good at apologies or explaining himself to anyone, much less a beautiful woman he'd come to regard almost like a sister.

A sister? You don't lust after your sister like a horny sailor. Aaron frowned. But that was at the heart of his problem with her. He didn't see her as another one of his women. She was more. Different. The idea that a woman could be, first and foremost, a friend and confidante wasn't a foreign concept to him. He'd heard of it happening to other men.

Other men, not him. He liked having no attachments, no strings, no responsibility.

From the corner of his eye, Aaron saw Luke walk into the dining room. He realized Luke had pegged him with a stare and glanced up. Aaron met his brother's icy glare. "What?"

"You screwed her, didn't you?" Luke's tone and word choice grated Aaron's raw nerves. He tensed his jaw and looked away. He was in no mood for Luke's surly preaching.

Luke stepped up beside Aaron's chair and shoved a hand in Aaron's chest. "Answer me, you prick! Did you sleep with her?"

He caught the edge of the table to keep from falling backward, then lunged to his feet. "No!"

"Bull! If you didn't screw her, then what was she doing in your room naked? Huh?" Luke jabbed him with one finger.

Aaron clenched his teeth, fed up with Luke's hostility and persecution complex. "None of your business."

"I'm making it my business. Someone has to look out for her. Have you forgotten what that ass back in Texas did to her?" Luke stepped closer and stuck his nose in Aaron's face.

Aaron fought for patience. He didn't want to fight Luke. "Nothing happened."

"She was crying when she left your room, for God's sake! Something happened. What the hell did you do to her?"

"Butt out."

Luke poked his finger in Aaron's chest again, and Aaron's typically slow temper swelled. Even he had his limits.

"What the hell possessed you to screw around with Ab—"

Aaron shoved Luke, cutting him off mid-sentence. Fed up with Luke's temper and righteous attitude, he aimed a finger at his brother and growled. "Cut it out, man! I'm sick to death of your bitching and pouting. What happened between me and Abby is none of your business. I won't justify myself to you!"

Luke set his jaw and met Aaron's defensiveness with a simmering glare from one narrowed eye. "You couldn't keep your grubby paws off her, could you? You bastard! You used a vulnerable woman and broke her heart because you couldn't keep your pecker in your pants!"

"She came to me!" Aaron shouted.

Luke lunged for Aaron's throat, and he raised an arm to block his brother's assault.

"Stop it!" Abby appeared from nowhere and wedged herself between the brothers. "Have you both lost your minds?"

Luke spun away and stormed out, and Aaron sighed and yanked a chair out from the table. He dropped onto the chair and put his head on the table with a moan.

"I could hear you all the way into my room. You were fighting about me, weren't you? And about what happened last night?" Abby's voice sounded calmer, but still heavy with grief.

He hesitated, then sighed. "Yeah."

"Swell," she groaned miserably.

Aaron lifted his head and met her eyes. "Abby, I have some explaining to do."

Abby tucked a wisp of hair behind her ear as she sat down across from him. She shook her head. "No, I put you on the spot last night, and it was unfair."

"Abby." Aaron reached across the table for her hands. "I'm no good at apologies and even worse at explaining myself, but I wanted—"

"Then don't apologize."

"Abby, will you let me talk? This is hard enough."

She nodded.

"I've wanted to make love to you. Truly I have. You're a sexy woman, and I don't know why Steve cheated on you like he did. But when I think about seducing you, I… have an attack of conscience. You… you mean more to me than just a roll in the sheets."

He flexed his hand and cracked his knuckles while

searching for what else he needed to say. "I, um…
don't want to screw up the friendship we have by
complicating it with sex. The women I've slept with
in the past were just warm, willing bodies who only
wanted a good tumble like I did. I never meant to hurt
you. I hope we can still be…"

Aaron stopped when he heard the cliché that was
coming from his mouth. Abby deserved better that a
lame, trite line like that.

Abby tilted her head to the side, and the corner of her
mouth twitched. "Still be…?"

"You know."

"Sparring partners? Roommates? Kissing cousins?"
Abby smiled. "Partners in crime? No, I know! You want
to take our singing act on the road!"

Aaron laughed and rose from behind his chair to pull
Abby into his arms for a hug.

"Friends!" he finished, chuckling. "Very special
friends. There. But remember you made me say it."

Abby buried her face in his chest and squeezed him
tightly. "I'd like that."


"Abby, do you need anything from the drug store? I'm
going to pick up a few things." Aaron bounced his keys
in his hand and waited for a reply.

Abby looked up from her magazine, and a devilish
smile curved her lips. "Tampons."

She cut a sideways glance to Luke, who silently
stared out the window at the beach, but not even her
attempt to rattle Aaron cracked the steely glower on
Luke's face.

"Not a chance," Aaron returned as he trotted down the stairs toward the front door.

She noticed the brothers hadn't so much as acknowledged each other's presence. She felt responsible for the rift between them but knew the best thing she could do was let them work it out for themselves. She turned her attention to her magazine while Luke continued brooding. Despite his display of kindness the night before, or perhaps because of it, she sensed a new awkwardness between them. A new hurdle to knock down before they could progress in his therapy. Maybe today would be a good day to work on getting Luke out of the house. He had to get used to being seen in public.

"Want to go for a walk?" she asked.

"No."

"Hey, you spoke to me! That's an improvement."

"Bite me," Luke grumbled.

"Where?"

Luke turned a sour look to Abby, then got up to wander into the kitchen. He rummaged through the refrigerator then a cabinet. "There's not jack for food in this house."

He slammed the cabinet door, and she jumped, startled by the bang.

"Geez, Luke! Would you give it a rest?" She took a calming breath and continued in a gentler tone. "Why don't we go out and get something to eat? I'm in the mood for some mint chocolate chip ice cream."

When his expression wavered, she added, "I'll buy."

He responded with a quick, brusque nod and started for the door. "I'll drive."

Abby halted mid-stride. She knew he had to be kidding, yet when they reached his Wrangler, Luke climbed in the driver's seat. Hesitantly, she took the passenger seat and buckled her seat belt, curious what Luke was up to.

He backed the Jeep out the short, straight driveway, and with her heart pumping anxiously, she gripped the seat.

Luke shifted gears, glanced at her with a grim face, and pulled the car forward slowly. After a block, when he stopped at a stop sign, he swung toward her and barked, "Would you call my bluff already? Or do you like the idea of me getting us both killed?"

She released the breath she'd been holding in a whoosh. "Thank God. I was mentally writing my will."

After putting the car in park, he climbed out and circled to the passenger side while Abby clambered over the gearshift.

When he was settled, she grinned at him. "Remind me never to play poker with you. You're harder to read than a Tolstoy novel sometimes." Luke remained silent, his head turned toward his side window for most of the drive.

Despite his arguments, she insisted they eat their ice cream in the store. She slid into a booth and dug into her dish of ice cream with relish, and he sat across from her, glancing warily at the other patron in the store.

When a family with young children came in, Abby watched in dismay as the oldest girl, a child of about five, pointed at Luke and asked loudly, "Mommy, is he a pirate like Captain Hook?"

The woman glanced at Luke, flushing with embarrassment, and shuffled the girl away, whispering in her ear.

Luke's jaw tensed. Abby held her breath.

The blue of his good eye grew dark and stormy. Without waiting for her, he slid out of their booth and stomped toward the door. Abby scurried to follow him, while Luke dumped his unfinished dish of ice cream in the trash.

By the time she got to the car, he was waiting for her in the passenger seat of the Jeep. His face was drawn taut, and she could see blood vessels standing out on his neck.

"Luke, she was just a child. She didn't mean to—"

"Cut it out!" he growled. "It's the truth! I'm a goddamn freak!"

"No, you aren't. Luke, people are going to look, yes. People may even whisper and children may make comments, because you stand out. But there is no reason to—"

"Would you just drive!" He pinned her with an arctic glare. "I want to get the hell out of here!"

Sighing, she started the car, then turned to him. Reaching for his chin, she tried to angle his face around to her. "Luke, look at me."

He jerked out of her grip. "Drive, damn it!"

"You have to get used to the attention. You can't hide out the rest of your life like a hermit."

"Drive!" Luke barked, whipping his face toward her with a ferocity in his expression that made her heartbeat slow.

She let the matter drop for the time being. He wouldn't listen to anything she said to him in the mood he was in.

As she drove home in the stony silence, she replayed the wounded expression on Luke's face when the girl called him a pirate, and her heart broke for him.

While she puzzled over what she could say or do to ease his pain, they became embroiled in a traffic jam. Abby looked ahead to the intersection where police and ambulance lights flashed, and she groaned, knowing it would be several minutes before the accident was cleared and traffic would move again.

Then she spotted the crumpled red Mustang, and her heartbeat stilled. "Aaron."

# Chapter 12

"OH, MY GOD! THAT LOOKS LIKE AARON'S CAR," Abby cried.

Luke brought his head up with a jerk. Icy fear coiled inside him. "What?"

"Look." Abby pointed toward the intersection in front of them, and he followed the direction of her finger to the wrecked Mustang.

"Oh, hell," Luke whispered, feeling the blood drain from his face, leaving him light-headed. *Please, God, not Aaron.*

In a heartbeat, he unbuckled his seat belt and bolted from the Jeep. Luke raced past the line of stopped cars toward the intersection, running full-tilt, and scanned the area for Aaron.

He spotted his brother standing in the median talking with a policeman, and relief surged through his body, leaving his limbs weak and trembling. Slowing his pace, he jogged toward Aaron.

"Luke!" Abby called, and he turned to find her running to catch up to him. She'd parked his Jeep on the shoulder of the road.

Aaron turned, apparently having heard Abby's voice, and ran a hand through his hair. Together, Luke and Abby crossed the highway to join him. They hung back until the policeman finished talking to him, then Abby ran to Aaron and threw her arms around him.

"Are you all right?" she asked breathlessly.

Aaron met Luke's gaze and nodded. "I'm fine. Just sore muscles. A little bump on the head."

"What happened?" Luke wondered if his voice sounded unsteady to anyone besides himself.

"I was on my way home from the drugstore, mindin' my own business, and this guy in a white truck sideswiped me and pushed me off the road."

Luke cast his gaze around the intersection to look for a white truck.

"Don't bother looking. He ain't here. The guy never stopped. Took off hell-bent for leather, tires squealing. I wrapped my car around that light post head on." Aaron rubbed his temple. "Thank God for air bags."

"Geez, you scared me, man. When I saw the car, I thought that… I thought…" Luke ran his fingers through his hair, blowing a deep breath out through pursed lips.

"You thought you were going to inherit my share of the business?" Aaron asked with a teasing grin.

Luke frowned at him. "That's not funny!"

"No, it isn't." Abby hugged herself and turned to stare at the crumpled car with knit brows.

"Damn, my insurance rate's gonna skyrocket." Aaron sighed. "I'll need a ride home."

"Sure." Luke watched Aaron walk away, then swung his gaze to the red Mustang. A prickle of fear rose on the back of his neck, realizing how close of a brush with death Aaron had had.

A rush of confused emotions crashed down on him, and for a moment he thought he might throw up. He bent over, holding his knees as he sucked in several deep breaths, fighting for his composure.

"Luke? Are you all right?"

Abby stroked a warm hand over his back, and her touch helped soothe his frayed nerves. "I'll be fine. Just a delayed reaction to the hit of adrenaline, I guess."

But later in the afternoon, Luke still hadn't shaken the eerie sense of doom that twisted him inside out.

He could have lost Aaron.

In the blink of an eye. A heartbeat. A failed air bag. He could have lost his brother.

Images of Aaron's wrecked Mustang flashed in his mind over and over again. Each time a chill crawled up his spine. He quelled the shivery dread by reassuring himself that his brother, his best friend, was safe. Not a scratch. That reminder brought relief washing through him.

Aaron, the lucky dog, always escaped unscathed, it seemed. He could live life on the edge, recklessly tempting fate, but fate had yet to catch him.

*But I toe the line and pay with an eye and a thumb.* Luke scowled, pricked by disgust, some aimed at Aaron and some at himself for begrudging his brother's good fortune. What if Aaron hadn't been so lucky? And the crumpled car would flicker in his mind's eye, and the cycle of emotion would begin again.

Luke rubbed his temple, trying to ease the throbbing there. He needed a refuge from his thoughts, quiet time alone to calm the whirlwind of emotions battering him.

Seeking the isolation of the back deck, he stretched out on a lounge chair and stared up at the sky. The last traces of evening sunlight still hid his stars, but soon they would appear in the twilight.

*His stars.* That's how he thought of them. His private escape and refuge. A passion Bart and Aaron had never understood, and he'd never wanted to share.

He managed almost an hour of privacy before Abby found him. Or maybe she knew he was there all along and gave him some time and space to think before joining him. She seemed to know him so well, seemed to see through all his bluster and bull.

Abby's insights to his feelings both intimidated and warmed him. Knowing he couldn't hide anything from her, that she saw through his guises, unsettled him, while knowing she understood him—and cared about him— reached deep into the loneliest part of his soul.

She acknowledged his presence with a gentle smile, then silently stepped to the railing to inhale the fresh evening air. He watched her close her eyes and tip her face toward the sky. The gulf breeze ruffled her short, chocolate-brown hair and pressed her T-shirt to her body. The soft material conformed to the swell of her small breasts and delineated the subtle dip at her waistline.

Last night, he'd caught a glimpse of what her clothing hid before she closed her robe. Creamy flesh and perfect, pink-tipped breasts. A sexy mole beside her belly button. Plenty of fodder for his private fantasies.

Before meeting Abby, he'd have sworn he was into big tits and lush curves. Nothing about Abby fit the stereotyped image of the sexy woman he pictured in his X-rated fantasies. Lately he'd been re-writing those steamy scenes to include pert breasts that just fit his palms, eyes that flashed like emeralds, and a small, slender frame.

She paused from savoring the evening long enough to cast a glance over her shoulder. "Mind if I join you, or is this a private party?"

He shrugged. "Suit yourself."

With a nod, she turned back to face the beach. "I love this view. It's so beautiful."

"Mm. And it got a little better when you came out."

For a moment, she seemed not to have heard, then as if the compliment finally struck home, she turned a startled glance to him. She opened her mouth as if to protest, then closed it again slowly. A smile blossomed on her face, and a deep pink blush, the shade of the sunset, stained her cheeks. His heart thumped a little harder. God, she was easy on the eyes!

Last night proved that she fit his arms just right. Given the chance, he could make a career of holding her, comforting her, protecting her from hurt.

For all her bravado and tough-as-nails posturing, he saw her vulnerable heart, the woman afraid of having her stubborn optimism doused by reality. Her fiancé had left deep scars, and Luke yearned, like nothing he'd known in his life, to cradle this woman close and help heal her wounds. Maybe because he understood the pain of being disillusioned by someone you loved and trusted.

As quickly as the memory of his mother's final words to him rose to haunt him, he quashed it again. He locked the hurt away.

Whatever his reason, the desire to protect Abby from further pain stayed foremost in his mind.

"You okay?" she asked.

He raised his gaze to meet the concern in Abby's face. Had his own expression given away his thoughts?

"I'm fine."

She nodded but continued to regard him with those perceptive eyes. "You know, maybe Aaron's close call today is just what he needed to make him slow down a bit and drive more carefully."

He snorted. "Are you kidding? Aaron never changes. He's always pushed the envelope, lived on the edge. I think he has a death wish."

"Hm." Abby bit her lip and knit her brows. "And how does that make you feel?"

He sighed and shook his head. "Don't start playing Freud with me."

She pivoted on her toe and walked to the side of his lounge chair. "When you saw his car, you turned white as a sheet. Admit it, Luke. You were scared spitless."

Narrowing his gaze, he crossed his arms over his chest. "And you weren't?"

"We're not talking about me."

"And why aren't we? I'm getting kinda sick of our one-sided conversations. You poke and prod me, want to dissect me like some kid's science experiment, but your life is taboo." He heard the edge of irritation that colored his tone and regretted it. She didn't deserve his hostility. He was tired of keeping Abby at arms' length, sniping at her at every turn. Yet last night when he'd tried to comfort her, she'd closed him out, pushed him away. Not that he blamed her. He didn't have the silver tongue, patience, and understanding Aaron had.

She wet her lips, looked down at her hands. "I've never been so scared in all my life."

Abby's softly spoken confession twisted inside him. He'd only been turning things around on her to take the heat off himself. Now her poignant admission hung between them. The weight of her honesty lodged in his chest. He didn't want to care that she'd been frightened. He didn't want to feel the pull to comfort her and take comfort from her. Caring too much left him open, vulnerable. Feeling anything for her was too risky. She'd proven last night she didn't want his sympathy, and he wouldn't offer something she had no interest in. He'd learned that lesson years ago...

"Those few minutes before I reached his car and knew he was okay," she continued, "were the longest of my life. I don't know what I'd have done if he had been hurt or..." She met his gaze. "Maybe it seems strange to you that I'd be that upset over someone I've only known a few days, but I... I've never had to deal much with personal loss. Even when my dad went overseas in Desert Storm, I had this sense of assurance that he'd be okay. Nothing would happen to my dad. And sure enough, he came home safe and sound. So I don't have a lot of experience with losing people I care about. I—"

"It scared me, too." The words spilled from his tongue before he could stop them. Maybe to keep her from baring any more of herself. Maybe to reward her openness. Maybe because Abby seemed more and more like a safe place to unload his grief and unburden his soul.

Her knowing eyes bore into him, and he heaved a deep sigh. He'd opened the door now, and he knew she'd want to be let inside the barrier he'd kept up until now. He chose his words carefully, not wanting to reveal too much. Maybe he could just test the waters first. "Well, he is my brother after all. I'm not completely without feeling."

Her hint of a grin encouraged him.

He rubbed his sweaty palm on the side of his shorts. "When I first saw the car, I, um... thought about the fact that we'd fought this morning. I didn't want that to be the last thing he knew of me."

Speaking the words, voicing his fear, brought a rush of feelings to the surface. His throat ached, tightened. Luke clenched his teeth and fought down the rise of guilt. A voice in his head warned him he was treading near dangerous territory.

"He knows you love him." Abby's voice flowed through him like warm honey.

Still, the personal direction of the conversation set him on edge. He shifted his weight restlessly in the lounge chair. He turned his head to gaze out at the waves, which appeared only as whitecap ruffles in the encroaching darkness, and he cleared his throat. "But that's a moot point, 'cause he's fine. They'll fix his car, and he'll live to wreck it again another day."

"Loving your family is never a moot point, Luke."

"Can we talk about something else, please?"

When Abby fell silent, he hazarded a glance in her direction. She hugged herself and chafed her arms above the elbow.

"Cold?"

"Maybe a little."

He held out a hand to her. "Come here."

When Abby put her hand in his, he drew her down into the chair with him and pulled her to lean back against him. She stretched her legs out beside his and rested her back on the left side of his chest, her head on his shoulder. His arms covered hers, and he rubbed his good palm on her cool skin to warm her.

"Better?"

"Mm-hm."

He didn't know about her, but the press of her soft tush against his outer thigh and the satiny softness of her skin under his fingers were definitely making him warm. The heat collected in the pit of his stomach, then shot electric bolts to any part of his body she happened to touch even briefly. His knee, where her hand rested. His chin, where her hair tickled him. His chest, where her shoulders leaned lightly, as if she were afraid she'd hurt him if she put her weight against him.

He settled that question for her by stretching an arm across her chest and pulling her more snugly against him. The minor discomfort of pressure against his healing burns paled in comparison to the pleasure of having her close.

She held her body stiff and straight at first. But as he stroked her arms, she relaxed by degrees, sinking into the angles of his body. Like last night, he noted the way she fit him. Like two pieces of a puzzle. That realization started a bittersweet ache in his chest.

She'd be leaving eventually, going back to Texas.

*Don't get attached to her.*

To distract himself from the track his thoughts were taking, he searched for a safe topic of conversation. "The breeze from the water can make the beachfront cool, even in the summer."

The same breeze caught a wisp of her hair and blew it in his face. The strands caressed his lips, and he inhaled the sweet scent of coconut from her shampoo.

"So if seeing Aaron's crumpled car scared you, imagine how he felt when you got hurt. He saw the explosion happen, knew you were on the boat—"

He groaned. "Are we back on that again? You are like a dog with a bone. I don't want to talk about my accident or Aaron's."

"But I want you to understand that what happened to Aaron affected you. In the same way, your accident affected Bart and Aaron. Something tragic can't happen in a family as close as yours without everyone feeling the pain and fear and worry."

"So I should feel guilty or responsible for what happened to me, because I screwed up their lives, too?"

She huffed impatiently. "I didn't say that. You're not to blame for what happened to you. Your family doesn't blame you either. But they need your under-standing just like you need theirs. Maybe not as much or in the same way, but... well, if you could cut them a little slack, it would go a long way. You've really been abusing them at a time when they are pretty stressed out, too."

She'd begun drawing little circles on his leg with her finger. It was a nervous, unconscious act on her part, he felt sure, but the sensation drove him nuts. Her deli-cate tracing on the one small area of his leg brought his every nerve ending to life. His skin tingled, and his blood thickened. His groin, just a whisper away from her elbow, grew heavy and hot, ached with need.

"So what do you say, Luke? Will you try?"

Hell, what had she asked? She had him so worked up he'd forgotten to listen.

"Uh... yeah?" God, what had he just agreed to try?

"Good." She tipped her face toward him and smiled. Whatever he'd agreed to made her happy. Making her happy made him feel good. Her smile seeped into him and warmed his heart like a blanket on a cold night. The odd combination of lust and emotional comfort didn't war within him like he'd have imagined they would. Instead they twined together and fed each other.

"I've seen families like yours fall apart because each member focused only on themselves and their needs," she added, turning back to look out at the beach. "Don't let that happen to your family, Luke."

Her warning slapped him like cold water. She'd struck far too close to a raw, sensitive spot in his soul. His heart slowed as he considered what she'd said.

His family could fall apart. Icy dread slithered up his spine like it did when he thought about Aaron's crumpled car. What would he do if he lost Aaron or Bart? Losing his mother had been hard enough. Having her leave the family had nearly destroyed them…

He sighed.

Abby was right. His parents' divorce had rattled the foundations of his family because they'd each wrapped themselves in their own grief. He and Aaron had seen Bart's suffering but had been too young, too hurt themselves to help their father. Instead they'd rebelled. Though he and Aaron had banded together, neither discussed their mother as if by mutual silent agreement. As if she'd died.

"Luke?"

"Hm?"

"You're being awfully quiet." She tipped her head to peer back at him again.

"Yeah. Just thinking."

"About what?"

He shrugged. "Lots of stuff."

"You're not going to tell me, are you?" He heard a note of disappointment in her voice, and it plucked at his conscience.

"Not tonight. I'm not ready to talk about it. I'm still sorting some things out for myself."

"But that's why I'm here. To listen. To help sort things out."

He turned his gaze up toward the darkening sky, where the first stars were finally visible. He changed the subject to avoid answering her. "Clear night. A good one to see the stars."

Abby tilted her head back and looked up at the stars. "Yeah. They're beautiful. I don't see nearly this many in Dallas because of all the city lights." She stared at the sky quietly for a moment while he watched the peaceful contentment on her face. "Oh, look! You can see Orion's sword. At home, all I can see are his belt, shoulders, and feet." She sighed and glanced at him. "My knowledge is pretty much limited to the Big Dipper and Orion, but the stars fascinate me. I wish I knew more."

As Abby turned back around and rested her head on his shoulder to gaze at the heavens, a satisfied thrill spiraled through him. She'd hit upon a topic where he knew he excelled, and he intended to strut his stuff. After weeks of feeling clumsy and inept because of his injuries, he could at last feel at home, in control, with the subject at hand.

"So what do you want to know?"

"I'd be happy if I could just point to another constellation and say look"—she pointed a finger at the sky—"there's Taurus the bull or Gemini the twins or whatever."

A grunt of acknowledgment rumbled in his chest. He slid his hand along her arm and redirected the aim of her finger.

"That's Taurus. Right next to Orion. See the three stars that make up the head? And then up for the horns."

She didn't answer immediately, but when she did her voice was filled with wonder. "Yeah, I see it."

Still holding her hand, he pointed her finger in a new direction. "The red star, Orion's left shoulder, is called Betelgeuse. And over there's the Big Dipper. If you follow the stars on the short side, there's the North Star. Polaris. And the Little Dipper. You know, they say the pyramids in Egypt are laid out according to the constellations."

She turned to look at him instead of the sky. "How do you know all this?"

He shrugged casually, barely containing a smug grin. "Astronomy is kinda a hobby of mine."

While she stared at him with a look of disbelief, he closed his hand around hers and folded her arm against his chest. He caressed the back of her hand with his fingers, savoring the smooth skin and the chance to hold Abby close.

"Your hobby? You... the telescope! It really is yours. I thought..." She didn't finish her sentence. Her mind was obviously clicking off what she knew about him and readjusting her perceptions.

"You thought what?"

"I, uh... I just figured the reason you had a telescope was to... spy on female neighbors."

He angled his head and scowled. "You assumed I was a pervert?"

"No! Uh, well… Kinda." She shook her head, and he enjoyed watching her fumble.

Finally he brought her hand to his lips and brushed a chaste kiss on her knuckles. "My father raised me to be a gentleman. I promise you the 'scope is not for 'I Spy'."

A chagrined smile tugged the corner of her mouth, and her gaze dropped to their joined hands. She squeezed his hand gently. "Forgive my assumption, sir. I'll think twice before jumping to conclusions about you next time."

He grinned. "All right. You're forgiven."

Her expression became deeply thoughtful. "So how did you get interested in astronomy?"

"Hm. Hard to say. It just happened."

She relaxed against him once more, resting her head on his shoulder as she looked up at Orion. "Beltug—what?"

"Betelgeuse." Luke stared at the red star, and memories flood back to him. The Christmas before his mother left when he got the telescope he'd wanted so much. Summer nights after his mother left when he spent hours on the deck alone, staring at the night sky.

Some internal tug prompted him to voice that memory. "After my parents got divorced, I spent a lot of time just looking at the stars. When everything in my life was falling apart, it gave me a kind of… peace… stability knowing that the stars would always be there for me. Night after night. Constant. Ageless. Unchanging."

Her only response was to squeeze his hand.

"Right after the explosion, I couldn't see the stars because of the swelling in my left eye. It's better now, but they're still dim." He sighed as a restlessness and frantic sort of longing clawed at his chest. "I hate—"

He stopped himself, realizing he was revealing too much. Abby's warmth and honesty, the intimacy of the moment, almost lulled him into spilling his guts.

That would never do. How could he give so much of himself to a woman destined to leave him in a matter of weeks, days?

"You hate what?" she asked.

"Never mind."

"You can tell me." She peeked up at him, her green eyes bright and encouraging.

"Forget it, okay?"

Disappointment darkened her expression, but she nodded.

The wind blew another wisp of her hair in his face, and he caught it with his left hand and rubbed the short, silky strands between his fingers.

His chest tightened. God, he'd miss her when she left. How had she gotten so deep under his skin so quickly?

"Think you might show me your telescope one night?"

He considered a crude retort but dismissed it in deference to the amiable mood between them. Somehow shocking and antagonizing Abby didn't feel right tonight. He wanted this quiet, intimate rapport to last as long as possible. She'd be battling him again about his therapy soon enough. "I'll show you my telescope or anything else. Pick the night."

"I'm free tomorrow."

"You've got a date."

She flashed him a smile, and the moonlight played across her face, making her fair skin glow and her eyes sparkle.

Aaron had always been the impulsive one in the family, but when the urge to kiss her struck Luke between the eyes, he didn't stop to question it. Without a second thought, he caught her chin with his left hand and brought his lips down on hers.

Luke's kiss startled Abby, but not nearly as much as her body's reaction to his warm mouth. The mere brush of his lips on hers sent jolts of electricity charging through her. The stunning potency of his kiss immobilized her momentarily, and she could only cling to him for stability while her head swam.

Luke plowed his fingers into her hair, holding her head between his hands while he explored the shape and texture of her lips with his own. The gentle pull as he drew on her mouth caused tendrils of pure pleasure to unfurl inside her. The moist heat of his tongue seeking entrance to her mouth sent powerful waves of carnal hunger coursing through her. Like a rip tide. She'd been warned about the powerful tidal currents that could overwhelm even a skilled swimmer, and now she knew the feeling of going under, of being sucked down by a force stronger than she was.

She heard a whimper, realized it was her own, and knew at some level she'd lost control of her senses.

Her senses, but not her mind. With extreme effort, she dragged herself from the sweet turbulence that temporarily numbed her conscience and flattened her palms against his hard chest. She pushed against him and yanked her head from his grip, gasping for a breath. "No."

She pressed a hand to her lips, which tingled from his tender assault and skillful manipulation, and she raised a wary glance to meet his gaze.

His expression reflected hurt, confusion, and lingering passion. "No?" With a short humorless laugh, he shook his head. "The way you just kissed me didn't say 'no.'"

Trembling, she clambered to her feet and spun to face him. "I can't… we can't let that happen again. It's too soon. I can't risk… You're too…"

She struggled to regain control over her ragged breathing. Steve's kiss had never affected her so dramatically. No man's kiss, not even her first kiss in junior high, had been as mind-blowing as the staggering kiss she'd just shared with Luke.

Why *wouldn't* Luke be good at kissing? He'd had years of practice with a legion of women. Reason enough to protect her heart. He wasn't looking for anything permanent, and she had a life back in Texas. Falling for Luke could only lead to heartache.

"I'm too what?" Luke's face grew as dark as a gathering storm.

Abby held up a hand as if to ward him off as she backed slowly toward the door to the house. "I'm sorry. I just can't…"

When words failed her, Abby spun away and raced inside. She wasn't ready to risk her heart again. It surprised her, scared her, how easily her feelings toward Luke had shifted, intensified.

Intensity. Yes. Intensity was at the heart of her fear. Everything about Luke was more powerful, more intense than she'd ever known with Steve. It only stood to reason Luke held the power to hurt her more deeply than Steve had. She had to be more careful. She couldn't fall for a man like Luke. Especially when she knew she'd be leaving in a few weeks.

In her bedroom, she sank onto the bed and closed her eyes. In her mind's eye, she saw the constellations and the glow of pride on Luke's face as he shared his secret passion for astronomy. She recalled the touch of sadness in his voice as he described his parents' divorce and what the stars had come to mean to him.

With a bittersweet pang, she realized he'd finally let her past his defensive wall, shared a glimpse of his gentleness and intelligence. Yet a peek was all he allowed her. A tantalizing snatch of his soul. A crumb that made her hunger for more. No wonder she'd lowered her own guard. That hint of Luke's warmth and intelligence had mesmerized and enchanted her. Her instincts told her he still withheld a treasure of love and complexity. She longed to bask in that love and explore his soul.

She shivered, remembering the tenderness of his caress as he held her and chased away her chill. Her body pulsed when she thought of his sexy kiss. She hugged herself, fighting the dull ache that bloomed in her chest when she considered the sweet security and sense of belonging she'd felt in his arms.

"What are you doing?" she whispered into the dark room. "You just got out of a broken relationship. This is just a rebound reaction. It must be. You can't fall in lo—" She stopped before the word formed on her tongue. Love? Was she falling in love with Luke?

Rolling over, she buried her face in the pillow.

No. Don't do that to yourself. You're asking for heartache if you fall for him while you're still vulnerable because of your last relationship debacle. Luke's not the one-woman kind.

Didn't the fact that he stopped short of sharing his inner thoughts, refused to expose his deeper needs and feelings, prove he wasn't willing or ready to commit himself? She could accept no less than full commitment, heart and soul.

A tear leaked from the corner of her eye onto the pillowcase. She wished…

Abby sighed.

Wishing didn't make it so. She had to put any thoughts of herself with Luke out of her mind. Permanently. No matter how difficult or how much it hurt.


The next morning, Abby looked up from the newspaper in time to see Luke heading out the door to the deck, his expression deeply thoughtful, even troubled.

"Luke?"

He turned toward the kitchen as if startled by her voice. "Oh, I didn't see you."

"You didn't look," she returned, grinning. "Where are you headed with that preoccupied mind of yours?"

"Just out for some exercise. I'm getting soft in the middle from hanging around the house so much."

Abby angled her head as she gave his muscled legs and firm torso a leisurely scrutiny. "I'll be darned if I see anything soft."

Her compliment earned a mischievously lifted eyebrow and the beginning of a grin. Success.

She set down the paper. "Care for some company? I wouldn't mind some exercise myself."

He shrugged. "Think you can keep up?"

"I know I can." She sent him a cocky look.

As she followed Luke down the deck stairs, she noticed the extra caution he used, holding the railing and stepping down each stair slowly, conquering them one at a time. Once he reached the bottom of the steps, Luke walked across the sand with quick, long-legged strides. Abby hurried to catch up and keep his pace.

After a short distance of walking, Luke lengthened his strides enough that Abby had to take two steps for each one of his. A few seconds later, he cast her a quick sideways glance and accelerated the tempo again. She jogged a few steps, vowing not to let him shake her.

Tugging up a corner of his mouth, Luke began jogging. Her heart pounding from exertion, Abby doggedly matched his speed. Then Luke eased into a run. Abby pushed her short legs to stay even with him, then poured on all she had to pull in front of Luke briefly.

He answered her unspoken challenge by taking off down the beach at top speed. Abby could never match his long-legged pace and athletic ability. Instead, she staggered to a stop, panting for breath, and watched Luke race down the beach.

Her heart turned over seeing him fly across the sand. Did he feel he had to prove a point to her? To himself?

Finally he stopped, bent over at the waist with his hands on his knees to catch his breath, and she walked up the beach to meet him. When she halted a few steps from him, he peeked up at her and smiled proudly. "I win."

"Why are you so competitive?" she asked between gasps for breath.

"Am I competitive?" He sat down in the sand, and she dropped on her knees beside him.

"As all heck. Especially with Aaron."

He glanced her way. "Aaron's different. We're brothers."

"So?"

"So weren't your brothers competitive?" Luke squinted in the bright morning sun as he looked at her.

"A little I guess, but nothing like you two."

Luke shrugged and turned his gaze out toward the horizon.

She contemplated Luke's profile while he watched the waves. The sun made his blond hair shine like gold, and the stubble darkening his cheeks gave his face a hard, rugged appeal.

Abby balled her hands and exhaled deeply. *Don't go there.*

He cast a quick glance at her. "I'm the younger brother, and I guess I've always tried to do whatever Aaron did, then be better at it."

Abby shifted to sit in the sand beside him. "And are you?"

"Am I what?"

"Better at things than Aaron."

A dark intensity settled in Luke's expression as he faced her. "You tell me."

An uneasy prickle chased down her spine, and she eyed him warily. "Meaning?"

But she had a hunch she knew exactly what he meant. She kicked herself mentally for opening the door with her ill-conceived baiting.

His gaze zeroed in on her lips, sending electricity tingling up her spine. Memories of Luke's kiss sent hot fingers of desire across her skin, through her blood, deep into her marrow. What little oxygen she'd recovered following her sprint snagged in her lungs.

"I saw you kiss Aaron after your... *date*." The bitter emphasis he put on the word spoke for the hard feelings that lingered over Aaron and Bart's deception in hiring Abby. Luke paused and glanced out at the water again before adding, "Did Aaron's kiss affect you even half as much as mine?"

Abby's mouth dried. The answer was easy. *Nowhere close.*

Couching a proper response proved far more difficult. "Why does that...? The two of you aren't... I can't just—"

Luke chuckled. "That's what I thought."

Abby snapped her mouth closed and gritted her teeth. Tossing a handful of sand at his feet, she growled her frustration. "Don't gloat. Egotism is not becoming."

He snorted. "Like I have so much to gloat about." He lifted his injured hand and, giving his compression glove a sneering glance, tucked his hand out of view again.

"Luke—"

He whipped his head toward her. "Don't. I'm not interested in another count-your-blessings lecture right now, okay?"

Abby folded her arms on her bent knees and stared out at the waves. "Fine."

Luke lapsed into a glowering silence for several minutes before asking, "I'm too what?"

Her heart kicked. She could play dumb, pretend she didn't know what he meant, but evasion had never been her style.

"You're too everything. You're too much, too soon. I'm not ready to even think about another guy yet."

"You were ready enough for Aaron," he challenged.

Abby shook her head. "Give it up, Luke. Aaron isn't even on my radar screen, okay? We're just friends."

He grunted his skepticism and fell silent again.

"So... have you heard from Steve?" he asked quietly a few minutes later.

Abby's gut tensed, shockwaves rippling through her as if he'd kicked her. "What?"

"You heard me. If I'd screwed up and lost a fiancée as special as you, I'd have at least called to apologize. Has the jerk even had the balls to do that much? To apologize for hurting you?"

Abby swallowed hard. Luke's choice of topics had caught her off guard, her defenses low. Her mind flashed back to Steve's groveling excuses and denials the night she'd caught him cheating. She'd been too angry, too hurt to hear him out at the time, and since then, when his number popped up on her cell phone's caller I.D., she'd ignored his calls.

"Even if he is sorry, I don't care to hear it. It doesn't change facts. I won't go back to him, no matter how good it was before he..." She waved a hand, not bothering to finish the thought.

She felt Luke's stare as she contemplated the repetitive motion of the undulating waves. She inhaled the salty breeze deeply and blew out a calming, cleansing breath. The pain of Steve's betrayal passed more quickly this time. *Progress.* Maybe Bart's advice was taking hold.

"Was it good?"

Luke's question pulled her out of her meditation. "Pardon?"

"What you had with Steve—was it really that good? I mean, you were going to marry him, so there had to be something about him you found worthwhile."

Abby gave him a stunned laugh. "Of course there was."

Luke angled his head a fraction. "Such as?"

"Why do you care?"

He shrugged and flipped up his left palm. "Curiosity mostly, I guess. And I thought maybe you could use someone to talk to." He lifted one eyebrow in challenge. "Or is all that business you've been feeding me about opening up to someone and sharing your *feelings* only go one way?"

She leveled her shoulders and returned an unflinching gaze. "I have shared my *feelings*"—she repeated the word with the same mocking tone he'd used—"with my best friend, Brooke." Once her gut reaction to Luke's less-than-endearing approach eased, she paused, struck by what he was offering.

Commiseration. A listening ear. Kindness.

Warmth blossomed deep inside her, and she bit back the wiseass response forming on her tongue. Swiping her wind-tossed hair out of her eyes, she narrowed an assessing gaze on Luke. "Are you sure you want to hear about my ex?"

He didn't answer right away, but he gave her a level look. Finally, with another shrug, he turned back toward the water. "I'm game… if it will help you sort things out. Put him behind you. Get some perspective."

She actually thought she was doing all right putting her relationship with Steve in perspective, especially since talking with Bart. But because she was curious to hear Luke's take, she said, "Okay. I'll play."

Abby scrunched her nose, squinting against the bright morning rays, and let her thoughts go back over memories she'd carefully avoided in recent days. The stab of betrayal and loss came, but with less sting than she'd expected.

"We met through mutual friends in college and hit it off right away. Steve was smart and funny, and we had enough in common that we had a good time together. When we started dating, we used to sit up late and talk and talk and talk. About politics, and classes, and our families, and movies, and... anything really. He was a good listener, and when we disagreed on something— and we did disagree on a lot of issues—he could debate a topic without demeaning my view."

But when was the last time she'd had one of those late night conversations with Steve? Abby wrinkled her brow, and her pulse stumbled. When was the last time Steve had really listened to what was on her mind?

She shoved the niggling question aside for the moment and continued, "We both like traveling, camping, hiking, that sort of thing, so we spent our first summer together hiking in the Rockies and rafting down the Colorado River. And he took me skiing over Christmas the next winter. We talked about going biking in Europe, but he decided to take summer classes instead and we never made that trip."

They'd never made any other trips other than weekends to visit his family or hers around the holidays. They'd blamed their schedules and tight finances, yet Steve had found the time and money to go on a golfing trip with some buddies last fall. Another restless jab poked her.

Maybe she and Steve had been drifting apart long before she caught him in bed with Buxom Blondie.

When she grew silent, Luke nudged her with his elbow. "What were you thinking just then? Your face got so serious and dark."

She shook her head. "Nothing. I was remembering... nothing."

He scoffed. "Bull. That look wasn't nothing. You'd never let me off that easily." He wiggled his fingers in a give-it-up gesture. "Spill."

"Fine," she said tightly. "I was thinking how everything I've told you was true of the first year or so we were together, but not so much the last few months. Something had changed, and I hadn't really noticed."

A bubble of dismay popped in her chest, and she stared down the beach, stricken by her revelation. "I was so busy planning my wedding I never realized my fiancé was pulling away." She swallowed hard, forcing down the bile that rose in her throat. "Maybe this is my fault. Maybe, if I'd paid attention, I could have saved our relationship."

Luke caught her chin with his left hand and angled her head toward him. His hard gaze and the warmth of his fingers against her skin scrambled her thoughts, stirred heat in her belly.

"And maybe some relationships aren't meant to be saved. The guy cheated on you. Don't make excuses for him or take any of his guilt on yourself. The guy was an asshole who hurt you. As far as I can tell, that's all the perspective you need. Forget him."

Abby held her breath, studied the fire in Luke's expression. The passion that ran just beneath the surface of this man intrigued her. If she could tap into that conviction and fire, channel it…

His loosened his grip and trailed his fingers along the curve of her lips.

Pulling back from his intimate touch, she cleared her throat, forced a laugh. "Hey, you brought him up. Not me."

He balled into a tight fist the hand that had caressed her. Turning away, he clenched his teeth, and the muscle in his jaw twitched. "Yeah. My mistake."

"Luke—"

As soon as she put her hand on his arm, he shoved to his feet and stalked several steps down the beach. "I'm going to finish my run now. Alone." He sent her a glare full of hurt and frustration. "Sorry I brought up Steve. I just thought…" He shook his head. "Never mind. I was wrong."

With her heart in her throat, Abby watched as he jogged away.

Luke headed down to the beach, needing an outlet for his pent-up energy and frustration. He licked his lips, remembering the taste of Abby's kiss last night. Mouthwash and starlight. If temptation had a flavor, it tasted like Abby. After several minutes of pushing his body to punishing speeds, he staggered to a stop. Dropping to sit in the warm sand, he propped his arms on his knees and hung his head.

Why did her kiss have to be so sweet? Why had she run from his kiss like it carried the plague?

*You're too much, too soon.*

Bull. He was too damaged. Not good enough somehow. Just like when his mother abandoned him.

He bit out a scorching curse. He should have left well enough alone. Shouldn't have let down his guard. Now he'd always know exactly what he was missing, living without Abby's kisses. She would leave soon, and all he'd have would be the memory of those precious seconds with her soft lips against his.

With a frustrated sigh, Luke pushed himself to his feet. He sprinted down the beach. He punished his body for its response to Abby's kiss, trying to exorcize the memory of the short-lived bliss from his mind.

But the memory wouldn't leave him and never would, he knew. How could a man ever forget the taste of a woman like Abby?

"Brooke, I kissed Luke. Or rather he kissed me. But… either way, it was a mistake." Abby flopped across her bed, clutching her cell phone, her link to Texas and the life she knew she had to go back to soon.

"Why do you think it was a mistake?" Brooke asked on cue.

"Because now I want to kiss him again!" she groaned.

Brooke chuckled, "And this is a bad thing?"

"Yes! It would be totally reckless of me to get involved with another guy so soon after breaking up with Steve."

"Maybe. Unless…" Brooke drew out the last word. "What if he's the guy you were meant to be with? What if that's why you broke up with Steve and why you went down to Destin? What if it's fate or kismet or karma or something that you are down there with him?"

Abby pulled the phone from her mouth and stared at it as if it had just burst into flames. Shaking her head, she tucked the cell back to her ear. "Brooke, don't you ever get tired of being so disgustingly optimistic and happy all the time?"

Brooke laughed. "Why shouldn't I be?"

Abby smiled. "No reason. And don't change. But seriously, don't you see a problem in me getting involved again so soon? Does the word *rebound* mean anything to you?"

"If rebound is what it is, yes. That could be a problem. But you have too good a head on your shoulders, you're too sensible to fall for a guy on the rebound. I mean the fact that you're worried about it tells me you're on top of the situation. If you like this guy and have feelings for him, why shouldn't you pursue it?"

"Well, there's the he-lives-in-Florida-and-I-live-in-Texas factor to consider."

Brooke laughed. "Oh, Abby! Don't you ever get tired of being so pragmatic and responsible?"

Abby sighed. She did get tired of second-guessing her every move, of planning…

"Hey, that reminds me," she said, shoving to her feet and crossing to her suitcase. "I need a favor from you."

"I'll do it if I can. You know I will."

Of course, Brooke would. Brooke would climb Mt. Everest to help someone she loved.

"You're the greatest. I need you to gather up some more of my things and ship them down here to me. I only packed for a few days, and I don't know how long I'll be staying. Maybe even a month or two." She mentally inventoried her closet and debated which clothes in particular she wanted Brooke to send. "Be sure to get my blue dress. You know, that new one?"

"A month or two at the beach." Brooke sighed. "God, that sounds glorious. What I wouldn't do—Hey! What if I drove your things down to you?"

"What? Brooke, I can't ask you to do that. You have a baby and a husband to consider and—"

"You didn't ask, I volunteered. I want to come… if I wouldn't be in the way. Oh! Matt is supposed to be in Houston for some kind of conference starting Thursday. I can come then! I'll bring Chad and your things, get in a couple days of sun and a visit with you, and… oh, I like this!" Brooke's voice grew animated, and Abby grinned.

"You know I'd love to see you, but don't do this because of me. You can mail the boxes and—"

"I'm doing it because of me. I haven't been out of this stupid house in months. A trip to the beach sounds like heaven!"

Abby heard her friend sigh happily, could almost feel Brooke's rejuvenated energy flowing through the phone line. "Okay. Then I'll see you Thursday?"

"Mmm, probably Friday afternoon, I'll take two days to drive it, because of Chad."

"This kind of spontaneity isn't like you, Brooke."

"I know. That's why it sounds so fun!" Her friend's infectious laughter filled Abby with warmth.

"Well, take care, and tell Matt 'hi' for me." After disconnecting the call, Abby laid out a clean shirt and shorts and headed into the bathroom to shower after her sandy jog with Luke, his question echoing in her head.

*Was it good?*

Yeah, her relationship with Steve had been good once upon a time. That's why losing him hurt. And how she knew falling for Luke could hurt even worse when it ended. Despite Brooke's cheerful assessment, Abby couldn't imagine she was Luke's type. She was a diversion. Convenient. Temporary.

And he was a heartache waiting to happen.

# Chapter 13

LATER THAT MORNING, ABBY KNOCKED ON LUKE'S bedroom door, and, receiving a low "What?" she stepped inside. "So… it's lunchtime, and I'm starving."

He glanced up from the courtroom-meets-reality-television program he watched and arched an eyebrow. "And this concerns me… how?"

She crossed to his TV and snapped off Judge Whoever-it-was. "I've been in Destin for a week, and I've barely scratched the surface of the local fare. I want you to take me out for lunch."

He scoffed. "Because our last trip out went *so well*." He pulled a face. "I don't think so."

She sat on the foot of his bed and gave his leg two sharp pats. "Come on, Grumpy. I don't like to eat alone in public, and I bet you have the inside track on some great little place tourists don't know about."

He stared at her, twisting his mouth in thought.

*Better than the usual scowl and dark glare.*

"I am getting sick of PBJ," he muttered.

She sprang to her feet and rewarded him with her best smile. "Yeah. Let me just get my purse, and I'll meet you at the Jeep."

Twenty minutes later, he instructed her to pull into a small strip mall along the main drag through town. She scanned the signs above the doors in the strip. Only one was an eatery. A regional chain pizzeria.

She gave him a pointedly disappointed look. "Uh, not the local mom and pop treasure I had in mind."

"Maybe the secret is that they really do have the best pizza in town." He unbuckled and opened his door.

She shrugged. "At this point, I'm not picky. I'm so hungry I could eat… peanut butter and tuna!"

He tried to hide the grin that tugged at his lips, but his sudden need to rub his cheek didn't fool her.

His amusement was a positive omen. She needed him in a good mood for what she had planned.

The scents of fresh yeasty crust and spicy meats greeted them, and Luke picked a table in the back corner, away from the flow of customer traffic. They ate their fill of arguably the best pizza she'd ever had, surrounded by garishly colorful walls and folksy murals.

Luke's good mood held through their meal, and he responded to her casual questions about the growth of Destin in recent years, the baseball team on the overhead TV, and his favorite movies.

By the time they left the restaurant, she was optimistic that he'd be agreeable to their second stop.

He frowned at her when she passed the turn to his house. "That was your turn back there. You can hang a U up here at the light."

She chewed her bottom lip, her pizza sitting in her stomach like a rock as she fretted over her trick. "We're not going back to the house quite yet."

"We're not?"

She took a deep breath. "You have an OT appointment with Joyce Harris."

His glare grew stormy. "Like hell I do. You're my OT now."

Abby shook her head. "No, I'm not. I thought I made that clear. I'm just a friend helping you follow through on what Ms. Harris—"

Luke cut her off with an earthy obscenity. "You tricked me. Lunch was just a ruse to get me out of the house, wasn't it?" The angry undertones in his accusation didn't upset her nearly as much as the hurt she detected.

"Not entirely. I do want to try more of the local—"

"Cut the crap! You tricked me, and you know it. I thought you prided yourself on your honesty." He smacked his left hand on the dashboard. "God, Abby! I thought you were above this."

"I'm sorry, Luke. But would you have come with me if I'd told you where we were going?"

His nostrils flared as he clenched his teeth and sent her a black scowl. "Guess we'll never know, huh?"

She turned in at the occupational therapy center and parked his Jeep. "I know you're mad, Luke. I deserve it. But don't blow off this appointment because you're pissed at me. I handled this badly, and I'm sorry. But you need to work with your therapist. For *you*. Do it because you want to get better. Do it because you don't want to lose the progress you've already made. Do it because you want your life back. Do it because—"

Luke shouldered his door open, and growling angrily, he swung out of his seat. "Don't deceive me like this again, Abby. Ever. I would have come with you if you'd asked. But *friends* don't stoop to this kind of behind-the-back manipulation."

The slam of his door reverberated in her soul. She'd expected anger and stubborn resistance, had been set for a battle of wills. But his hurt and disappointment chafed and left a raw wound inside her.

He'd offered her his tentative trust and respect, and she'd destroyed it. Would he have come with her to the appointment as he said? She might never know.

But she was sure she'd injured the friendship they'd been building. And that hurt her most of all.

"Tell me if I hurt you. I know the skin is still tender." Abby held Luke's injured hand in hers the next evening and massaged the scar tissue with her thumbs to increase the blood flow and promote healing. Through hours of intense therapy the next day, neither of them had mentioned their kiss, or their talk on the beach, or her trickery to get him to his OT appointment—a fact that relieved Abby immensely.

"I can take it." He glanced up and met her eyes. "After the debridements at the hospital, this is a piece of cake."

She winced. "I bet."

She'd heard how painful the treatment of burns could be, using a brush to remove the dead skin from the burn wounds in a whirlpool setting. Her heart hurt for him and the pain he'd suffered. "The worst is behind you, you know. You've survived more pain in the last few weeks than a lot of people deal with in a lifetime. You deserve a lot of credit for that."

He seemed surprised by her encouragement. For once, he didn't have a smart-alecky retort. She prayed his silence didn't mean he was still mad, though she couldn't blame him if he was. She hadn't forgiven herself for her poor judgment.

She could see progress in the healing tissue and no signs of a late infection. At his appointment with Joyce

Harris, the OT had shown her how to help desensitize overly-sensitive nerves in his hand. They were making progress, increasing flexibility in his hand and arm, but needed to continue the passive stretching, the daily massages, and the strengthening regimen. Joyce showed Abby new exercises for Luke to practice grasping small objects with his right-hand fingers and shifting domi- nance for daily tasks to his left hand. Buttons would be a challenge, as would tying his shoes. They had their work cut out for them.

The deck door slammed shut, and she jerked her head around to see Aaron walk into the living room. "Anybody out there want to join me in a beer?"

Abby flicked her gaze to Luke in time to see him cringe.

"Not me. I may never drink again."

Aaron mumbled something that sounded like "wimp," and Abby grinned. "I'll take an iced tea while you're up. And I put a plate of dinner in the fridge for you."

"Thanks, Ab. If I were the marrying kind, I'd snatch you right up."

A shadow crossed Luke's face, and she wondered what about Aaron's comment had disturbed him.

"You don't think you'll ever marry?" she asked Aaron as she turned her attention to Luke's hand, helping him flex and extend his fingers in their daily routine of passive stretching.

"Nah." Aaron walked into the living room with her tea.

"Thanks. Would you put it there?" She nodded her head toward the coffee table. "What do you have against marriage?"

Aaron shrugged. "Doesn't work."

"Not all marriages end in divorce, Aaron. My parents are still happy after forty years. My friend Brooke and her husband will last. I can feel it. They're so much in love."

"I'm not saying I wouldn't give it a try if I met the right woman. Just that, until then, I'm having too much fun auditioning Mrs. Right."

"How are you supposed to know when you've met Mrs. Right if you only do one-night stands?" She realized her tone held a preachy quality she hadn't intended, and she frowned.

"When I meet the right woman, I'll know."

"And how do you think you'll know?" Luke asked, giving his brother a skeptical glance.

"I'll just know. When I meet her, she'll blow me away," Aaron said glibly.

"Meaning…" Luke prompted.

"Meaning nothing." Abby glared at Aaron. "There's no such thing as love at first sight. Love takes time and work and sacrifice."

Luke made a clicking sound in his cheek and shook his head. "Time, work, and sacrifice… all things that are foreign to my brother."

Aaron scowled. "Yeah, you're real funny, Luke."

The microwave beeped, and Aaron headed back to the kitchen to retrieve his dinner.

"Does this hurt? Where are you most sensitive to touch?" Abby lightly dragged her fingernail across Luke's palm.

His fingers twitched in response. "It's mostly my palm. Your finger felt more like a blade."

"We can work on that. Can you distinguish different surface textures?"

When he hesitated, she nodded. "Let me work up a little test for you to see how much you can recognize. We'll save that for tomorrow."

"Are we about done with this session, then?" Luke sounded tired, and no doubt he was.

She'd subjected him to an extensive session of tedious exercises, but the session proved productive as well. When Luke set his mind to a task, she'd found, he was a force to be reckoned with. If he stuck with his therapy and met each challenge with the determination he'd displayed today, she felt sure he'd reach his therapy goals ahead of schedule. Though his daily exercises would continue for at least a year and maximum use of his right hand was still months away, Luke was making dramatic strides through the most difficult and painful part of his therapy. He was making up for lost time and putting his rehabilitation on the fast track. Soon he wouldn't need her to walk him through the daily regimen.

That thought should have pleased her. Wasn't his success her objective? Of course it was.

Then why did the idea of finishing her job here leave such a hollowness in her chest?

Before she could answer Luke, the telephone rang, drawing his attention away. Aaron snatched up the cordless phone in the kitchen. "Yo."

Abby glanced over her shoulder to watch Aaron's expression for some clue about the caller, just as Luke did.

"Nah, this is Aaron." He listened for a second, then a wide, sultry grin spread across his face, and when he spoke again, Aaron used his smooth, Mr. Charming tone of voice. "Hey, there, Kelly. What's goin' on, dollface?"

He turned to Luke and mouthed, "The hot redhead." He wiggled his eyebrows, but Luke sent him a bored look.

"Yeah," Aaron said, "Luke? Oh, he's healing up great. Yeah. He'll be good as new in no time. Yeah, that was pretty scary."

"Kelly is the chick Aaron was hitting on when the explosion happened. Her family's got a boat in a slip down from ours," Luke explained, and Abby nodded. Luke turned his focus back to Aaron's end of the phone call.

"Well, he lost his thumb and an eye. Yeah, a tough break. So what have you been up to? I haven't seen you around the pier lately. Paris? Cool. Nah, never been there. Maybe you could tell me all about it. I'm free tonight. What do you think—" Aaron stopped mid-sentence and lifted his gaze to Luke.

Abby continued bending Luke's fingers slowly back and forth to stretch the tendons and skin at the joints, but she watched the proceedings with interest.

Aaron's expression reflected a bit of surprise then confusion. He knitted his brows as he looked at Luke. "I don't know if he has plans... well, he's right here. You can ask him. Hang on."

Covering the speaking end of the receiver with his hand, Aaron carried the phone across the room. He scowled at Luke as he thrust the phone toward him. "She wants to know what you're doing tonight."

Luke arched one eyebrow, and a small gloating smirk hovered at the corner of his mouth as he took the phone from his brother.

Abby's heartbeat stumbled, and jealousy pricked her with its fangs. She released Luke's hand and sat back on her heels to listen.

"Hello? Yeah, hi, Kelly. Sure, I remember you." Luke wiped the palm of his left hand on the leg of his shorts.

Was he nervous about talking to this woman?

"Uh, not too bad. Thanks. Yeah, me too. Tonight?" Luke glanced up and met Abby's gaze briefly before looking away. "I can't tonight, Kelly. Sorry. I have other plans."

Abby exchanged a curious, concerned look with Aaron. Luke had no serious plans that she knew of. Her own jealousy aside, she knew Luke needed to start dating again. He needed to get back into his old routine, start seeing people, and stop hiding out. A date with a pretty woman might be good for his morale.

Even if the thought of him with another woman irritated her like all heck.

She reminded herself that she had no claim on Luke, was better off staying away from him personally. She needed to keep his best interests in mind.

"Yeah, maybe another time. Sure, you too. Take care." Luke punched the button to disconnect the call and handed the phone back to Aaron.

"Are you crazy? Kelly Winslow is a babe! She's gorgeous. And you turned her down?" Aaron sounded truly stunned, and his expression seconded the opinion.

"Yeah, she's all right. But like I told her. I have plans."

Aaron looked skeptical. "To do what? Jerk off in the shower?"

Luke glowered at his brother with impatience and disgust. "There's a lady present."

Aaron brushed off the chastisement. "I can't believe you just passed up a chance to go out with one of the hottest women in the state."

"Believe it. I promised Abby I'd show her my tele-scope last night, but it rained. So we postponed until tonight. Looks like a good night for it, too."

She jerked her head around to give Luke her own disbelieving stare. "You told her no because of me?"

"Yeah. When I make a promise, I keep it. That's what *friends* do." He furrowed his brow. "You're not standing me up, are you?"

"Uh, no. I just…" His emphasis on the word "friends" didn't escape her. Did this mean she was forgiven?

"Your telescope? Geez, Luke. You'd rather spend the night with your telescope than with a gorgeous woman? What a geek." Aaron shook his head in amazement.

Luke lifted his chin and met his brother's ribbing with an unflinching glare. "I *will* be with a gorgeous woman, thank you."

Her breath caught. She wished she could believe his compliment was more than a retort to his brother, but she didn't dare.

Aaron cast Abby a sheepish grin. "I didn't mean that the way it sounded. Sorry."

She shrugged. "Luke, if you'd rather go out with Kel—"

"I'd rather not." He narrowed an intense, sincere gaze on her, and a thrill skittered down her spine. "Why can't you believe that I want to keep my promise? I want to show you the telescope and the stars."

"But I—"

"Abby, I want to be with you tonight. Not Kelly."

Though she opened her mouth to speak, no sound came out. The look on his face brooked no resistance. Not that she wanted to resist. She wanted to spend the evening with him, too. She wanted to learn more about his love of the stars and build on the tenuous trust and forgiveness he offered. His loyalty to the promise he'd made her, his flattering deferral to her over the red-haired bombshell, stirred something inside her.

He chose her over another woman.

He couldn't have given her wounded spirit a greater gift. The thought almost brought her to tears, she was so touched. She blinked back the moisture in her eyes and cleared the emotion from her throat. "Thank you, Luke."

He glanced down at his right hand and moved his fingers slowly. "I'll get the 'scope set up, and let you know when it's ready."

He rose from the sofa and headed out to the deck.

When she glanced at Aaron, he wore a strange, amused expression.

"Mm-hm. Very interesting," he muttered as he walked away.

She started to deny to Aaron that he'd witnessed anything but a friendly exchange between her and Luke. But she couldn't. Something more was happening between them. He knew it. She knew it. Even Aaron knew it.

She was getting in too deep with Luke, and somehow she had to save herself before it was too late.

The next day, when Aaron took his lunch break, he found Abby elbow deep in sudsy dishwater.

"Do you guys do nothing but dirty dishes all day?" She scowled at him as he took a glass from the drying rack of dishes she'd just cleaned.

"We didn't hire you as a maid, Abby. Leave those. I'll wash 'em later." He reached in the refrigerator and took out the carton of orange juice.

"I don't mind. Besides, I have a friend coming in a little while for a visit, and I wanted to straighten up a bit before she got here."

"A friend? What sort of friend?" Aaron slurped his glass of juice.

"What sort of friend?" Abby cocked her head.

"Yeah. The type that is secretly hoping for a chance to jump your bones, or the type that I can hope will jump mine?"

She sent him the disgusted look he'd been fishing for. Man, he loved yanking her chain! God knows, he needed something to lighten things up around the place lately. He was on disaster overload. Luke's accident, his car wreck. Geez, what next?

At least Abby had made headway with Luke. His brother had been less grumpy and had an aura of purpose surrounding him now. And he could see something happening between Abby and Luke that intrigued him. By his guess, they were on a fast track to a hot fling.

He grinned, thinking of his brother making a go of things with Abby. He liked the idea of Luke finding someone. He'd always pegged Luke as the type to make a relationship with one woman work, and Abby seemed like the perfect lady for the job.

Aaron glanced into the living room where Luke was writing in a notebook using his left hand, his brows knit in concentration. Luke's serious expression softened as he stole a glance at Abby when she wasn't looking.

Aaron's smile broadened.

Luke and Abby. Some guys have all the luck.

"There will be no jumping of anybody's bones." Abby sent him a stern look. "Understand?"

"Why? Is she a dog?" Damn, he loved baiting Abby.

She shook her head in disbelief. "You're incorrigible!"

"That means you're a pain in the ass," Luke chimed in.

"As a matter of fact, she's quite pretty, but she's off limits. Not only is she married, she's a mother. She had a baby a few months ago, and she's bringing her son with her. So you stay away from her, hot shot," Abby warned, wagging a finger in his face.

Aaron pushed further, enjoying the fire in Abby's disgruntled gaze. "Hey, if she's hot, I can't make any promises. Women find me irresistible. What can I say?"

Abby responded with an unladylike snort. "Spare me."

Aaron headed out of the kitchen, grinning. "If you need me, I'll be in the shower."

The doorbell rang as he passed the front door on his way to his bedroom. "I got it."

When he opened the door, the woman on the front porch raised her eyes to his, and for the first time in Aaron's memory, the sight of a woman left him feeling as if he'd been kicked in the lungs. He stared like a star-struck school boy, his voice gone. Then the woman smiled.

And Aaron was blown away.

"You must be Aaron." She said his name with a Southern drawl, and to his ears the word had never sounded sweeter.

For the span of a heartbeat, Aaron gawked, trying not to gape at the auburn-haired beauty. He drank in her voluptuous figure, high cheekbones, and silky, thick hair that swept in gentle waves just past her shoulders. On the second pass, he noticed her luminous ivory skin, lush coral lips, and slender nose.

She was perfection.

"This is the Morgan residence, isn't it? I'm looking for Abby Stanford."

"Uh, yeah… I…" His voice failed him again when he met her eyes. The woman's eyes were the amber shade of whiskey and just as intoxicating.

"Brooke!" Abby's high pitched squeal shook him from his stupor.

"Abby!" Brooke returned, her eyes lighting with joy.

As Brooke stepped forward, she thrust something at him, and he instinctively accepted the bundle. He dropped his gaze to what he held, and his stomach tightened. A dark-eyed baby with brown fuzz for hair looked up at him and gurgled.

A baby! He was holding a baby!

He held the kid away from him, his hands under the child's armpits, the baby's arms and legs dangling. He'd heard that baby's sometimes hurled with no warning. While Abby and Brooke hugged and exchanged enthusiastic greetings, Aaron eyed the rugrat warily.

Suddenly, over the women's noise, he heard a familiar snicker. The snicker grew to a chuckle then erupted into a full-fledged roar of laughter. He pivoted toward the stairs in amazement, as did Brooke and Abby.

Luke was laughing. Laughing until he cried, until he had to sit down on the steps and hold his side. The sound of his brother's laughter was music to his ears.

"I thought you said he was always in a foul mood," Brooke said to Abby.

"He has been." Abby's voice reflected the same disbelief—and relief—that Aaron felt. "What, pray tell, is so all-fired funny?"

Luke gasped for a breath and pointed at Aaron. "My big brother… holding that kid… like it was… a ticking time bomb! His face—" Luke dissolved into peals of laughter again. When Abby and Brooke swung around to look at Aaron, their giggles joined his brother's.

Luke stepped forward and stroked the baby's head. "Thanks for the laugh, little fella. I owe you one."

Aaron scowled and foisted the baby into Luke's hands. "Ha, ha, ha. Let's see you hold him, then."

Luke took the baby, though his hold was just as awkward. The infant giggled and squealed and kicked his legs in glee.

"Hey, he likes you, Luke." Abby moved up beside Luke, and Aaron took his cue to leave.

He frowned as he marched down the stairs toward his room.

Hell. Leave it to his brat of a brother to humiliate him in front of a gorgeous woman.

No, he'd done that on his own. He'd bumbled like an adolescent and passed off her baby like it had cooties.

Her baby. Great. The auburn-haired bombshell was married. The woman of his dreams had a husband.

Some guys have all the luck.

# Chapter 14

"Wow, you weren't kidding when you said these guys were hunks!" Brooke whistled and set Chad's diaper bag on the end of Abby's bed in the guest room. "Whew. And Luke's smile... well, be still my heart, you belong to another man."

Abby chuckled. Her own heart pitter-pattered remembering the brilliant smile Luke had worn, laughing at Aaron's awkwardness with Chad. As she'd predicted, Luke's face came alive when he smiled. He'd vibrated with the energy and virility and warmth that she'd caught glimpses of in recent days.

"He does have a great smile, huh? That was the first time I've seen him really use it."

Even the memory of his radiant expression left her breathless.

She sat down on the edge of the bed and watched Brooke lay out a clean diaper for Chad. "Oh, Brooke, I'm in trouble."

Brooke glanced up with a frown. "Trouble?"

"I think I'm falling for Luke." Abby sighed and picked at a loose thread on the bedspread.

Brooke looked up from Chad's dirty diaper. "Falling for him. As in, in love with him?"

"As in." She broke off the stray thread and rolled it between her fingers.

"Wow. You don't let the moss grow, do you?"

"Trust me. Finding a new man was at the bottom of my list when I got here. Falling in love with a ladies' man like Luke is especially crazy." She flopped back on the pillows and put her arms behind her head.

"So tell me about him. How did this happen?"

"It snuck up on me. But there's always been something about him that flustered me, made me tingle just to look at him, you know." Abby chewed her bottom lip thinking of Luke's sensual stares, as if he mentally undressed her, and the magnetic pull that drew her to stare right back. Her pulse picked up, and she breathed deeply to quell the flutter in her veins.

"Hold still, Chad. You can see Abby in a minute."

Abby peered over at the four-month-old, who twisted to roll away from his diaper change. His tiny hands reached for her, and she stuck her finger out for him to grasp.

"Go on," Brooke prompted.

"Well, last night, he showed me his telescope. He's an astronomy buff, it seems. In fact, he passed up a date with another woman because he had promised to show me the telescope."

"Gotta like that. So what happened?"

"We looked at the stars and moon and planets... for hours."

"Huh? That's it? You actually looked at the stars. No making out?" Brooke's teasing grin made Abby chuckle.

"No, I think he's still mad about something I did yesterday. Or he's gun-shy because I pushed him away the last time he kissed me. I don't know. Not that I'm ready to escalate things between us. I'm still worried about getting in over my head."

Her friend's grin widened. "No guts, no glory."

Abby gave her a snort. "Look who's talking, Mrs. Only-dated-one-man-my-whole-life."

Brooke settled on the bed beside Abby and unbuttoned her shirt to nurse Chad, who'd begun to whine. "I'm just saying you won't know if you could have something special with Luke if you don't give him a chance. I know the timing is bad, but life doesn't always work on our schedule."

"So you think I should throw caution to the wind? Is this my Brooke I'm talking to?" Abby said.

"It's what you'd tell me if our roles were reversed, isn't it?"

Abby stared up at the ceiling. "Maybe. All I really know is, I spent three hours with him last night, huddled around his telescope with his aftershave driving me wild, watching his handsome face glow with pride as he talked about his hobby and movies and our jobs and his therapy and baseball and Texas and tourists and—" She stopped to catch her breath. "When all I really wanted to do was rip his clothes off and have my way with him."

Brooke chuckled and wiped a tear of mirth from the corner of her eye. Chad protested when her movement jostled him away from his meal. "Sorry, pumpkin."

Turning to Abby, Brooke tipped her head and asked, "What do you think you should do? You know him better than I do. You know what your heart is telling you."

"Maybe that's what worries me. I'm not sure I *do* know him. The thing is, as much as we talked last night, as well as we hit it off, he only talked about *things*. If I ever tried to turn the conversation toward more personal subjects, he deflected the topic back to safe, neutral territory. He wouldn't open up to me, wouldn't share anything of what he felt, what he dreamed.

"Bart told me days ago that Luke was closed, reserved about sharing himself. I guess I shouldn't be surprised he won't let me in, but…"

When she hesitated, Brooke finished the thought for her. "But you want him to let you in. You want to feel he trusts you with what is deep inside him. You want the emotional intimacy that he's holding back."

She turned her gaze toward Brooke. "Yes. No. I…" She rolled onto her side and propped her cheek on her hand. "I do want him to open up, but at the same time, I can't afford to get close to him. Not when I'll be leaving before long. Not when we live so far apart."

Abby grew quiet.

"Not when Steve just ripped your heart to shreds."

Leave it to Brooke to cut to the chase. "Yeah. I have a feeling that if I ever let myself love Luke, really love him, I'd be lost for good. He could hurt me so much worse than Steve did, because everything about Luke, everything I feel when I'm with him is more intense, more powerful… more wonderful. That's what makes it so scary."

Abby reached for Chad's foot and stroked his baby toes. A pang lodged in her chest. She wanted a sweet little bundle to cradle and nurse and wrap in her love. She wanted the lifetime commitment and promise of a man who would love her and make love to her.

Only her.

*When I make a promise, I keep it.*

Luke had kept his promise to spend last night with her. He'd been sweet and thoughtful and proved a good listener. He'd been eager to share his hobby with her, and their conversation had given her new insights to his sharp mind. And he'd behaved himself, too, honoring her stipulation that they had to keep the evening platonic. Abby bit her lip, her body thrumming, when she remembered the crackling tension, the electricity that had hummed between them nonetheless.

For a moment she indulged the fantasy of Luke as her lover, of her own baby with Luke's blue eyes, of promises of love and forever.

"Abby?" Brooke nudged her.

She roused herself from the daydream and sighed. "I poured myself into my relationship with Steve and got nothing back but betrayal. I won't do that again. I have to know he's as committed to me as I am to him, or I want no part of him." Her tone rang with determination, and she set her shoulders to match the conviction of her words. Now if she could only convince her heart to cooperate, she'd be fine.

But she feared for her heart, it was too late.

The next morning, Abby arrived in the kitchen before anyone else and assumed the responsibility of making coffee. She filled the coffee maker with water then hunted for the grounds. She found them on the top shelf of the cabinet. No problem for the six-feet-plus Morgans, but the can sat just beyond her reach. Undaunted, Abby stood on her tiptoes and stretched as far as she could, batting futilely at the can of coffee. She was just about to resign herself to standing on a chair when a warm body pressed against her backside and a tanned arm reached passed hers to lift down the coffee.

She turned in the tight space between the cabinet and the wall of masculinity and raised her gaze to Luke's. "Thank you. You're handy to have around."

Luke's mouth twitched with the hint of a smile. "Am I?"

Tipping her head back to meet his probing blue stare made Abby feel especially tiny compared to his brawn. Tiny and feminine.

She started to answer that, yes, he was useful, when his hand settled at her waist, and he locked his fiery blue gaze with hers. He stripped away any pretenses and peered into her soul. Her heartbeat fluttered, and her knees grew weak under the power of his hot, penetrating stare. With his body, his heat pressed so close, wild, primitive urges assailed her. The longing to feel his hands, his lips against her skin crashed over her with the strength of a tidal wave. She wanted him... inside her.

An image of Luke's body, joined with hers, flickered through her mind, and she gulped for air. The prickly heat of arousal stung her cheeks, her breasts, and her breathing grew shallow and rapid.

Abby forced herself to speak, though her voice sounded strangled to her own ears. "Excuse me."

Rather than moving, Luke murmured softly, "Tell me you feel it, too."

Abby's eyes widened, her pulse quickened to the point she felt dizzy.

"I can't... I..." Ducking under his arm, she pushed away and scurried from the hypnotic spell he cast over her.

Luke stayed in the same spot for several more seconds, his head down, and when he turned to her again, his jaw was rigid, the glare he gave her cool and cruel.

"Morning, all," Bart said as he entered the kitchen, and Abby welcomed his diversion. "Looks like the weatherman was right for a change."

She glanced out the window at the rain splattering on the wide pane.

"Well, this rain spoils any plans for snorkeling, but it gives me an excuse to catch up on paperwork." Bart gave her a forced smile.

The creases beside his eyes and his tight-lipped smile hinted at the stress and lack of sleep he'd suffered lately. It seemed to Abby that Luke's father handled crises by sweeping his troubles under the rug and plugging on. He didn't deal with problems; he neglected them. But putting a bandage on a festering wound didn't allow it to heal. She made a mental note to talk with Bart later.

"Gonna close up the shop or just cancel the tours?" Luke asked, his voice showing none of the chill Abby had seen in his expression just seconds before.

"If it were later in the season, I'd feel compelled to keep the shop open, but this early in the year business is slow. What do you think, Luke?"

He seemed startled by his father's deferral to his judgment. "I'd say since Brooke's in town, it'd be nice to close the shop and not have to worry about it today. Besides, Aaron's earned a vacation."

Bart flashed him a smile that was full of pride. "It's decided then. How about a proper breakfast this morning?"

"What do you have in mind?" Abby sat down at the bar and rewarded Bart's effort to include Luke in the business with a secret grin.

"Morgan omelets." Bart took out the frying pan and a carton of eggs.

Luke turned his gaze to Abby. "You're in for a treat. His coffee sucks, but his omelets are the stuff of legends."

Bart paused in his preparations. "My coffee sucks?"

"Hell, yeah. What have we been telling you for years?" Luke opened the refrigerator and began taking out ingredients for his father.

"Should we be expecting Brooke this morning for breakfast?" Bart asked Abby.

"If it's not an imposition. She's an early riser because of the baby, and I told her rather than hang around the hotel alone to come on over here."

"No problem. Glad to have her." Bart began cracking eggs with surprising finesse.

When the doorbell rang, Abby tore herself away from the fascinating production and hurried to let Brooke in.

Once she and Brooke settled Chad with his baby monitor in Abby's bedroom, they joined the men for breakfast.

After eating, Bart excused himself to his office while the rest of the group voted to rent a few videos to help pass the rainy day.

"Come on, bro. If we go to the store, we get to pick the flick." Aaron jabbed Luke in the arm as he got up from the table. "Besides, with my car in the shop, we gotta take your Jeep."

Abby released a sigh of relief when Luke readily agreed to accompany Aaron to the store. More than the chance to choose the video, she suspected he missed hanging out with his brother, and she knew the time together would do them both good.

"Nothing too violent," Brooke pleaded as Aaron searched the kitchen counter and his pockets for his car keys.

"And nothing pornographic," Abby added, poking Aaron with a finger.

"What else is there?"

Abby sent Aaron a warning glare then turned to Luke. "We're counting on you."

"Trust me." Luke's tone was even and deep, and the confident expression he wore was shockingly sexy.

A thrill spun through her middle, and she paused before she nodded. "I do."

Luke stooped to pick Aaron's keys from the coffee table. "Hey, Stupid, catch."

Aaron turned just in time to catch the keys Luke flung at him. "Where…?"

Luke pointed to the end of the coffee table, then headed out of the living room.

Abby noticed that Aaron cast a long lingering look at Brooke before he left. Rather than salacious, his gaze seemed wistful.

And was, therefore, far more disturbing.


"You've got a serious thing for Abby, don't you?" Aaron asked without preamble as he drove Luke's Wrangler to the video store.

Stunned by Aaron's abruptness and insight, Luke hesitated a beat. "Okay, put down the crack pipe. You've started hallucinating."

"Geez, you can't even deny it without looking guilty!" Aaron slapped the steering wheel as he laughed.

"You're out of your mind," Luke grumbled and sent his brother a menacing glare. If Aaron had picked up on his feelings for Abby, why did she remain so unyielding, so reluctant to see what was happening between them?

Rather than discuss his feelings for Abby, Luke chose diversion. "Yeah, and what about you?"

"Naw." Aaron shook his head. "We're just friends. I've told you that we talked and—"

"Not Abby!" Luke said impatiently. "Brooke!"

Aaron jerked his head around, turning an incredulous stare to his brother. "What!"

"You've been drooling over her ever since she got here." Luke grabbed the armrest as Aaron wheeled into the parking lot of the video store. "Slow down, man. Try not to wreck my car, too!"

"May I remind you she's married and has a kid?" Aaron said calmly, ignoring Luke's comment on his driving.

"May I remind *you* that she's married and has a kid? Don't mess with her, Aaron. Married women spell trouble."

"Who's messing with anybody?" Aaron returned defensively. "Sure, I noticed that she's a babe. Kinda hard not to notice. But I know better than to try anything with a married woman."

"I certainly hope so."

"How'd we get onto me? I asked you about Abby." Aaron unbuckled his seat belt.

"Don't change the subject."

Aaron huffed. "Don't *you* change the subject."

"Abby's made it clear nothing's gonna happen between us." Luke turned to get out of the car.

Before he could escape, Aaron grabbed his arm. "Then you've put the moves on her, and she turned you down?"

Instead of gloating, Luke heard surprise and sympathy in Aaron's question. He sighed. "Yeah, all right? I kissed her, and she ran like hell away from me. Satisfied?"

"And so you're giving up?"

"I'm not a glutton for punishment!"

"I think you could melt her ice if you tried." Aaron's tone was low and sincere.

"Are you forgetting my new woman deflectors?" Luke held up his right hand for emphasis.

"You don't really believe that matters to Abby, do you?" Aaron shook his head slowly, his face dark with concern and disbelief.

Luke turned away from the compassion and worry reflected in his brother's face. "She was ready enough to get it on with you. What else am I supposed to think?"

Rather than pursue the uncomfortable conversation, Luke bolted from the car. Aaron followed Luke into the store and marched up behind him as he scanned the rack of new releases. "Fine. Give up on her if you think she's not worth the effort. But if you love Abby—and I think you do—then you'd be an idiot to let her go without a fight."

Luke stalked silently over to the horror section, blatantly ignoring his brother, but Aaron didn't relent.

"You saw how miserable Bart was when Mom left—or have you forgotten?"

Luke spun around and nailed his brother with an icy glare. "I haven't forgotten."

"He sat back and let her leave, Luke. Didn't do a damn thing to stop her. And you're gonna lose Abby unless you wise up pretty quick."

His brother's brutal honesty kicked Luke in the gut. He crossed his arms over his chest, channeling the unwelcome pain into a defensive attack. "What do you know about relationships with women? You don't even hang around for the morning after."

"I know that to make it last, you have to be willing to work at it. You have to give something of yourself. That's why Bart lost Mom. He didn't do anything to stop her from leaving."

Luke's temper snapped and years-old agony flooded back. "There was nothing he could do! She didn't want us! I asked her—no, *begged* her—not to go. I swallowed my eight-year-old pride and pleaded with her to stay. And do you want to know what she said?"

Aaron's face had grown pale. He stared at Luke with his own sorrow and years of pain etched in his face.

Luke lowered his voice, but his tone remained hard and unforgiving. "She said there was nothing left for her here." He swallowed, loosening the emotion choking him. "I poured out my heart to her, and she told me it was worth nothing. Do you know how that felt? Do you have any idea how much it hurts to hear your mother say you mean zilch to her?"

"She didn't mean you," Aaron rasped.

"Like hell she didn't." Luke clenched his jaw so tight his teeth hurt. "I'll be damned before I make that mistake again."

With that, he left Aaron standing in the aisle and stormed from the store.

# Chapter 15

THE RAIN STORM CONTINUED THROUGH THE DAY, ADDING to Luke's already dark mood. The subject of their mother had always been taboo between him and Aaron. The fact that his brother had broached the forbidden topic that morning bothered Luke more than he wanted to admit.

Occasionally, as they watched the video Aaron had selected—an action-adventure flick that seemed to satisfy the women—Luke caught himself watching Abby instead. She played with Chad throughout the morning and cuddled the baby when he dozed off just before lunch. Abby would be a great mother someday.

He frowned, wondering why in hell he'd thought in those terms. Was he comparing her affectionate nature to his own mother's neglect? And why did the idea of Abby with her own children cause a sensation like the flow of warm molasses to fill his chest? God, this weather made him maudlin.

Restless, Luke got up from the sofa and stalked into the kitchen to prowl through the cabinets. He found a pack of peanut butter crackers and fumbled awkwardly to open them.

"Try holding the pack in your right hand and ripping with your left."

He glanced up to find Abby standing across from him, watching his efforts with keen interest. Instead of following her suggestion, he ripped the pack open with his teeth.

Abby grinned. "Whatever works. Ingenuity and adapting is the name of the game."

"I don't consider my life a game." He brushed past her, and she followed.

"No, and I don't either. It was just an expression."

Luke dropped back down on the sofa and popped a whole cracker sandwich into his mouth.

He stared at the television but had lost interest in the video. Sighing, he began drumming his fingers on the arm of the couch.

Aaron scowled at him from his post in Bart's recliner. "Would you stop? That's annoying as hell."

A bitter retort came to mind, but he swallowed it in deference to Brooke and Abby.

"Luke." Abby stood and crooked her finger. "Come with me."

Intrigued, he arched an eyebrow and followed her down the stairs to his bedroom.

For a moment, a quiver of expectation washed through him, but it died quickly when she crossed the room to his computer and pulled off the dust cover.

"I think it's time you got back to business."

Luke narrowed a suspicious gaze on her. "What are you talking about?"

"Aaron told me about your web page design work. I see no reason why you can't get back to that, or even working the business end of Gulfside Snorkeling, until you get the okay to drive the boat again."

Luke tried to tamp down the eager enthusiasm that burst to life inside him. He didn't want to seem desperate and pathetic. His excitement had an edge of anxiety. Although there was no reason why he couldn't get back to his computer work, a kernel of doubt still lessened his zeal.

He shrugged and tried to sound noncommittal. "Why not? Got nothing else to do."

Abby patted the back of the desk chair. "Let's go, then."

Luke rounded the chair and sat down. The compression glove he wore to help his scars heal made working the mouse with his right hand uncomfortable. He waited for the computer to boot up, then clicked on the icon to get onto the Internet.

Abby knelt beside him. "Do you think you can use this mouse, or should we consider getting one for your left hand?"

"Depends. How much movement will I have in my hand when all is said and done?" He glanced over his shoulder at her and met a warm smile.

"Depends. How hard are you willing to work at your therapy?"

The challenge she tossed him fired his competitive drive. The prospect of getting back to work, of feeling useful, and of being part of the family business again fueled a sense of hope he'd believed dead. He tugged up one corner of his mouth. "Try me and see."

"I talked to Matt earlier," Brooke said as she and Abby sat in the sand that night and watched the waves in the moonlight. "He said he saw Steve at his conference, and they had dinner together."

Abby's stomach somersaulted. "Oh?"

"He told Steve you'd come here to Destin on your own. Apparently Steve didn't know."

"I had no reason to tell him."

Brooke hummed her agreement. "He says he's sorry. He wanted Matt to tell you how terrible he feels about what happened."

Abby scowled and snapped a narrow-eyed glare at her friend. "Brooke, if you're building up to a speech on how I should forgive him and take him back, then I'm going back inside."

She held up a hand. "Not a chance. I know how you feel about his cheating, and I have to say I'm on your side. I'm just passing on Matt's message from him. Don't shoot me."

Abby dug her toes in the sand, cooled by the day's rain. "Coming here has been good for me. You know, this morning when I woke up, my breakup with Steve wasn't the first thing I thought of."

Luke had been.

Her pulse kicked up remembering the sultry dream that had teased her just before dawn. Luke was edging Steve out of her head in numerous ways, and while putting her breakup behind her was a relief, she couldn't help but wonder if she weren't just trading one heartache for a different one.

"Is it going to be a problem, us still being friends with Steve, now that you're not a couple anymore?" Brooke asked.

Abby shrugged. "You're not planning on forcing us together in awkward situations when I get home, are you?"

Brooke scoffed. "No. I'm not mean."

"Then I don't see a problem. Just don't become best friends with Cindy and abandon me, okay?"

Brooke snapped a startled look toward her. "He's... not with Cindy. He calls her his one-night mistake."

Abby blinked at Brooke. "Really?"

"Really."

She wasn't sure how that made her feel. Perhaps a bit vindicated? Cindy's taunt certainly held less sting. Clearly her blond competition didn't satisfy whatever Steve was looking for, either.

But it rattled her to think that one night, one mistake could so radically change the course of her life.

Just as one moment, one tragic event had altered Luke's life.

Abby shuddered. She had to guard against making just such a life-changing mistake where Luke was concerned. Already he was wearing down her resistance, sucking her deeper into his lure every time he sent one of his hypnotic, seductive looks her way. Every time he touched her or murmured her name in his low, sexy voice.

Like the moon's pull on the tides, Abby found herself more and more drawn to the youngest Morgan's magnetism. Was it fate as Brooke suggested, or was Luke a disaster waiting to wreak havoc on her peace of mind?

Brooke nudged Abby's foot with hers. "Hey, you okay? Sorry. Guess I shouldn't have brought up Steve."

Abby aimed a finger at her friend. "Don't start dancing around subjects trying to protect me. I'm doing all right. In fact, I'm really getting a lot in perspective here. The change of scenery, the challenge of helping the Morgan family work through their struggles…" Abby released a cleansing breath. "Marrying Steve would have been a mistake. I can see that now. We were already drifting apart, having trouble talking to each other about what really mattered. It'd be nice to think that someday we might be friends again, but I'm starting to believe we were never meant to be a couple."

Brooke's eyes widened. "Wow. And you're okay with that?"

"Yeah, I am. Steve's infidelity saved us from making a bigger mistake. Knowing that, despite the pain of disillusionment, eases the sting of his rejection and his betrayal."

Smiling broadly, Brooke wrapped an arm around Abby's shoulders and squeezed. "Have I ever told you how much I admire your wisdom and strength? I want to be you when I grow up."

Abby snorted. "Only if we get to trade, and I'll have your body, your happy marriage, and your cute kid."

Brooke chuckled. "Hmm, I do have it pretty good, don't I?"

"You're the charmed one, Brookie."

Humming her agreement, Brooke lapsed into silence, and Abby's thoughts drifted to Luke again. His life had been charmed before his accident.

Or had it been? Appearances, as with her relationship with Steve, could be deceiving. Had there been something Luke had lacked in his life? Something elemental missing? Something he was still searching for?

Abby longed to know Luke's true soul and deepest heart. She ached to find that soft spot where his real self could shine through.

But what she needed most was the very part of himself he guarded the most fiercely.

Brooke left the next morning with a standing invitation to come back and visit any time. Abby hugged her friend goodbye and made her promise to call when she got in. Then turning to Luke, she put her shoulders back and assumed a stance that meant business. "Time to get to work."

Over the next several days, Luke learned the meaning of the word work in ways he never had before. Abby subjected him to endless exercises prescribed by his OT, intended to strengthen his grip and fine motor skills and learn to do tasks with his left hand. Transfer training, as Abby called it.

One evening, as she massaged his fingers and he fought the erotic urges her healing touch always stirred in his blood, Luke glanced over at Bart, who studied a printout of the month's receipts. Looking for a distraction from the sensual stroking of Abby's fingers along his fingers, he interrupted his father's concentration. "So how'd we do?"

Bart peered over the top of his reading glasses. "Not bad, considering."

"Considering what?"

"That we've been operating short one team member." Bart held his son's gaze briefly before dropping his attention back to the printout.

He debated for a moment whether his father meant the comment as an indictment or not. "I've been a little occupied with the therapy you insisted on. Only so many hours in a day, Bart."

His comment brought Bart's gaze back up.

Abby thumped Luke on the forehead and scowled.

Bart pulled off his reading glasses and regarded Luke silently for several moments. "I realize that. Abby tells me you're making progress, too. That's good. But when you are ready to come back to work, we're ready to have you. Gulfside is a family business, son, and we need you."

*We need you.*

The words caught him off guard and caused a quick tightening in his chest. For a moment he didn't know how to respond. His instincts told him to return the sentiment, to tell his father how much being part of the business meant to him. But just as quickly, he pushed the inclination down, as had become his habit over the years. Emotionalism set him on edge, especially remembering how his affection and his needy pleas had been rejected by his mother.

Instead, he nodded to Bart and turned to watch Abby manipulate his joints. She raised a meaningful glance to him, her brow puckered and a mild scolding in her green eyes. Then, flicking her gaze toward Bart and back to him, she silently made it clear that she thought he should do or say something more to Bart. The expectant lift of her eyebrows, the "Well?" she mouthed urged him to make some overture toward his father.

Averting his gaze, Luke pressed his lips into a stubborn frown. She obviously didn't understand how difficult it was for him to express himself. Either that or she didn't care how much it cost him, the struggle it was to confront— much less vocalize—his feelings for his family.

Once burned…

He felt her emerald eyes boring into him. The oppressive weight of the silent room reminded him of a black hole, where the gravitational pull of a collapsed star sucked in everything, even light. But just as nothing escaped the force of a black hole, Abby's silent pressure pulled at him with unrelenting power.

Or maybe his own conscience, his own buried need to reach out to his father, loosened the stranglehold his pride and his misgivings had on him.

Drawing a slow breath, he turned back to Bart. "I can help out on the morning tour tomorrow if you want. That is, if the drill sergeant will give me the morning off."

"Take the whole day."

He heard satisfaction and pride in Abby's voice, and somehow, pleasing her was its own reward.

Bart set his papers aside and met Luke's gaze.

"I'd like that. Very much."

"Then I'll be at the boat at ten."

"Good. Welcome back."

An awkward silence ensued, during which Luke appraised his father and considered the hell he'd been through in the past weeks. The explosion had hurt the business as well as Bart's son, eliminating the pontoon boat for tours.

Though Bart's style was to ignore problems, the strain of his current situation clearly showed in the slump of his shoulders, the weary expression he wore, and the deep lines of worry on his brow.

He remembered the points Abby had made to him the night after Aaron's car accident. Tragedy didn't affect just one member of a family. The ripples moved outward to touch everyone.

*They need your understanding just like you need theirs.*

His chest tightened with compassion for Bart and regret for his self-centeredness. His heart thumped an anxious rhythm as he searched for a way to broach the sensitive topic of the family's current crises.

"Uh… how are things going with you, Bart?"

He received a puzzled look from his father in response.

"Oh, well…" Bart sank back in his chair, and his expression reflected both his surprise that Luke had raised the subject and his reluctance to delve into the matter. "Fine, I guess."

Luke grunted an acknowledgment, more of Bart's discomfort with the issue than of his vague answer.

Then Bart returned the volley. "How are you handling things?"

"Okay."

"You're doin' all right, then?" Bart nodded as he asked, answering his own question.

"Yeah, sure." Luke cut a glance to Abby who was following the lame exchange with a peculiar quirk in her brow. What did she expect from him? At least he tried!

He pulled his hand away from her massage and stood from the couch. "I'm going to bed."

Abby sighed her obvious disappointment with his feeble attempt to connect with Bart and slumped back against the couch.

"Good night, Luke," Bart called to him as he crossed the living room toward the stairs.

Luke stopped at the top of the stairs and turned back to face Bart. "Good night… Dad."

Bart raised a stunned glance.

Luke hurried out of the room before he or Abby could comment on his parting gesture, but as he headed to his room, he felt good. Damn good.

For the first time in months, he looked forward to the morning.

❖ ❖ ❖

When Luke reached the back deck after helping with the morning snorkeling run, Abby lay stretched out on a lounge chair in the sunshine.

In a bikini. A tiny bikini.

The sight of her skin glistening with tanning oil stopped him in his tracks and caused a heat to rush through him that had nothing to do with the noonday sun.

"Does Bart know he's paying you to sunbathe?" he asked as he climbed the last steps up to the deck.

She raised her head and lifted her sunglasses to peer at him. "It's Saturday. Even prisoners get time off for good behavior. Besides, you were gone."

"Well, I'm back now."

"So I see."

Luke took a seat, choosing a chair in the shade provided by a table umbrella. Sweat trickled from his brow, due in part to the necessity of wearing the compression vest for his scars under a long-sleeved shirt in ninety-plus heat. He'd been headed to the refrigerator for a cold drink when his plan had been diverted by a certain hot pink bikini.

"If we talk about what's on your mind, I can call it work." Abby slid her sunglasses back into place and settled back on the lounger again.

"You want to know what's on my mind?"

"Sure. Shoot." Abby wiped away a bead of perspiration that slid between her breasts, and he swallowed a groan.

"I'm thinking that if you'd paid just a little more, you could have gotten some bikini to go with that string."

Abby peered over the rim of her sunglasses. "Funny. I bought this for my honeymoon. Modesty was not a contributing factor in my selection."

Luke's gaze roamed the abundance of visible flesh, the curve of her hips, the damn sexy mole by her belly button, and his muscles tightened. "Obviously."

"How was the tour this morning?"

"Fine. Are you wearing any sunscreen?" He wouldn't let her best him at the art of changing the subject.

"Why?"

"Because the Florida sun isn't kind to skin as fair as yours."

"Thanks for the concern, but I came prepared." Reaching in the bag beside her chair, she produced a bottle of coconut oil.

"SPF 4?" Luke twisted his lips in wry amusement. "What the hell good is that going to do? You might as well use corn oil. You're going to fry!"

She made no reply. Instead, she slathered another handful of oil on her stomach, and her skin shimmered in the sun. The scents of coconut and body heat greeted him in the breeze.

His libido responded in full force, and he tore his gaze away before he got hard.

"Are you going to answer my question?" Abby flipped down the lid on the bottle with a click and dropped it beside her chair.

"What question?"

"About the tour? Your first day back on the job?"

Luke sighed. He didn't feel like talking, but maybe an honest answer to her question would keep his mind off her body and what he'd like to do with that coconut oil. "It was good to be back on the water. The sea has a way of getting into your blood." *So do green eyes and sexy little moles.*

"I'm glad. I know it meant a lot to Bart to have you back."

Luke didn't try to deny it. He'd noticed a difference in Bart today as early as breakfast. His father had seemed... hopeful. Genuinely so, not the pseudo-cheer that had irritated Luke in the past weeks.

"I like what you did for him last night." Her voice mellowed, and the soothing timbre slid over him like a gentle summer rain.

Her insight and caring rooted themselves deep inside him. Like the night of Aaron's accident when he'd warmed her from the cool air, his lust twisted and merged with the tug her kindness and compassion evoked from his heart. The combination of the sexual and emotional created a potent blend. His whole being hummed with a desire to be closer to her, to fill her the way she filled him.

Although they were hidden by her sunglasses, he imagined her flashing emerald eyes and knew from experience the soul-searing way they studied him. As before, her gaze caused a physical reaction deep inside him, leaving him feeling vulnerable, totally at her mercy. Yet somehow the prospect didn't unsettle him as it had weeks ago when they first met. He couldn't believe, wouldn't believe she didn't sense the same connection between them. So why did she fight it so hard?

When she turned her head away without further comment, Luke closed his eyes and refocused his thoughts. He tried to ignore the seductive coconut scent wafting to him, reminding him of his sexual fantasy.

Why was he torturing himself like this when she'd made it clear she wanted no part of him? At least, her

words and her actions said no. Her body, her eyes told
him yes, emphatically, whenever they were close. She
was waging an internal war against her desires just like
she'd forced him to.

But perhaps with the right coaxing…

Aaron didn't have all of the seductive charm in
the family.

Luke relaxed in his chair and began to scheme. Her
movement and the squeak of the lounge chair caught his
attention, and he peeked over at her again. Abby lay on
her stomach now, her chaise flat, and she fumbled to untie
the strings of her bikini across her back. He glimpsed the
curve of her breast briefly before she stacked her hands
under her cheek and returned to her sun worship.

He got hard in an instant. She had to be deliberately
taunting him, tempting him. She had to know what she
was doing to him and how he'd react. Didn't she?

Luke wet his lips as his gaze darted to the bottle of oil
beside her chair. The need to touch her skin overrode the
voice in his head that advised him to leave well enough
alone. He rose from his chair and grabbed the bottle,
flipping up the lid. He squeezed a liberal amount on her
back without warning her, and Abby gasped when the
sun-heated oil hit her skin.

"Worthless as it is, SPF 4 is better than nothing." He
straddled her and the chair. Propping one knee on the
edge of the lounger, he began smoothing oil over her
sexy bare back.

She angled her head to glance up at him. "Uh, thanks."

He worked slowly, luxuriating in the sensual feel of
slippery oil on soft skin. Not an inch of her skin went
untouched. He wasn't about to miss this opportunity to

have his hands on her, explore the dent at the small of her back and the ridge of her spine. He even dipped his fingers under the top edge of her bikini bottoms.

"Hey, watch it, buster! That's good enough, thanks."

Good enough? No way. He'd only gotten started. He'd slept with dozens of women over the years, but the sum total couldn't equal the arousing and satisfying act of caressing Abby. No chance he'd stop now.

She remained suspiciously still throughout his massage, and the rapid rise and fall of her back as her breathing grew shallow told him that his touch turned her on. He squeezed her shoulders, and a tiny moan, almost a whimper, escaped from Abby's throat, ricocheting through Luke's heated body like lightning.

He made another pass low near her fanny, and he heard the hiss of her breath. "Stop it, Luke. Y-you're not funny."

Her voice cracked, assuring him of her faltering composure.

"I'm not trying to be funny." He rubbed the small of her back with his left hand, massaging deeply, working the muscle.

"Luke, I… I'm warning you!"

His hand stilled obediently. "What are you going to do, Ab? Deny what you're feeling? That fire licking your veins?" His throat was tight, his voice thick with his desire. "I know you feel it. I know you want it as bad as I do. Why are you fighting it?"

"I've told you why. The timing is wrong for me. I'm not ready…" With a huff, she snagged her T-shirt from beside the chair and clutched it to her chest as she rolled over to face him. "I'm not looking for a relationship right now, and I don't do casual flings." Her mouth firmed into an uncompromising line. "We both know I'll be leaving eventually, so there's no point starting something we can't finish. Understand?"

He watched her turn and disappear inside while his body throbbed with unfulfilled passion and his pride stung from her dismissal.

"Yeah. I understand more than you think," he mumbled.

In recent days, she'd seen too much of his scars, his handicap, his disfigured hand to see him as anything but a freak of nature. Flirting and clothed cuddles were one thing. Hot and sweaty sex, naked full-body contact with his injuries was another. Even he had a hard time facing what the mirror showed him.

The humiliation of her rejection was bad enough. Luke refused to even acknowledge the pain lodged like a spear in his heart. To do so would mean recognizing what she meant to him. That could prove the most dangerous endeavor of all.

# Chapter 16

AROUND DINNERTIME, ABBY FOUND LUKE PUTTERING around the snorkeling office, where he'd been killing time, sorting through the store's inventory and rearranging the display of snorkeling merchandise.

"Hey, am I interrupting anything important?" She handed him the next box of swim goggles from the stack he was shelving.

"Nothing critical. The store's just suffering from a bad case of Aaron-itis. These shelves are disorganized and dusty. Thought I'd straighten things up a bit for Bart."

And he'd been more than a little restless, exceedingly bored with the tripe on TV and looking to escape his circular thoughts regarding Abby.

Abby chuckled. "Anal-retentive much?"

He pulled his head out of the display cabinet and arched an eyebrow. "What did you just call me?"

"Ever study Freud?"

Luke sat back on his haunches and shrugged a shoulder. "The guy who came up with the Oedipus complex and penis envy?" He snorted derisively. "Yeah, I put a lot of stock in his theories."

"Freud aside, you have to admit you are a little bit of a perfectionist."

He grunted. "Hardly. I'm far from perfect. Especially now."

"I didn't say you *were* perfect. No one is. Only that you have a drive in you that wants to be better all the time. An internal fire striving for as close to perfection as possible." She paused. "Am I wrong?"

He worked to keep the cold ball of apprehension that rolled in his gut from showing on his face. Her perceptiveness about him was eerie and unsettling sometimes. Like she'd dissected him and knew what made him tick. His deepest fears and strongest desires were exposed and vulnerable around Abby.

Dangerously so.

Schooling his face, he went back to work without responding.

"Anyway, I came to find you because I thought we could squeeze in another therapy session, but if you're busy…"

Kneeling in front of the display case, he stuffed the stack of masks back on the shelf. "Nah. This'll keep. What did you have in mind?"

"Oh, whatever. Some left hand work?"

Luke sighed. Re-learning basic skills like shaving and tying his shoes with his left hand dominant frustrated him no end. He felt like a child fumbling with such elementary tasks as writing the alphabet and using scissors. "Only if you promise me a massage afterward."

The wary look she gave him said she'd not forgiven him for his bold advances on the deck. "Only the therapeutic kind."

"Naturally." If she heard his sarcasm, she gave no indication. "If you're waiting for an apology, you won't get one, Ab. I make no excuses for the way I feel. I know what I want. And one day you're going to realize you want me just as much as I want you. You're fighting what you feel, but one day I'm gonna win."

Her throat convulsed as she swallowed. "Maybe so. But if that day comes, it will be the day I have to leave."

"Leave? Why?" He rose to his feet and faced her with his hands on his hips.

"Because sex would only complicate what could be a great friendship between us. Your family has grown important to me, but my home is in Texas. I'm only here to help your family while you get back on your feet. Even though you and Bart and Aaron are dear to me now and I love it here, if my presence complicates things for your family instead of helping, I have no business staying."

The finality of her assessment drilled cold spikes of dread through his chest. Just like that. No questions asked. No reprieves or alternatives.

He was nothing but a complication to her. When her job was done, she would leave him. Like his mother had left. Proof positive that giving his heart to Abby would be a fatal mistake.


Over the next several days, Luke showed marked progress. Abby's pride in Luke's rehabilitation efforts had a dark side, however. Her work was nearly finished. Not that Luke wouldn't need to continue his weekly sessions with Joyce Harris to maintain and improve on the skills, strength, and flexibility he'd acquired in recent weeks. But his attitude toward his rehabilitation had improved considerably, from stubborn resistance to begrudging compliance to willing effort with an eye toward getting back his old life.

Now that Luke had begun working in the store and helping with tours again, her assistance with the business was less needed as well. Luke had even begun piloting the boat again, as long as Bart or Aaron accompanied him, and he had learned to compensate for his limited field of vision. Soon he would be driving his Jeep again.

One morning in early July, Abby tested Luke's ability to recognize objects and textures by touch alone, measuring the sensitivity of the healing nerves in his fingers and comparing the results with those she'd gotten a few weeks earlier.

Blindfolded, Luke sat on the sofa in the living room, rubbing with his right hand the small object she'd given him.

"It's rough and bumpy. Curved. Smooth on the other side. A shell. Half of a clam shell." He passed the shell back to her with a self-assured grin.

"Yes. Very good. How does this feel?" She set out a piece of sandpaper and guided his hand to it.

"Flat. Rough. Either sandpaper or… no, sandpaper. I'm sure."

"Right. Try this." She switched the paper for her next test object.

"Hm. Interesting." Luke scrunched up his face in concentration, and she held her breath. "Soft. Smooth. Kinda slippery… no, silky. Kind of… I don't remember having this one before. What—"

When he reached for his blindfold to peek, she knocked his hand down "No cheating."

"It's some kind of silk or satin, I think. Am I right?"

She snatched the silk camisole from the table where he fingered it. "Yes."

Turning, she grappled in her pile of test objects for the next item. Luke reached past her for the camisole, and she looked back at him to find he'd removed his blindfold. "Hey! Put it back on!"

"Not till I check this out." He unfolded the lingerie and arched an eyebrow. He whistled his appreciation of the lacy pink garment. "Very sexy. Yours, I take it?"

"Give it back, Luke."

His gaze scrutinized the camisole then raked over her with clear intent. He was picturing her wearing the lingerie. Luke ran his fingers over the lace trim slowly and wet his lips. His pupils dilated, and his gaze grew hot.

Abby's pulse fluttered, but she mustered the composure to grab the garment from him and scowl her displeasure with him. "Quit fooling around and put the blindfold back on."

He gave her a sultry grin. "You and me, a blindfold, sexy lingerie… all the right ingredients are there, darling. What do you say?"

Her shoulders sagged, and she sighed. "I'd say I'm getting nowhere anymore. You're bored with this routine, and rightly so." She gathered up her collection of items with a sinking sensation in her chest. "I'll call your OT to set up your next appointment and fill her in on your progress, but I don't see where we have much work left to do."

He blinked his surprise. "What? We're not done. I can't… there are still so many things I can't do, that I haven't mastered yet. What about that exercise with the sticks where I pick 'em up by pinching them between my fingers. I still have trouble with that."

She stood, the test items clutched to her chest. "I know, and we can work on that some more. You'll keep working with Joyce Harris in the coming months, but I just don't see that you need me for your daily routine anymore."

"What about what you called late stage contractures? Didn't you say the tendons in my hand might tighten up if I didn't keep them limber?" Luke stood too, concern and confusion darkening his expression.

"You'll have to keep exercising your hand, of course, but you don't need me to do that. Your nerve cells are obviously healing well, and your scarring is minimal and—"

"But I'm not ready—"

"Luke." She caught his hand and squeezed. She met his worried gaze. "You are ready. You're going to be okay without me."

He hesitated a beat. "So you're leaving?"

Abby drew a deep breath before she answered. The truth she'd avoided, but now saw clearly, pressed down on her chest.

"Soon. Not yet. I want to talk with your OT first, make some evaluations, double-check some things with your doctor before I go, just so I'm sure…"

Wrenching his hand from her grasp, he stalked away, stopping to stare out the window with a hard frown on his face. His uncertainty and consternation were normal. Being released by a therapist often frightened her patients. Facing rehabilitation challenges alone could seem daunting.

That knowledge didn't make Luke's distress any easier to accept. She wished she had some way to reassure him without seeming blatantly placating or patronizing. She thought about his birthday coming later that week, and an idea began to take shape in her mind.

Planning Luke's special birthday present proved her easiest task over the next few days. As he had in the beginning, Luke refused to cooperate with his therapy and seemed withdrawn most of the time.

Abby guessed that his gloom and reserve were rooted in his apprehension regarding her leaving, his fear of failure rearing its head again.

When she wasn't battling Luke, she spent much of her time planning, shopping, and scheming with Bart and Aaron in order to bring her idea to fruition and still surprise Luke. She wanted her present to be ready for his birthday, and with Bart's and Aaron's help, it was.

Luke ate his birthday dinner somberly. He was in no mood to celebrate. His every instinct told him Abby was preparing to leave Florida and walk out of his life for good.

After eating cake, Bart and Aaron presented Luke with a handheld GPS and a MP3 player for his Jeep. While he played with the buttons and settings of his new toys, Abby faced him with a mysterious smile.

"Now it's my turn. Follow me."

He cast a curious glance at his brother and father, who both shrugged. Intrigued, he followed Abby downstairs to the door of his bedroom.

"Close your eyes. I'll guide you."

"Why? What—"

"Do you ever follow directions without arguing? Just trust me, okay?"

She slipped her hand in his, and the contact of her warm fingers sent a rush of pleasure through him. She led him to the side of his bed.

"Now lie on your back, but keep your eyes closed."

"No chance this means I'm about to get laid, is there?"

"Get your mind out of the gutter, Morgan."

He heard her flip the light switch, turning off the lights, then felt the bed sag as she climbed up beside him. Despite her denial that sex was her intent, his body tingled with expectation as she made the atmosphere more intimate and settled beside him. His senses came alive, his body alert to every detail around him. The floral scent of her perfume wafted to his nose, leaving him intoxicated with its sweetness. The heat from her body blanketed him with comforting warmth. The gentle whoosh of her satisfied sigh carried his thoughts in erotic directions. What sounds would she make in the throes of passion?

That particular daydream made his muscles taut and his groin throb. With a tremendous effort, he pushed the tantalizing thoughts aside and reined in his body's escalating tension.

"Okay, open your eyes," she said.

He did. Then he blinked in bewilderment as tiny spots of light came into focus before him. He stared at his ceiling in awe.

"Your own private night sky. Now you can have the stars overhead every night as you fall asleep. Anytime you want them, really. What do you think?" She snuggled closer and rested a hand on his chest.

Luke's voice stuck behind the emotion that closed his throat. Instead, he nodded as his gaze drifted over the strings of white Christmas tree lights affixed to his ceiling. She'd even arranged some in constellations.

Words escaped him. He studied the tiny lights in fascination and disbelief for long minutes before he could form a coherent thought.

"Abby," he rasped. "I... It's the best present I ever got."

"Then you like it?"

Luke angled his head to face Abby, who watched his reaction apprehensively. He swallowed hard to clear the constriction in his throat. "I love it."

Abby smiled. "Bart and Aaron helped me. I figured out how to attach them, but Aaron helped with the electrical part. See over here. This is the toggle switch to turn them off and on."

He off-handedly noted what she was telling him, but most of his attention stayed focused on the golden glow that played across the curves and planes of Abby's face. She'd gone to a great deal of trouble to do this for him, he knew without asking. But it was the thought behind the project that he treasured most. Her kindness and generosity touched him, filled him with an indescribable sense of peace.

"Watch this." She grinned playfully and turned off the star-lights. "Oops, cloudy night." She flipped the stars back on. "Ah, clear night."

She giggled, a clear, sweet sound like a wind chime, and the humor lighting her face brought a smile to his own lips.

"Want to see me make it rain?" She held up the matches she'd used to light his birthday candles and pointed to the sprinkler system.

"This is your show." His smile brightened, daring her. But when she stood up on the bed, he seized her around the waist and pulled her back down on top of him. "Now who's incorrigible?"

His laughter joined hers. Abby rolled over so that she looked down into his eyes, her face scant inches from his. Her eyes sparkled and danced, and longing wound around his heart. How could he ever let her go?

"Happy birthday, Luke." Her whispered words flowed like a gentle balm to soothe the turmoil inside him.

"Thank you, Abby." His own voice sounded strange to his ears, and apparently she heard the difference, too.

Her smile dimmed, and her gaze became more intense as if she were trying to read the emotion that choked him.

But more than one emotion swirled inside him, and even he couldn't sort them all out. He stared up at the woman who'd waltzed brazenly into his life, challenged him, stood up to him... changed him.

She'd brought him laughter when his world was at its darkest, hope when he was lost, friendship and under-standing when he was alone. She'd given him the stars when his life seemed a perpetual night.

And he'd fallen in love with her.

Aaron had called it right. Maybe his brother wasn't so dim-witted where women were concerned, after all.

They exchanged searching gazes for another moment before she pushed away and flopped back on the second pillow with a soft sigh.

"So," she said without preamble. "It's too bad you didn't have these lights up before now. All your women would have loved this special effect, huh? Sex under the stars?"

She sounded jealous, and her tone piqued his curiosity. "Perhaps."

"Exactly how many women are we talking here?"

"Several," he said, being deliberately vague. In truth, he hated to think of how many nameless, pointless encounters he'd had. They all left him with nothing to show.

"Could you be more specific?"

"Why should I?"

Abby remained silent for a while. When she spoke, her tone chastised him. "I guess you and Aaron were absent from school the day they gave the lecture about the dangers of promiscuity?"

"I was always careful." He rolled on his side to look into her eyes and repeated emphatically, "Always."

"And Aaron?"

"You'll have to ask him, but I know he's not stupid."

Abby became oddly still, her expression pensive.

"What are you thinking?" he whispered.

"Why won't you tell me how many women you've been with?"

He sighed. "Because I honestly don't know. Not any that matter to me now." He looked away, uncomfortable with the wounded expression she wore, the honesty in her gaze. Yet he felt compelled to level with her concerning his past. "I'm not proud of my history, Abby. But I gave up meaningless sex a long time ago. I'd trade all my past flings in a heartbeat for just one woman that really meant something to me."

*For you.*

Luke drew a slow breath. "How 'bout you? How many men have you been with besides Steve the jerk?" His chest tightened with apprehension, not sure he really wanted to know. The idea of another man touching Abby fired a jealous rage inside him.

"Zero."

Relief whizzed through him, and he released his breath in a whoosh. He should have guessed. A woman with Abby's integrity would be faithful, patient, careful concerning her lovers.

Without thinking about his actions, he reached for her cheek and stroked her delicate skin with his fingertips. She shivered and turned away. Her withdrawal, even when their conversation and the mood between them had grown so intimate, landed like a sucker punch in his gut.

"It's probably just as well, too," she added. "I wasn't very good at it."

Luke furrowed his brow, shaking off his dejection to focus on the grief he heard weighting her tone. "Why would you say that?"

"The facts speak for themselves. If I had satisfied him, why would he cheat? Why take a gorgeous blond lover even for one night?"

"Abby." Luke gripped her jaw and turned her face to meet his gaze. "I've told you before that Steve was a jerk, unworthy of you. If your sex life was lacking, it's for damn sure not because you were undesirable."

He seized her hand and pressed it to the rock-like evidence of her effect on him that strained against his fly. Abby gasped and tried to pull away, but he anchored her hand in place.

"This is what you do to me, Abby. With just a look. By just walking into a room. Don't tell me you're unde-sirable. I want you so bad it hurts. I want you like I've never wanted any woman before, sweetheart, and don't you forget it."

Her eyes were wide with panic, a veil of caution darkening their depths to a deep emerald hue.

"Don't you dare run from me, Abby," he whispered. "Trust me to take care of you. Just once I want to hold you and feel you respond to my touch."

He rolled toward her and trapped her body beneath his. "I want to bury myself inside you and get lost in the taste of your kiss."

"Luke, wait. We can't…"

He felt the tremor that shook her and brought her fingers to his lips to brush a kiss on her knuckles. "Don't be scared. I'll take care of you."

When he moved his kiss to her brow, she shoved against his chest, struggling to free herself from his imprisoning hold.

Defiant sparks lit her eyes as she glared up at him. "Luke, I've told you how I feel about sleeping with you. This is a mistake. We can't—"

"Why can't we?" he interrupted. "We're both consenting adults. You can't deny that we've been building toward this moment for weeks. So why fight it?" Luke nuzzled her neck and trailed kisses to her ear.

"Because… sex will change everything between us! Oh!" she gasped when he nipped her earlobe. "We should at least talk first. So we know…" Her breath snagged in a sexy hiss when he teased the hollow behind her ear with his tongue.

"We've done nothing but talk since the day you arrived. It's time to follow through, time to act on what we both know we've got happening between us."

Her muscles relaxed a fraction, and he sensed her weakening resolve, saw the flicker of doubt and hunger in her gaze.

"But Luke, I can't… let myself—"

He cut off her reply with his kiss, sealing his lips to hers and gathering her closer in his arms.

Abby tensed when Luke kissed her, willing her body not to respond to the sensual caress of his lips. She knew making love to him now would seal her fate. She couldn't give him her body without also giving him her heart. Yet he hadn't once shown her any reason to hope that he cared for her as deeply as she'd grown to love him.

Her resistance to his magnetism merely offered him a challenge, provoked his competitive spirit. She was nothing more to him than a test of wills he was determined to win, and when matched against his powers of seduction, the strength of her resolution crumbled.

Still, she couldn't walk away without at least trying to make him understand why she had to turn him down. Wrenching her head from his grasp, she gulped for air. She worked to assemble a coherent thought while Luke nibbled her earlobe and traced her jaw with the tip of his tongue.

"Luke, please. I… I—"

He pressed a hot, open-mouthed kiss at the pulse point of her neck. The rest of her sentence became lost in the moan that escaped her throat. She found herself panting for breath and once more tried to gather her composure and mount some resistance.

"Luke, sex has to mean something for me, and… I…" He feathered his tongue along the shell of her ear, and she lost her train of thought. "Luke, I… can't think straight when you do that. Please, I…" She pushed against the solid wall of his broad chest, but he only captured her hands and pinned them above her head.

"Then don't think. Just close your eyes and feel. Enjoy. It will be good, Abby. I promise." He looked deep into her eyes, searched her face, waited as one silent second after another ticked by with only the sound of her ragged breathing between them.

"Please," she whispered hoarsely, the word a squeaky plea. But was she begging him to stop... or to continue? Suddenly she couldn't be certain of anything. Her head spun, and her skin burned as if on fire.

Luke released her hands, levered his body off her, push-up style, so that she could scamper out from under him if she chose. Then he ducked his head to seize her lips again.

He'd given her the freedom to leave, the chance to walk away, yet she lingered to savor his drugging kiss. The heat of his insistent mouth melted her mutinous bones and left her weak with need. His persuasive kiss stifled the arguments her conscience screamed, and her treasonous lips parted to accept the Trojan horse of his tongue. And she knew the battle was lost.

He tenderly explored her mouth, teasing each surface with seductive strokes. Lowering his body beside her, he insinuated a hand between them and plucked at the buttons of her blouse. One by one, he unfastened the tiny disks with his left hand. As he released each button, he blazed a moist trail in his wake, easing down between her breasts with feathering strokes of his tongue. After he peeled back her blouse, he unhooked the front clasp of her bra. Luke cupped her breasts and teased her nipples with his fingertips. A sensation like liquid fire shot through her and quickened her pulse.

She experienced the helpless sense of falling, and she grabbed hold of Luke's shoulders, clinging to him for all she was worth. If losing her heart to Luke devastated her, as she expected, at least she'd go to her demise in ecstasy.

He moved his hands lower to massage her ribs and coax her hips to grind against his, and he gave her nipples attention with his mouth and tongue. A heady rush of tingling heat whooshed through her.

With impatient hands, Luke unsnapped her shorts and tugged them and her panties below her knees in a swift motion. She kicked off her shorts and fumbled at the zipper of his jeans with a similar eagerness. While holding himself above her, allowing her hands access to finish their work, he captured her lips again, treating them to a passionate assault. With his fingers, he stroked the moist heat between her legs, and her body ached with need. She arched into his touch, wanting to feel him deeper inside, hurtling toward the blissful completion he promised with his touch. Finally, Luke pushed her trembling and ineffective hands aside and opened his fly for himself. He shoved his jeans down, releasing his steely erection from the restrictive denim. She felt the heat and weight of him nestle between her legs, and she caught her breath, reeling in fresh waves of tingling anticipation. Curling her fingers into his hair, she drew his head closer, matching the fevered frenzy of his kiss.

Like a primed pump, the flow of their passion escalated quickly to dizzying heights. He rubbed his rigid length along the juncture of her thighs and drew on her lips with deep, mind-numbing kisses until she gasped for a breath.

"Say you want me," he murmured in her ear. "I want to hear you say it."

She nodded and panted for oxygen.

"Say it."

"I want you, Luke. You know I do."

The instant the words left her mouth, he rolled off her and walked away.

# Chapter 17

WITHOUT LUKE'S BODY AGAINST HER, ABBY FELT BARE, bereft, and a chill washed over her. She wondered for an agonizing second if he were punishing her for all the times she'd run from his attempts to seduce her.

Instead, he disappeared in his bathroom, emerging seconds later with a small foil packet. With haste and finesse, he opened the condom with his teeth and sheathed himself for her protection. Returning to her, he looked into her eyes with his now familiar intensity burning in his gaze.

Relief washed through her and left her limp, giddy.

He moved on top of her, and she opened herself, body and soul, to accept him. She wrapped her arms around his neck and clung to him as he sank into her, groaning his satisfaction. She felt herself stretch to accommodate his size.

The slow stroke of his body inside her sent sweet, hot pleasure spiraling through her. The sensations collected in her womb. She raised her hips to meet his thrusts, feeling the frantic search for fulfillment building inside her. Her heart thumped wildly, and she heard her own mewling sighs. The warmth of Luke's labored breaths caressed her cheeks as he held her gaze with his piercing stare. Perspiration slickened her skin and shimmered on Luke's brow.

The pulsing need inside her climbed higher, and when her completion came within reach, she closed her eyes, tipped her head back, and clamped her legs around Luke's.

He claimed the arch of her throat with his mouth, hugged her body closer to his, and drove deeper, harder. She cried out as he carried her into the turbulent maelstrom of her climax, and she shattered in a glorious burst of white-hot sparks.

In the midst of her nirvana, she heard Luke's savage growl, felt him shudder and tighten his grasp around her before sagging against her with a satisfied sigh. He nuzzled the curve of her neck, trailing small, shivery kisses in a path to her cheek, then rested his forehead against hers.

Abby lay motionless, bone-tired and apprehensive about what might happen now, in the wake of their frenzied coupling. He pressed his lips to her closed eyes, and the tender gesture wrenched her heart.

Luke had so much love and gentleness inside him. If only he would offer her some piece of that inner self, share his heart and open his soul to her, she could believe they had a future together.

A future together. With a pang, she realized Luke had never mentioned anything about the future, much less a commitment of forever. His only interest, it seemed, was in the here and now. Immediate gratification. Just sex, no strings attached.

A challenge to be conquered.

"Well, sweetheart," he murmured in a voice with a low, sexy rasp. "I'd say I've proven my point. You can't deny now that we've got something pretty amazing happening between us."

His words only confirmed what she suspected, and

pain shot through her chest. She opened her eyes and peered up at him.

He gave her a wickedly handsome grin.

Her voice lodged behind a lump in her throat. When Luke withdrew from her body, she experienced a sharp sense of loss.

He must have read her disappointment, because he ran a finger down the length of her nose and gave it a tweak. "Don't look at me that way. I'll be right back in a second for round two. Just let me change rubbers."

Giving her a quick kiss, he climbed off of the bed. Abby cringed, realizing they'd been so anxious, they hadn't even gotten completely out of their clothes. Luke still wore his shirt and compression vest, and her blouse and bra had simply been shoved aside.

At least Luke had had the good sense and courtesy to stop long enough to put on a condom. What would she have done if she'd gotten pregnant because of her recklessness? And reckless was the only word that could describe such an impetuous mistake.

Her stomach churned, rebelling at the thought of the caution and prudence she'd ruthlessly tossed aside because she couldn't control her raging desire for Luke. She'd negligently sold her heart down the river for a few minutes of pleasure. No, better than just pleasure. Heaven. Pure bliss. Sensual Eden.

But now her heart would suffer through Hell.

Already the pain of knowing Luke didn't return her love raked through her chest like shards of glass. Abby hugged herself, chafing her arms as a chill of despair and self-reproach skittered through her.

She had to leave. Now. Today. Before she sank any deeper into the mire of mistakes and bad decisions.

She couldn't work with Luke any longer. She couldn't stay and allow her heart to be battered any further by his unwillingness to open himself to her. She'd made a royal mess, and the best thing she could do now was leave before it got any worse.

Her arms trembled as she pushed herself up and began re-buttoning her blouse. Scooping her shorts from the floor, she tugged them on, then sat down on the edge of the bed to put on her shoes.

"What are you doing?"

The sound of Luke's voice stilled her hands on her sandal straps.

"Dressing."

He grunted. "Why? I told you I'd be back. You don't doubt my stamina, do you?"

Humor laced his tone, but she also heard a hint of concern.

"I'm sure you have tremendous stamina, Luke." Her own voice sounded thready, tremulous.

A pregnant silence followed in which she couldn't bring herself to face him. She finished fastening her sandals and stood to leave.

"Why are you leaving?" Now his voice was hoarse, unsteady.

"I have to pack."

"Pack?"

"I'm going home, Luke. My job here is finished."

Another long silence ensued, and her throat tightened with unshed tears.

"Unusual brand of therapy you practice. Do you

screw all your patients as the coup de grace or just a lucky few?"

She spun to face him, humiliation and fury roiling inside her. "You bastard!"

A single tear escaped her lashes, and she swiped it away with an angry brush of her hand.

Luke's face contorted with misery, and he bit out another scorching curse. Lifting a remorseful gaze to her, he sighed. "I'm sorry, Abby. That was uncalled for, I know. I…" He drew a hand down his face, then closed the distance between them. "I just don't understand. What just happened between us was great. It was mind-blowing and hot and—"

"Wrong."

"Huh?"

"It was a mistake." She raised a hand to forestall his objection. "Look, it boils down to this. You've made tremendous strides in your recovery in the last few weeks. All I am now is a nag, telling you to do your exercises and reporting back to your OT. You don't need me."

"So what! So you're not helping me with my therapy anymore. What we've got now is better." He pulled her against him and locked his arms around her. "I'm not ready to give you up, Abby."

The warm, solid strength of his body muddied her thoughts and made her knees wobble. Garnering her wits took a tremendous effort, but she did. She backed away from him, shaking her head. "If I have no job here, then there is no reason to stay. We always knew I'd leave one day. That's why I didn't want to complicate our relation-ship with sex. It only makes it harder to say goodbye."

She wondered for a moment if it was Luke or herself she was trying to convince. "Back in Texas I have a job, an apartment, friends, responsibilities, plants…"

"Plants?"

"I have a fern at home that probably hasn't been watered in weeks. Brooke promised to take care of it but…"

He sent her an incredulous look. "You're gonna give up incredible sex because of a fern?"

She huffed her frustration and took another step away from him. "Amongst the other reasons I named. Luke, my life is in Texas. We knew that from the start. That's why I said what just happened was a mist—"

He pressed a hand to her lips. "No. It wasn't a mistake. I don't want you to regret it."

The tears she'd fought down rose again in her throat. "Oh, Luke, don't make this harder for me than it already is."

His fingers closed over her shoulders, and he pulled her into his embrace. He held her with a fierce, protective grip that almost convinced her he loved her after all. A spark of hope flickered to life and shimmered deep in her soul, taunting her. Luke grew eerily quiet, and his breathing became deep and harsh.

"Don't go," he said at last. "I want you to stay… with me."

She wanted desperately to believe she'd heard a glimmer of emotion in his plea. Her tears leaked onto her cheeks. "Then give me a reason," she whispered. "Just one reason to stay."

*Tell me you love me. Please, Luke, just give me one little piece of your heart!*

Shadows danced in Luke's blue eye. His mouth set in a grim line. "All right."

With slow, deliberate care, he slid his hand behind her head and lowered his lips to hers. His kiss started tender and grew savage. His mouth staked his claim to her, his tongue possessed her and spun his magic web around her. His passion and confidence left her trembling, wanting more, aching inside. Then, gentling his kiss, he soothed her ravaged lips with a tender caress from his mouth before raising his head. He fixed an intimate gaze on her, looking deep into her eyes.

She waited the span of an eager heartbeat—then another—for his profession of love, for him to tell her the things she needed to hear. But he only stared at her with a smug satisfaction curving his lips.

"Well?" she prompted.

"Well, what? That seems like a pretty good reason to me."

With a sinking sensation in her chest, the spark of hope burned out. Even with her on the verge of walking out of his life, all he offered her was his kiss. Just sex. Drawing back her shoulders, she struggled to tamp the swell of disappointment rising in her. "That's not a good enough reason, Luke."

His brow furrowed, and a dark scowl clouded his face. With a firm thrust, he pushed her away. Hurt and anger set his jaw with rigid tension. Blue fire lit his eye. "Fine. Leave then. I hope you and your fern will be happy together."

With that, he snatched his jeans off the bed and stormed into the bathroom, slamming the door behind him.

The resounding thud echoed in the bleak emptiness of her soul. Despite her best intentions, her noblest efforts to prevent it, Luke Morgan had decimated her heart.

With that pervading thought uppermost in her mind, Abby fled Luke's bedroom.

She had a plane to catch.

*That's not a good enough reason.*

Luke ducked his head under the icy shower spray, torturing himself with the frigid water and the memory of Abby's response to his plea. Pain sliced through him.

It was just like before, when he was eight. He'd asked Abby to stay, offered her his love, and she'd rejected him. Flat out turned him down.

*That's not a good enough reason.* Translation: *You are not a good enough reason for me to stay and give us a shot.*

Luke pounded the wall of the shower with his fist.

Why had he bothered? Hadn't he learned anything the first time he'd begged a woman to stay with him? Not to leave him alone and frightened of the future?

*Please, Mom. Please don't go. Don't you love me anymore?*

*Oh, Luke, don't you understand? There's nothing left for me here.*

Nothing. Her son meant nothing to her.

He lifted his face to the stinging spray, wishing he could wash away the bitter memories. Fool that he was, he'd repeated his mistake with Abby. He'd asked her to stay with him. For him. For all the feelings he had for her. He'd thought that kiss said everything about his love that he *couldn't* put into words.

Hadn't she experienced the soul-deep connection that he had when they made love? Their union had been a mountaintop high for him, and he'd seen forever from its peak.

*That's not a good enough reason.*

Damn her! What more did she want? How could she choose a job, an apartment—*a fern*—over him? Why wasn't his love good enough?

Luke slumped against the wall of the shower, despair wringing his heart. He'd found the woman he wanted to spend his life with, and she'd rejected him. She would walk out of his life in a matter of hours, minutes, if he didn't stop her. If she left him, she'd take a piece of his soul with her. He felt the empty ache already. It consumed him with black grief.

But what could he do? He had nothing left to give. All he could do now was salvage his pride, make a clean break, and shut her out of his mind. Just one more loss in his life.

Luke turned off the water and dragged himself from the shower. A chill seeped deep into his bones.

Abby was leaving.

Painful as it was, he'd have to find a way to live without her.

# Chapter 18

BY THE TIME LUKE FINISHED HIS SHOWER AND DRESSED to head upstairs, Abby's luggage sat by the front door. The woman could pack faster than he could shower! He tried to find some amusement in that fact, but couldn't.

Aaron met him at the top of the stairs.

"Care to tell me what the hell's going on?" His brother waved a hand at the bags on the landing.

"Looks like Abby's bolting."

"Yeah, but why? You left with her a couple of hours ago to see the lights she put on your ceiling as a gift—a rather thoughtful gift, in my opinion—and next thing I know she's asking me to carry her suitcase downstairs." Aaron tailed him into the living room.

"Leave it alone, okay?" His tone brooked no resistance.

"Luke, what ha—"

"Well, guys, I think that's everything."

Hearing Abby, he and Aaron turned toward the stairs at the same time. Descending the steps from the third floor, she carried her purse and a small backpack, and Bart followed her, lugging a large garment bag.

Aaron spread his hands in disbelief. "So that's it? You're gone, just like that? Geez, when you get ready to go somewhere you don't fool around, do you?"

*My sentiments exactly, brother.*

"I'm sorry. I know I'm rushing off awfully fast. I called the airport and can fly stand-by on the flight that leaves in a couple of hours." She sounded winded, as if she'd been rushing around. Clearly she had been, if she was already packed.

Her haste to leave twisted the knifing pain deeper into his heart.

"I just don't understand the big rush. Did I miss something?" Aaron crossed the room toward Abby.

Her gaze shifted from Aaron to Luke, and he felt the impact of those green eyes on him like a physical blow.

"I just... I just can't stay." Her voice quivered.

Both Bart and Aaron looked at her with concern for her distress, then to Luke as if seeking answers she hadn't provided.

"Better hurry. Don't want to miss that plane." His sarcasm hurt her, he could tell. Her face reflected the pain, even though she straightened her back and set her shoulders.

She stepped forward to hug Aaron, and his brother crushed her in his big arms for what seemed an inordinately long hug. He kissed her forehead as she pulled away. "Don't be a stranger, Ab. Okay?"

She nodded and glanced to Luke again before taking a tentative step toward him.

He drew a deep breath, plastered a false smile on his face, and cleared any emotion from his throat before he spoke. "It's been real."

He crossed his arms over his chest, silently telling her she'd get no hug from him. But the gesture helped him hold himself together, knowing when she left he'd likely fly apart at the seams. But he'd not show her his misery, not let her see the agony her leaving caused.

Tears glittered in her eyes, and she stared at him for excruciating seconds, her lips parted as if she was trying to tell him something.

*Don't say anything. Just go.* His expression must have voiced his final plea, because she turned without speaking and headed for the stairs.

Aaron helped Bart load her suitcases in Bart's Cadillac for the trip to the airport while Luke stood in the doorway and watched. When Bart backed out of the driveway, Luke steeled himself against the sharp ache that threatened to tear him apart.

Aaron found him a few minutes later standing in the guest room that Abby had used. Evidence of her hasty departure was everywhere. Coat hangers littered the floor of the closet, drawers stood half closed, and a bottle of blue nail polish sat on the nightstand, abandoned in her haste.

Luke picked up the bottle, turned it over in his hands, and remembered the day he'd discovered the sassy shade of polish decorating her toes. They'd been on their way out to his doctor's appointment, and he'd fantasized about sucking those toes.

He closed his hand around the polish and sank to the edge of the bed. His weight rustled the sheets and stirred the faint aroma of Abby's floral perfume. Painful longing crashed down on him with an unexpected and powerful force. He buried his face in his hands and struggled for his next breath.

"Oh, God!" he groaned.

He felt a large hand on his shoulder and looked up to see Aaron staring down at him with worry clouding his eyes. "Hey, wanna tell me about it?"

Luke shook his head, and Aaron squeezed his brother's shoulder before removing his hand and stepping away. Aaron moved to the doorway of the bathroom and leaned against the frame. "I really thought you two were going to make something happen."

"Well, things don't always work out like we plan, do they?"

Aaron regarded him silently for another minute. "Did you tell her you love her?"

Luke sighed and met his brother's eyes. "I told you I don't want to talk about it."

"Did you tell her you love her?"

Luke groaned and looked away. "Leave it alone."

"Luke, did you tell her—"

"She knew. She had to know. How could she not know? God, it was in every kiss, every touch, every look. You said you saw it. How could she miss it?"

"Did you *tell* her you love her?" Aaron raised his voice, and Luke shoved himself from the bed with a huff.

"No! No, damn it!" He stalked across the floor to stare into her empty closet, squeezing the nail polish in his hand.

"What *did* you say?"

Luke whirled around. "I asked her to stay. Just like I asked Mom. And just like Mom, she said no. She said I wasn't a good enough reason to stay here."

Aaron winced as if he'd received the wound instead of Luke. "Surely she didn't mean—"

"Look around you!" Luke waved his hands at the desolate, empty room. "What do you think she meant?"

The muscle in his brother's jaw jumped as he clenched his teeth. "I know she loved you."

"That's crap."

"No. It's not."

"Leave me alone, all right?" Luke's tone held a chilly edge. He wasn't in the mood to debate Abby with his brother.

Aaron headed for the bedroom door but paused before he walked out. He cast Luke a sorrowful glance. "I'm sorry, Luke."

With that, his brother left him to fight his demons alone.


A pale blue glow from the dashboard lights provided the only illumination in Bart's Caddy. The darkness hid the silent tears slipping down her cheeks, and for that, Abby welcomed the blackness. She kept her face averted, feigning great interest in the scenery out her window so that Bart wouldn't see her crying.

One tell-tale sniff of her runny nose gave her away. But Bart had the good manners not to comment. He simply opened the glove box, took out a travel-sized package of tissues, and handed them to her.

When they turned onto the road leading up to the airport, he finally broke his silence. "Whatever he said, whatever he did, he didn't intend to hurt you. Luke just isn't like that."

Abby cleared her throat. "I know."

"Sometimes he loses his temper and—"

"This isn't about some argument, Bart. It's more complicated. I'm as much to blame as he is, really." She paused and blew her nose. "I needed more from him than he wanted to give. I knew from the start this could happen, and I…" She didn't finish her thought, and the car fell silent again.

Bart pulled the car into a parking space in the lot beside the terminal and cut the engine.

"Once, when Luke was a little tyke, maybe three or four, I guess, his mother and I took the boys to the park for a picnic."

She turned toward Bart, curious about his timing for telling a story about Luke's childhood.

"It was a beautiful day, I remember. He and Aaron played and played. Then Luke, headstrong child that he was, always trying to keep up with his brother, climbed the tallest slide at the park." Bart glanced at her and grinned. "We're talking tall slide. Really tall."

She smiled through her tears. She could imagine a young, towheaded Luke scurrying to keep up with his big brother. "And?"

"And he got to the top of the ladder, took a good look around at where he was—and froze."

Bart stared out the windshield, a smile playing at his lips as he recalled the event. "He just stood there at the top of the ladder, not going anywhere. Aaron finally called us to come get his brother, 'cause Luke wasn't about to admit he needed help."

He sent her a meaningful glance.

"Some things don't change, huh?" she murmured.

"Luke was too stubborn to climb down and admit defeat, and too frightened of what he'd gotten himself into to slide down. So he stalled out at the top, not going anywhere."

A strange quiver started in her stomach. "So what happened? How did you get him down?"

"We sent Aaron up to give him a push. He fought his brother, kicked and screamed, clung to the railing, but Aaron got him down. And do you know what he did once he came down the slide?" Bart looked sideways at her as he turned off the headlights and removed his keys from the ignition.

She thought for only a moment. She knew what a twenty-eight-year-old Luke would do and guessed a four-year-old Luke would have done the same. "He climbed right back up, didn't he?"

Bart answered her with a grin and got out of the car.

His story about Luke turned over in her mind throughout her flight home. She mulled over the implications, the truths about the man she'd fallen in love with, and the applications to her situation.

By the time her plane reached DFW airport, Abby had examined the story from a hundred different angles. None of them eased the ache deep inside her. In the end, Luke still hadn't given her the love, the commitment she needed to build a relationship on.

Steve had burned her with his infidelity. Before she invested her heart and soul again, she needed something solid, something lasting in which to root her faith.

She'd been home for several days, re-establishing her routine, throwing herself into her job at the rehabilitation hospital, when Brooke called one Tuesday and asked her to meet for lunch.

"Sure, where?"

"How about the little sandwich place across the street from the church where Chad goes to Mother's Day Out?

Then when we finish eating, I'll scoot across the street to pick him up."

Abby agreed, and they set a time that would avoid the bulk of the lunch crowd.

"Spill it," Brooke said as soon as they sat down in a corner booth.

"Excuse me?" Abby replied with a chuckle.

"You haven't said a word since you got home about Luke or what happened to send you running for home on a moment's notice."

"Because there's nothing to say. He couldn't, or wouldn't, commit. He didn't give me even a hint of his feelings for me—other than to tell me how 'amazing' we were in bed." She wiggled two fingers on each hand to draw quotation marks when she used Luke's word.

Brooke's eyebrows shot up. "You slept with him?"

Abby frowned. "Yeah. Once. The night I left."

"And?"

She sighed. "And what? It was a mistake to be that intimate with him, get that close. I should have known better."

"So you made a mistake and ran away rather than face up to it." Brooke sipped her iced tea through a straw but kept a level gaze on Abby.

Abby shifted her weight uncomfortably under her friend's incisive stare. "I didn't run away!"

"Then why are you here?"

Abby grunted. "My job was finished. There was no point in staying."

"What about Luke?"

"What about him?" She knew she sounded defensive, but Brooke was hitting too close to the simple truths

Abby had skirted since returning. An uneasy flutter started in her chest.

"You told me you'd fallen in love with him. Wasn't that avenue worth exploring? Even if your job was done, wasn't the relationship worth working on? You left just when things were getting interesting, just when you could have found what you were looking for." Brooke stirred the ice in her glass with her straw and pinned Abby with a questioning look.

Growling her frustration with the whole mess, Abby covered her face with her hands and rubbed her temples. "Luke didn't want a relationship, he wanted sex. He didn't love me. He'd have gotten bored with me eventually, and I'd have been back out on the street, just like with Steve."

"You're sure of that? He told you this?"

Abby opened a window between her hands to peer out at Brooke. "It was more what he didn't say when he had the chance that told me he wasn't in it for the same things I was. I don't need a billboard to read the signs."

"So you told him you loved him, asked him for a commitment, and he said no. Is that right?" Brooke's matter-of-fact delivery, the assured way her friend lifted one eyebrow as she looked at her told Abby that Brooke was leading up to a point she didn't want to hear. But if Brooke couldn't be blunt with her, couldn't be honest, what was their friendship worth?

Abby turned her gaze out the window and stared across the street to the church where Brooke had left Chad. In the churchyard, preschool-aged children chased each other around a small playground equipped with swings, a jungle gym, and a slide.

*We're talking tall slide. Really tall.*

"Abby, what is it? What's wrong?"

"I... I never told him how I felt. I expected him to give me something I hadn't offered him. I held back, because I was afraid of getting hurt."

Brooke remained silent but reached across the table for Abby's hand.

In light of her revelation, she saw Bart's story about four-year-old Luke with new insights. She'd asked Luke to take a leap of faith she hadn't been ready to make herself. What if Luke did love her but was afraid to step into uncharted territory without that push from her? His fear of failure had immobilized him on the slide as a child just as it had in the early days of his therapy. She remembered Bart telling her how Luke had withdrawn after his mother had left, how he'd withheld the love he'd once lavished on his family.

Abby chewed her lip. Was it possible Luke loved her but couldn't tell her? Was he stuck on that slide again, too stubborn to back down and too frightened to move forward?

The waitress brought their food, and Abby shook herself from her reverie.

"I know what you're thinking," she told Brooke. "I didn't give Luke a chance. I didn't tell him how I felt, so how can I blame him for holding out?"

Brooke took a bite of her sandwich and gave her a non-committal shrug.

"The thing is, I gave and gave to Steve and ended up with nothing but a broken heart. I need something, *anything* from Luke, just a token, so I don't feel like I'm the only one putting an effort into our relationship." She toyed with the pickle spear on her plate, but she'd lost her appetite. "Does that make me selfish? Am I wrong to expect Luke to make the first move?"

"I don't know. I understand how you feel. I don't blame you for being cautious. But Luke is not Steve. Deal with Luke in terms of Luke, not in terms of what Steve did to you."

Abby nodded. What Brooke said made sense. Her friend had given her a lot to think about.

"Abby, do you remember that saying you used to throw at me every time Matt and I had a fight in college and broke up for a couple of days?"

She met Brooke's gaze as Brooke began to quote, "If you love someone, set them free. If they come back to you, they are yours, if not…"

"It was never meant to be," Abby finished, then sighed. "I don't like that one so much when you toss it back at me."

Brooke grinned. "Don't give up. It ain't over till—"

"The fat lady sings. Yeah, yeah. You're all full of clichés today, aren't you?" She gave Brooke a teasing scowl.

"Sorry. You're a lot better at this than I am." Brooke chuckled and checked her watch. "Say, I've gotta run get Chad. The white-haired ladies get really upset if you're even a minute late."

Abby glanced at her own watch. "Yeah, I gotta run too. I start with a new patient this afternoon, and I hear he's a surly old codger. Wouldn't want to get on Mr. Gibbons' bad side."

Brooke gave Abby a quick hug on her way out the door. "Hang in there, kid."

She nodded. "I will."

❖ ❖ ❖

The days after Abby left seemed to move in slow motion. Though Luke buried himself in work, both for Gulfside and taking on new business designing web pages, his thoughts never strayed far from Abby. He replayed all the "what if's" and asked himself "why" a million different ways.

Each night, Luke stared up at the "stars" Abby had given him for his birthday and made love to her again in his mind. Holding her had felt so right. Losing her cut so deep. And facing his future without her left him with a hollow bleakness that took his breath away. Something had to give.

*Life is about choices.*

*I'm not going to give up on you. Are you giving up on you?*

The only bright spot in his life was the growing closeness he had with his father. He owed Abby for that, too. She'd pushed him to bridge the gap that had separated him from Bart for too long, and having that connection with his dad meant so much. Enough that when he ran out of answers, he mustered the nerve to turn to Bart for help. Reaching out for help wasn't easy, but he'd do anything to get Abby back.

Luke found Bart in his office one morning and knocked softly on the door. "Dad, mind if I come in?"

Luke stepped into his father's office, and Bart turned from his computer with an inquisitive glance.

"Of course not, Luke. Something I can do for you?" Bart flashed him an encouraging smile.

Nodding, he sat on the sagging sofa across from his father. He took a brass ship paperweight off Bart's desk and turned it over in his hands, fumbling for a way to begin. "I, uh… I need to ask you something. I need… some advice."

Bart drew back. Then with an uncertain grin, he laughed nervously. "I've always got plenty of friendly advice, free for the asking."

"No, that's… that's not what I mean. I don't need friendly advice." A knot swelled in his throat, and Luke swallowed hard to get rid of the tightness before he continued. "I need to talk… to my dad. I need my dad's advice."

He hoped Bart understood the subtle difference he meant.

The mast of the brass ship bit into his palm as he squeezed the paperweight and watched the emotions play across Bart's face.

He met his son's gaze. "I'm listening."

Luke felt a rush of satisfaction and warmth. And a yearning to be the son he'd denied Bart for years.

Taking a deep breath, he plunged in. "I've screwed up… with Abby. I don't know what I'm supposed to do now."

After studying Luke silently for a moment, Bart blew out a slow breath and leaned back in his chair. He gave his son a weak smile and shook his head. "Maybe Aaron should field that question. I haven't dated in too many years to count."

Luke suppressed the pang of disappointment and persisted. "But you've been married. You know about making a commitment to one woman."

A shadow flickered in his father's eyes, and his smile faded. "But I've also been divorced. I obviously didn't get it right."

An awkward silence grew between them. Luke rubbed the smooth side of the brass ship, and let his thoughts drift to his memories of his mother, of the days following the divorce when Bart had been beside himself with grief. He understood the pain his father had suffered all those years ago when the woman he loved walked out on him. He knew that pain now, first-hand.

Setting the brass ship back on his father's desk, Luke sighed. "So if you had it all to do over… your marriage to Mom… what would you do different this time?"

With a sad smile, Bart met his son's gaze. "That one's easy. I'd put up a fight."

Luke furrowed his brow. "Care to explain that?"

Bart bridged his fingers and propped his elbows on the paper-strewn desk. "When your mom left, she told me I didn't make her happy anymore and that she wanted out. She'd found another man who made her feel good about herself and told her the things she wanted to hear." Bart paused, the memory obviously still difficult for him to face. "Well, I loved her, so I wanted her to be happy. I figured if I didn't make her happy, who was I to stop her from finding it somewhere else?" His father met his gaze squarely. "And I let her walk right out of my life and my sons' lives. I've spent the last twenty years wondering if she might have stayed if I'd told her how much I loved her. That I needed her in my life."

Luke struggled to draw a breath, but his chest felt leaden.

"So… if I had it to do over, I would put up a fight. I'd tell your mother how I felt, what she meant to me, how much she meant in my life. I wouldn't let her walk out without trying to win her back."

Luke saw the torment in his father's eyes, and the weight on his chest pressed harder. "You're still in love with Mom, aren't you?"

Bart nodded slowly. "She's kinda hard to forget. I see her whenever I look at you."

Unable to meet his father's eyes any longer, Luke surged to his feet and crossed the room to stare sightlessly at the books lining the shelves along the opposite wall. The hum of the computer monitor and the thumping of his heart filled his ears with a lonely rhythm.

Finally Bart cleared his throat and spoke again. "Forgive me, Luke. Forgive me for not doing enough to keep your mother here. I know how much you've missed her."

Luke spun around, shaking his head. "I never blamed you. In fact, I wondered what I was lacking as a son that made her want to leave."

Bart sighed and closed his eyes. "Not a thing, son. Your mother loved you to pieces. But when you chose to stay with me and Aaron, she let you go, believing she was doing what was best for you, wanting you to be happy."

Luke shoved his hands in his pockets, mulling over the truths he was learning, seeing the family's history with fresh, more mature eyes. His parents had been lovers, bumbling through the rocky road of relationships, trying and failing, hoping and hurting, learning from their mistakes. Just like he was.

He fingered the coins in his pocket, jangling them.

"What about you?" Bart asked. "Is Abby what you want?"

He brought his head up with a jerk. "You know she is."

"Then if you want my advice, Luke, it's this: Get your butt on the next plane to Texas. And put up a fight."

# Chapter 19

WHEN HE REACHED DFW AIRPORT, LUKE TOOK OUT THE business card Abby had left with Bart. He showed the card to a taxi driver and told the man to drive straight to the rehabilitation hospital.

In the taxi, as on the airplane, Luke rehearsed over and over again what he would say to Abby when he saw her. He still wasn't exactly sure what she wanted from him, what words or promises or actions would convince her they were meant for each other.

When the taxi brought him to the front door of the hospital, his next move remained a mystery, and nervous sweat beaded on his lip. What would he do if she turned him down... again?

That thought almost sent him fleeing for the airport and Florida without finding her. He wasn't sure his heart could stand being rejected again. He must be a glutton for punishment to have come here. Yet the voice deep in his soul whispered to him that Abby was supposed to be with him, that he was doing the right thing.

Stepping into the lobby of the rehabilitation hospital, a chill skittered through Luke that he couldn't blame on the ultra-cold air conditioning. In the style of newer facilities, the hospital was decorated with homey, warm colors and comfortable furniture to make patients and families feel more at ease. The hospital reminded him of the numerous places Bart had taken him following the explosion. He had stubbornly walked out of every one, certain that his life could never be changed by any therapist or hospital.

But one woman had irrevocably altered his destiny and now held his future happiness in her skilled hands.

Luke approached the front desk and caught the receptionist's attention. "Can you tell me where I can find Abby Stanford, please?"

"Sure." The woman consulted a chart on the wall and turned back to him with a bright smile. "She's in workroom three, but she's with a client at the moment. If you'd like to take a seat, I'll let her know you're here and—"

"No, I don't want to wait. Workroom three?"

The woman's smile faltered. "Sir, you can't go back while she's with a client."

Luke flashed her a conspiratorial grin. "If anyone asks, tell them you tried to stop me, but I muscled my way through."

"But—"

He didn't hang around to haggle with the receptionist. Signs directing visitors and clients through the maze of halls guided him to workroom three.

The workroom turned out to be a large gymnasium with a high ceiling and a variety of equipment, from parallel bars to ramps and swings on pulleys. The room buzzed with activity. Patients grunted and toiled while the therapists, dressed in maroon golf shirts with the hospital logo, cheered and encouraged the attempts of their clients. The room smelled like rubber from the mats on the floor and the sweat of effort.

Luke scanned the busy gym floor for Abby. A strange, invigorating strength flowed through his body as his gaze passed from one toiling patient to the next. Men with missing limbs, children with braces on their legs, and one woman with a prosthetic arm struggled to overcome their condition and improve their lives. The room hummed with the positive energy of people fighting back against adversity.

If these people could battle against the odds, so could he!

Then he spotted Abby, and his breath caught. She was in her element and glowing with pride and purpose. Love and respect for his green-eyed spitfire filled Luke as he watched her. She knelt on the floor in front of an older man, who used the parallel bars to support himself as he shuffled his feet, one careful step at a time. Abby helped guide his feet in a straight path, smiling her motivation and praise to the man.

Never had Luke been so aware of his healthy legs as when he strode across the gym floor toward Abby. Curious gazes turned toward him and followed his movement to the far corner of the room. He stopped a dozen feet away from the spot where Abby worked and sucked in a deep breath.

His whole life had come down to this moment, it seemed. The urge to turn and run, to save himself from further rejection, battled with his need to stay and have his say. The threat of failure haunted him, but the hope that Abby had inspired in him rose to the occasion and held the fear at bay. With trepidation nipping his heels, Luke cleared his throat. "Abby?"

With a backward glance, she turned to see who'd called her. Her face registered joy, shock, and confusion in rapid succession. "Luke. Wh-what are you doing here?"

"Can we talk? In private?"

She glanced back at her patient. "I... I'm kind of busy right now."

"It's important."

She raised her eyes to him again, and the specter of mixed emotions swirled in their depths. "I figured as much, if you came all the way to Texas to tell me."

Luke crooked his head toward the door. "Then can we go outside?"

Her chest rose and fell as she drew a deep breath. "No."

The first niggling of misgivings crawled through him. "Please, Abby. Give me just five minutes."

Abby dropped her gaze to the floor but squared her shoulders. "I'm with a client, Luke. Mr. Gibbons has paid good money for my time and assistance, and I intend to give him every minute he's due."

"That's right," Mr. Gibbons said with a crackling laugh. "Hundred dollars an hour this lady's time costs. And I guess I don't have to tell you, she's worth every penny." The older man winked at Luke.

Luke gave the man a feeble smile, despite the downward spiral of his confidence in the outcome of his quest. "She's priceless."

His comment brought Abby's head up again. "I finish work at five, Luke. We can talk then."

He shook his head and reached in his shirt pocket for the two plane tickets he'd bought before he left Florida. "That's not good enough. Our plane leaves at 4:30."

She knit her brows. "What plane?"

"The one that's going to take us—both of us—back to Florida."

He showed her the tickets, but she gave them only a cursory glance. He noticed that her hands trembled, and he wondered if that was a good sign or not. Was he weakening her resolve or just aggravating her?

"I'm not going to Florida, Luke. I have a job here and friends and a home—"

"No, Abby. Your home is with me. You know it as well as I do. Come home with me."

She pressed a hand to her mouth and turned away. Then, straightening her back in the stubborn, decisive way she had, she faced Mr. Gibbons again. "Luke, please leave. I have work to do."

Luke glanced at the old man, and Mr. Gibbons shrugged.

Huffing impatiently, he searched for a way to extract Abby from her work long enough to reason with her. He fished in his pocket for his cash and withdrew a twenty dollar bill.

"Here." He held the money out toward the old man. "I'll buy some of your minutes with her. This should give me at least ten minutes, right?"

The older gentleman grinned and leaned on the parallel bars to reach for the bill. "Sure. Take twelve. I was lookin' to rest a spell anyway. She's relentless." He nodded to Luke. "Good luck."

Abby opened her mouth to protest, but snapped it shut again, dividing a stunned glance between the men. Luke stooped to put a hand under her elbow and bring her to her feet.

"Come on, honey. Clock's ticking."

She shook off his hand as she came to her feet and sent him an irritated scowl. "All right. You want to talk? Then talk."

She propped her hands on her hips, and green sparks lit her eyes.

"Outside."

"No, here."

Mr. Gibbons chuckled and lowered himself into his waiting wheelchair. "Young man, you sure you want to hook up with this filly? She's a mite headstrong. Seems to me you'd just be askin' for a headache."

Luke met Abby's glittering eyes with a level gaze. "I've never been more sure of anything in my life."

His response to the old man seemed to take the wind from her sails. Her hard glare softened, and moisture crept into her eyes. "You have twelve minutes, Luke."

"Nope. Ten now. Ya done wasted two arguing," Mr. Gibbons said and cackled.

Rubbing his palms on his slacks, Luke tamped down the flare of anxiety due to his dwindling time limit.

*Be calm. Just say what you rehearsed.* Taking Abby by the arm, he pulled her another few steps out of the old man's hearing.

"I want you to come back to Florida with me."

Abby rubbed her temple. "We've covered this ground already, Luke. I need more than that. I need a reason to go."

He tightened his grip on her wrist. "Aren't I a good enough reason for you?"

"I don't know what you want me to say, Luke! I need more than the offer of a sexual fling. What happens when you get tired of me, Luke? What happens if I can't satisfy you the way all those other women—" Her voice caught on a sob, and she stamped her foot as she squeezed her eyes shut and turned away.

"No other woman has ever given me what you give me, Abby. You mean more to me than just a fling. That's not what I want from you."

"Eight minutes!" Mr. Gibbons called, and Luke sent him an annoyed glare.

"But that's all you've ever offered me, Luke. Just sex. Just your body. But I need more. I need all of you. I need your heart and your soul. I need your promise of forever. I need to know what you hope, what you fear, how you feel—"

"Okay." Luke dropped her arm and took a step back, nodding. "You want to know how I feel?"

He flexed and balled his hands as he dug deep inside to find the words to give Abby her wish. "I feel… lucky to have met you. I feel… empty when I'm without you. I feel… alive when you smile at me."

She lifted eyes full of tears to him, and when one drop escaped her lashes and trickled down her cheek, his heart lurched. He reached for her and caught the tear on the pad of a finger. He heard an admiring sigh behind him and only then became aware of the crowd that had turned their attention to his exchange with Abby.

Spilling his guts to Abby was hard enough without the extra audience. But she was listening, and he wouldn't lose this opportunity for anything.

"Five minutes."

This time it was Abby who sent Mr. Gibbons a quelling look.

Luke took Abby's hand in his and laced his fingers with hers. Her thumb lay across the stub where his own thumb had once been.

Yet, with her hand joined with his, he didn't feel the lack. Rather, for the first time since the accident, he felt whole. Fulfilled. Inside as well as out. Abby filled the empty space that had haunted him for years, spread her sunshine and warmth to even the darkest nether regions of his soul.

His pulse raced with excitement and the need to tell Abby the truths he was finally learning for himself. But his thoughts tripped on each other, and his tongue tied. Where did he start?

"Luke?" She tipped her head giving him an uncertain but encouraging nod to continue.

"I… I feel…" The words tumbled about in his head, but nothing seemed to fit the depth of his affection and need for her. He stared at her helplessly, frantic to say something, but at a loss.

Disappointment darkened her expression, and she lowered her gaze, tried to pull her hand from his. Squeezing tighter, he blurted the first word that came into his head.

"Scared."

"What?"

"I feel scared, Abby. I'm scared as hell that I won't say the right thing, that I won't change your mind, that I could lose you forever because I can't find the words to tell you everything that's all tangled up inside me. I'm scared that when I show you the ring I have in my pocket that you'll still tell me no, and that, like my Dad, I'll spend the next twenty years wondering what I should have said to make you stay with me."

She blinked and wrinkled her forehead in confusion. "Y-you have a ring… in your pocket?"

He swallowed hard, trying to wash away the arid feel in his mouth. "Yeah. I have a ring. An emerald. I know a diamond is more traditional, but… the emerald reminded me of your eyes."

"One minute!" Mr. Gibbons called, and the crowd of spectators unanimously shushed him.

"So, is a ring a good enough reason to get on that plane back to Florida with me?" He held his breath expectantly. Full of hope.

Moisture filled her eyes. "No."

Pain ripped through his heart. Frustration and desperation clawed him.

A succession of tears dripped from her eyelashes. Each one drenched his soul with another drop of despair. "Why, Abby?"

"Luke, I've had a ring before. It did me no good when I found the man who gave it to me in bed with another woman." Her voice broke with wrenching sadness.

He grabbed her shoulders and pinned her with a stern glare. "I would never do that to you, Abby. You are the only woman I want. I'll be faithful, I swear it."

"You just don't get it!" she shouted, knocking his hand away and spinning away with a sigh.

"No, damn it! I guess I don't!" His frustration raised his voice as well.

"Time is up." She took one hesitant step back toward the parallel bars then a second. And a third.

Anguish tore him apart, raked across his heart, and shattered his composure. "Abby, don't do this! You know we belong together. You know we do! I don't know what else to say, what else I can do."

She kept walking.

"Abby, please! I love you!"

She stopped. Turned. Blinked.

His heart pounded against his ribs like a wild animal fighting to get free of its cage.

"There now," she whispered hoarsely. "Was that so hard?"

"Huh?"

She bit her lip, and the corner of her mouth twitched with a grin. She closed the distance she'd put between them in three long strides. "I love you, too, Luke."

He stared at her, dumbfounded.

When she slid her arms around his neck, a cheer went up around them.

"What time did you say that plane leaves?" she murmured as she hugged him.

"You mean you'll go home with me? But I—"

"I just needed to hear that you loved me."

He pushed her away and scowled. "What? Hell, woman! Why didn't you just say so?"

She groaned and shook her head. "Because then it wouldn't mean anything. It had to come from you or it would be worthless."

Luke dragged a hand through his hair. "You're a tough broad to figure out, sweetheart."

Abby flashed him a demure smile. "That's all right. You'll have the rest of your life to work on it." She pressed her body closer to his and drew her hands down his chest toward his hips. "Now, which pocket is that ring in?"

She slipped her hands in his pockets, and heat surged through him. He caught her wrists and growled huskily in her ear, "Better let me do that, sweetheart, or you'll start something these good people have no business watching."

Abby chuckled and raised eyes full of mischief to his. "We can be at my apartment in ten minutes."

The come-hither look she gave him was almost his undoing. With a great deal of restraint, he managed to kiss her lips once and step away. "What about Mr. Gibbons?"

His green-eyed spitfire tugged him toward the door and smiled. "He can't come."

# Chapter 20

AARON WAS RESTLESS.

He watched the clock mark the hours, waiting for Luke to return from Texas. With any luck at all, Luke would have Abby with him. He'd bet his share of the business she was. When Luke set his mind to something, his brother always seemed to win.

Aiming the remote at the television, he scanned the channels for the millionth time looking for something worth watching. He heard the front door open, and he rose from his chair to greet Luke.

"Hey! Anybody home?" His brother sounded happy, and Aaron's pulse picked up expectantly.

"Up here, Luke," Bart called.

A female squeal rang from the foyer, and Aaron grinned. Abby was with him.

His brother lumbered into the living room, carrying Abby in his arms. Both of them beamed like lighthouses.

"I'm home," Luke announced unnecessarily.

"No kidding?" Aaron sent him a wry grin.

"I'm home, too." Abby stared up at Luke when she spoke, and his brother answered with a goofy, slap-happy smile and smacking kiss.

"Get a room." He tossed a throw pillow at the couple, and Abby batted it away.

Luke wiggled his eyebrows. "Hm, not a bad idea. Abby?"

Laughing, she wiggled her legs loose from his grasp and put her feet on the floor. Luke kept his arms around her, though, as if he were afraid she'd flee again if he let go.

"Don't you want to tell everyone our news first?" she asked.

"If you insist. Then can we get a room?" His quip earned him a playful jab in the ribs.

"News? What news?" Bart scooted to the edge of the sofa and leaned forward, eyeing Luke.

Abby held out her left hand. An emerald ring winked in the lamplight. "Luke's bachelor days are numbered."

A strange sensation flowed through Aaron. A feeling like envy. "Well, I'll be damned."

Bart pumped Luke's hand. "Congratulations."

Luke turned an anxious look toward his brother.

Aaron curled up the corner of his mouth. "All the more women for me."

He moved his gaze to Abby and sent her a thumbs up.

The anxiety in Luke's expression faded, replaced by a satisfaction that lit his whole face. Love suited Luke, and seeing his brother's happiness gave Aaron an inner peace as well.

"I've already asked Brooke to come down for a few days later this month to help plan the wedding," Abby said. "We want to put this thing together quickly, shoot for maybe September."

"Why the rush?" Bart asked.

Luke shrugged. "Why not?"

"Touché," Bart replied with a laugh.

"Now, if you will excuse us—" Luke took Abby's hand and tugged her toward the stairs. "We have some unfinished business to take care of."

After Luke left, Aaron made his own excuses to Bart and headed to the privacy of his room. Flopping down on the bed, he shut his eyes and sighed.

Brooke would be coming back for a visit. And why not? She was Abby's best friend. She'd be at the wedding, too, and who knows how many other visits in the years to come.

*Damn!* Having her visit again would be hard enough without knowing she would be a constant in his life from now on. Watching her, wanting her, not having her would be torture. Seeing her with her husband—the lucky bastard—would be pure hell.

Aaron's chest squeezed with suppressed longing. How in God's name was he supposed to get over her?

Luke led Abby to his bedroom and closed the door behind them. When he crossed the room to her, Abby lifted her hands to his chest and smiled up at him.

"Finally. I thought I'd never get you alone." He flashed her a quick, lopsided grin.

"I appreciate your waiting while I finished my session with Mr. Gibbons. I wouldn't have felt right leaving before I arranged for someone to take over his therapy program."

He pulled her closer, savoring the crush of her soft body against him. "As much as I appreciate and admire your work ethic, love, I'm beginning to feel a little neglected. I have needs, too."

"Poor baby." She gave him an exaggerated pout. "I'm all yours now. What do you need?"

He gave her a wicked grin. "I need to see you naked. I

need to have my hands in your hair, on your skin. I need to taste your sweet kiss and—"

"And?"

Her eyes had grown smoky with desire, and their heat and promise set him on fire. Luke plowed his fingers into Abby's hair and tipped her chin up with his left thumb. He caught her lips with a deep, shattering kiss, and his mouth roamed over hers, searching for new angles, better positions to more fully claim what she offered. Abby unbuttoned his shirt until the cloth parted, and she slid her hands inside.

Abruptly, she pulled away from their kiss and opened the front of his shirt. Her eyes softened then rose to his. "Would you take your compression vest off for me?"

Remembering his scars with a flash of self-conscious wariness, he sucked in a sharp breath and pulled the cloth closed over his chest. "Uh… the doctor says I'll have to wear it for at least a year."

"But not every minute of every day. You take it off for the shower, so you can take it off to… make love." She smiled at him and tugged on his shirt.

He sighed. "I have to warn you. It's not pretty."

She stroked his face and smoothed his hair behind his ear. "When I say I love you, I mean as is. God knows, I'm not perfect. All I ask is that you let me love your imperfections as much as I love the perfect parts."

The love in her touch melted the cold apprehension gripping his heart. He knew she was right, and he wanted to trust her, to share himself with her. Odd as it seemed to him, the more he gave her, the more he felt fulfilled.

His grip on his shirt relaxed, and Abby guided the fabric down his arms until the shirt slithered to the floor. Together they worked the tight, stretchy vest off as well.

His pink and white scars stood out against the healthy tanned skin surrounding them. Abby brushed her fingertips over his chest, gently exploring the new skin. Her caress sent waves of pleasure rippling through him, and he shuddered.

When she ducked her head and kissed the flaws in his skin, his breath caught. Slowly her lips grazed him, moving from areas of scar tissue to uninjured skin with the same gentleness and passion for each. Her acceptance of his imperfections healed his wounded spirit and filled the aching void.

"I love you, Luke. All of you."

Circling her waist with his arms, he pulled her closer, and she sagged against him, molding her curves to his hard lines. The full body contact drove him wild. Desire coursed through him like a raging river.

He lowered her to the bed, and the distinctly feminine scent of her skin and her floral perfume filled his senses as he moved his kiss along her jaw.

Later when he joined their bodies, Abby met his lunges in a sensual dance and greeted his kiss with her tongue. His control shattered in a brilliant starburst, and he spilled his seed into her womb. The powerful erotic waves that washed through him were followed closely by an emotion so deep and true that tears gathered in his eyes.

"Abby, I love you. I love you so much." He trailed kisses across her cheeks and whispered in her ear. "You're a part of who I am. Promise me you'll never leave me."

"Never." The passion in her kiss echoed her vow.

He held her tightly, her head tucked under his chin, as the shockwaves that rocked him gentled. Her breath whispered in soft, moist pants against his chest. After a few moments, he reached for the toggle switch to turn on his Christmas-light stars. Under the glow of the twinkling lights, they languished in each other's arms. She tipped her face up to look at the homemade stars with him. Gazing at the heavens she'd crafted, Luke experienced the sense of peace and wholeness that he'd wanted for years and believed he could receive from the night sky.

But, with startling clarity, he realized the stars could never give him what he sought. He'd found blissful inner peace and completion with the woman in his arms.

Abby's love filled the void in his soul.

# Acknowledgments

Many thanks to occupational therapist Debbie Balch of Therapy Works in Monroe, Louisiana for her time and patience in answering my many questions about hand therapy and burn treatment. Your help was invaluable and most appreciated. Any mistakes regarding Luke's treatment and recovery are the author's and may be due to creative license I took for the sake of the story.

# About the Author

Georgia native **Beth Cornelison** worked in public relations before pursuing her love of writing fiction. She has published several category romances and has won numerous honors for her work, including RWA's coveted Golden Heart. Cornelison is active in her local RWA chapter and presents writing workshops across the country. She lives in West Monroe, Louisiana.